Blood Opal

~

Carole Sutton

Chapter One

Exeter – S.W. England

The call had come – the job was on.

A shadowy reflection in a shop window showed his tall heavy frame lumbering along the city pavement, a large tool-bag weighty in his hand. Next to him and typically out of step, marched his brother. Not as tall, and somewhat skinny, he carried only the mandatory clipboard and pen. Each wore identical dark blue overalls with the logo *City Carpets* emblazoned in yellow across their shoulders, their woollen caps tightly rolled up to their ears.

He slowed his pace, reassured, as they approached the automatic doors of Centurion House, a thirty-storey, newly renovated office block. The two of them looked no different from the workmen who'd been fitting carpets there all week. Only today was Saturday, the time 3.55p.m., and the carpet fitters had long since gone home. His stomach tightened as excitement stirred within.

The traffic noise abated once they were inside the giant doors. The only source of sound came from the far side of the deserted lobby where water, falling down the illuminated feature wall, created a soothing ambience. Now, they were out of public view, he quickened his steps over the black marble floor.

"C'mon, Dave, get your arse in gear, man," he said quietly, calling his brother by the name sewn onto the stolen overalls. His own labelled him, 'Bob.'

Dave hastened to catch up, glancing uneasily around. Sweat beads popped from his brow. "S'all right for you. I'm shitting meself. What if he's got a minder?"

"Cool it, for God's sake. You're shakin' like a kid on his first screw." Although irritated, he understood Dave's fear. This was the biggest job they'd tackled so far. Failure could have them banged up for years. He halted beside the central bank of lifts, lowered the tool bag to the ground and waited for his brother to get a grip on his nerves.

"What if the thing really is, you know – cursed?" Dave muttered.

"Jeez man, will you shut up? Don't be so bloody superstitious. We got a job to do." At the sound of footsteps, Bob shot a glance towards the main entrance. A woman dressed in a black business suit approached them. Her shoulder length, chestnut coloured hair obscured the shape of her face. She made no eye contact, but walked past them to study the building directory that stood in front of the water-wall.

As though her presence inspired confidence, Dave straightened himself and using the end of his marker-pen, pressed the button to open a lift door. Bob hefted his tool bag and stepped inside. They exchanged glances. Apart from Dave's last minute nerves, everything was going to plan.

Bob thought ahead as they rode the lift in silence. Their plan entailed getting out one stop early and walking up to the next floor to make sure the place was empty. Above that was the penthouse, a luxury apartment that included a pool and roof garden. Completed months ago, its owner, a wealthy entrepreneur, had already moved in.

They stepped out into a silent Floor 28. The painters had finished their job, but their scaffolding still awaited collection. Rolls of carpet stood ready for the real carpet fitters.   Bob hastened across the bare floor to the emergency stairway exit. He stopped to pull on a pair of latex gloves. Dave, already gloved up, opened the door to the stairwell. Their rubber soles made little noise as they climbed the concrete steps. They pushed open the door at the top and emerged into the vast empty area of Floor 29.

The public lift did not go up beyond this floor, which meant their target had to disembark here and change to a private lift for the penthouse. This is where the two of them had planned to wait.

Around the sides, open doors led to bare, vacant offices. Apart from the block of lifts in its centre, there was not so much as a pot of paint to hide behind in what seemed like acres of dusty space. The penthouse lift lay behind the closed door marked Private.

Dave pulled his phone from his pocket. "What if there *are* two of them?" he insisted. At that moment, the phone vibrated in his hand and he jumped as though stung. Fumbling, he opened the text message. "Alone. Lift 4," he read aloud.

Bob sneered. "Happy now?" He unrolled his woollen balaclava, adjusting the eyeholes. Dave followed suit, his beaky nose still prominent under its cover. Together they charged across the empty

4

space towards the lifts. They stood one each side of number four. Bob unzipped the tool bag and took out a steel wrench. He heard a faint whine as the lift raced up to meet them. Flattening himself against the neighbouring lift door, he waited for number four to arrive.

The door opened. A man clasping an attaché case chained to his wrist stepped out. Dave leapt in front of him. Bob swung behind and with a measured blow, landed his wrench on the back of the man's skull. The courier dropped to the floor.

Dave wheeled around to the tool bag and brought out a pair of bolt cutters, sliced through the chain links and freed the attaché case. Bob stuffed it into the tool bag, along with the wrench and the bolt cutters.

On the floor, the man never moved. Dave knelt beside him and touched his face. The man's head lolled to one side. Dave jumped to his feet. "He's dead!"

Bob only grunted. Killing had not been a necessary part of their deal, but it was one less tongue to wag. He glanced towards the private door, then pointed to one of the vacant offices. "In there – move it."

He took the courier's arms and Dave grabbed his ankles. They dropped him behind the door. A quick scan of the floor area showed no bloodstains. Bob collected the tool bag and ran for the lift. Dave grabbed his clipboard, pen and phone. He leapt in beside Bob and hit the button for the ground floor. Panting with exertion, he punched in a reply text. "Done."

"Hey, calm down," Bob urged him. "Gloves off, balaclava rolled up. Remember – walk slowly, like you're knackered after a hard day's work."

For a second or two, they would be in camera range on the ground floor lobby. Once out of the lift they ambled towards the back of the building, through a short passage and down a ramp to the emergency exit.

Bob checked his watch. The whole thing had taken less than twenty-five minutes. Dave's wife, the woman in the black suit, waited in a white Mercedes delivery van, with the engine running. Dave climbed in beside her. Bob dived in through the sliding side door and fell into the empty rear section. "Go, go, go!" He spun around to gaze out of the back window as the woman accelerated out of the underground car park.

Only the black plastic bag covering the CCTV camera fluttered in the breeze of their departure.

* * *

5

2

On Monday morning, Patricia Ursula Germaine, or "Pug," as she was more commonly known, spread the previous day's newspaper out on her shop counter. The Sunday papers were full of the violent robbery at Centurion House over the weekend. "The Blood Opal strikes again. Courier dead in gem heist," the headlines ran.

Excitement feathered in her belly. The coverage of the robbery had given credence to her latest brilliant idea. She would use the history of the Blood Opal for her TV series *The Story Behind the Stamp*. It was only a five-minute filler on the BBC's local program, but it was popular, and not only with stamp collectors. She had planned to use the stamps from Pitcairn Island depicting Fletcher Christian and the burning of the Bounty. Pirates and mutineers were always popular. But with the opal robbery happening not fifty miles from where she stood, it was too good an opportunity to miss.

With an effort, she pulled her mind back to business. She signed the evaluation she'd completed and returned the British Commonwealth stamp albums to the safe. As far as collections went, it wasn't bad, almost as good as hers. It should bring in a fair return for the beneficiary who wanted to get shot of it and pocket the money in the fastest possible time. An unfortunate trend she saw increasing year-by-year in her late father's old business, Germaine's World of Stamps.

The idea had come to her the previous night, when Dominic's snores had kept her awake. Most ideas that came to her in the darkness of insomnia turned out to be damp squibs in the light of day, but this one was different. With the world's eyes focused on their doorstep, it should prove popular with the TV program's producers. Who knows, they might even sign her for another series, and that would be good for business. People came to her shop for their stamp orders and accessories because they'd seen her on the telly.

She glanced around the shop. Somewhere, in these hundreds of small drawers, lay the sets of stamps called Infamous Gemstones, among which she'd find the Blood Opal. At least her filing system had improved over her father's shoeboxes piled one on top of the other, and yet he had always known exactly where to find anything. She smiled at the memory of her dad. She missed him greatly.

Sunlight streamed through the glass door, making the shop look dustier than it really was. A shadow blocked the light as the door opened and Celeste from next door breezed in. Her long blond hair hung in soft curls over her peacock-coloured caftan, a silver chain around her head glittered on her forehead. She brought in with her the perfume of oils and incense from her New Age boutique.

"Hi Honey Pug, just brought the rent over," Celeste said, in a breathy voice, waving her monthly cheque in the air. She slapped it down on the counter. "Had a quiet moment, so thought I'd pop in. Everything okay?"

Pug's ownership of the shop next door provided her with a useful income to supplement her business. Celeste was the ideal tenant, never a day late with her rent.

"You're just the person I want to see," Pug said, pointing a finger at Celeste. "With your knowledge of crystals and gemstones, what do you know about the Blood Opal?"

Celeste laughed and fluttered her hands in the air. "No, no, it wasn't me! I didn't take it. Honest."

"I know that, silly. I need some background. I'm doing this week's stamp story on it."

"Ooh, the curse of the Blood Opal – wonderful. Can't stop now, but I'll have a look and let you know. By the way – like the hair!" In a silky swish of colour, Celeste swept out the door, leaving traces of patchouli to mingle with the old stamp shop's papery essence.

Pug put her hands to her head and tucked her hair behind her ears. She'd forgotten about the streaks. Her hair was dark brown, straight and below shoulder length. The make-up girl at the TV studio had suggested she try foils to lighten it. The girl had said it would give her face a lift and emphasise her blue eyes. Not normally given to prettying herself up, Pug had resisted the suggestion until last Saturday, when some mad moment took her off to the hair salon.

Afterwards, she wondered why she'd bothered. Dom's reaction was to tell her she looked like a "bloody zebra." It was only a few dark gold highlights. Nothing like a zebra – it was more like a tiger, if he had to be animalistic about it.

She found the Blood Opal stamps nestled among the Pacific Islands' issues and laid one set out on the counter. According to the blurb, the black opal had a murky past. But the pictures on the stamps looked quite beautiful.

The first one showed a pear-shaped black *nobby*, its front cut open to show the brilliance of the fiery red colour bar in its centre. Others showed the opal in various stages of its history. The last one, an enlarged photograph on the souvenir sheet, showed the gem in the form of a pendant, encased in a gold filigree cage. From the open front, the stone's vibrant colour gleamed from its dark surround with flickers of blue, scarlet and yellow like the bed of a furnace. An accompanying leaflet described the stone as, "oval, with a good dome, a solid black opal with dimensions of 1.8 by 1.5 inches, weighing ninety carats."

She read everything available on the stolen gem, and shrugged off tales of opals being unlucky to make notes for the basis of her talk. It's true sometimes their colour faded, or their faces cracked, but as their consistency was similar to glass, it was little wonder some of them broke. It had nothing to do with luck. As for inanimate stones carrying a curse, that was bollocks, but she had to admit, it did sell newspapers.

Between customers, she dealt with the routine; opened the latest packet of stamps from the Crown Agents, sorted, filed and made up the orders, all the time turning over angles of the story for her TV talk. Five minutes was not long enough for a story this good.

According to one of the articles in the newspaper, the opal pendant had come under the auctioneer's hammer the previous week. The bidding reached its anticipated value of half a million pounds, then slowed and finally went to a telephone bidder for just under a million. The inflated price was said to be due to its curiosity value. The anonymous buyer was a wealthy entrepreneur – a recluse, who decorated his penthouse with the unusual, the remarkable and the bizarre.

Celeste came in with a handful of downloaded printouts just as she was closing for the day. "When you've read these, you might not be so keen to do a story about it," she said, with a smile.

"Don't tell me you believe in cursed stones," Pug said. "If that were true, why would anyone want to steal it, far less kill a man to get it."

"That proves the point, doesn't it? Bad luck for the courier, he's dead. If you have your head screwed on the right way, you'll leave this one strictly alone." Celeste's face was deadly grave. Pug was tempted to laugh, but she knew how seriously her friend took such things, and didn't want to upset her.

"Do you have any details of the Blood Opal's origin?" she asked.

Celeste held up a small booklet. "All in here, it's a potted history of famous opals. They started out millions of years ago, under the sea. The miners found this particular one in the 1930s, at a place called Lightning Ridge in Australia. You've heard of the gold rush – well gold wasn't all there was to be found in the Land of Oz back in those days. These guys mined for opals. In some places, you could pick 'em off the ground, but for others, you had to dig."

"Does it say who found it?"

"Found in a dead man's hand," Celeste read aloud. *"The Blood Opal was discovered by Seamus Kelly. He and his partner had dug a warren below ground without finding anything worthwhile. In time, they ran out of money, then out of food. In desperation, Seamus, working thirty feet below ground, took one risk too many. It didn't pay off. His tunnel collapsed. By the time they'd dug Seamus Kelly out, it was too late to save his life. In his hand he clasped the biggest, blackest nobby any of them had ever seen."* Celeste looked up triumphantly.

"Where does this so-called curse come in?"

"Read this," Celeste waved the booklet in the air. "Seamus wasn't the only one to die. The craftsman, who cut the stone open and revealed the colour bar inside, died in a bush fire not long after. They originally named it the Redback for its resemblance to the red and black spider of that name. Soon they discovered the opal had the same venomous bite and they renamed it for the 'blood' it spilled. And that's just the start of it." Celeste handed over the booklet. "Gotta fly, see you tomorrow."

Pug let Celeste out and locked the door after her. Home was half an hour's drive away, but she was in no hurry. Dom had been edgy for days and she had a feeling another row was brewing. God only knew what it would be about this time.

Her curiosity took her back to the booklet. In her imagination, she could see the miners working two to a shaft, one below ground, the other hauling up the dirt with the windlass, could smell the sweat of men, the heat, dust, dirt and flies. It was far too good a story to leave alone. She absorbed everything she needed for her TV talk then packed the information into her briefcase, ready to go home. Tonight, she'd write it up.

3

Pug turned the Volvo into her road with a growing sense of unease at the thought of spending the evening with Dom in one of his bad moods. After seven years of marriage, she noticed the rising disenchantment. Sometimes, she thought they were going through a rougher than usual patch, other times she wondered if there was someone else. The cold atmosphere, the bad temper, the loveless bed told of his discontent. And it was getting worse; he wouldn't even sit down and talk the problem over.

Was it money? Dom liked the high life. He shuffled credit cards with the same dexterity as playing cards. They lived in a beautiful home on Mullion Road – Millionaire's Row some called it – on the banks of the Tamar River near Plymouth. They had a boat moored downriver and expensive cars.

Back in the early halcyon days, she would have been happy to share a mud hut with him. But Dom's philosophy included the old adage, "start as you mean to go on." She had agreed to use her business as collateral for the house mortgage when Dom assured her his salary was adequate for the monthly repayments. If the problem *was* money, she needed to know about it. And that would lead to confrontation. She hit the button to silence the radio music – the blare in her head was drumming enough.

In the soft evening glow, she could see lights from the next-door house between the trees. No lights shone from her home. Dom was probably upstairs in his study at the back of the house. He did a lot of his insurance company's computer work from home.

She slowed down and swung around into her drive. The remote opened the garage door on her side. She braked suddenly. Another car stood inside the garage, parked in her place. Not a car she recognised.

"Bugger!" Visitors had not been on her agenda tonight. It was probably a client seeking insurance advice. Why hadn't they parked outside Dom's garage? Reversing, she pulled over onto Dom's side to give the caller room to move out.

Laden with her briefcase, bag and jacket, she walked towards the front entrance. The potted palm had toppled over, partly blocking the hallway. Not like Dom to leave it like that. He was the house-proud one, the one who would write "fuck" in the dust if she left it more than a couple of days. The one time she'd retaliated and added "you" to his message, he wouldn't talk to her for a week.

She walked down the passage to the kitchen. In the doorway, her case and bag fell from her hands as she surveyed the chaos. Open drawers, cutlery and kitchen tools were scattered over clean tops, table and floor. Cupboard and fridge doors left open. Contents of her soup jug spilled thick red capsicum and tomato soup across the tiled floor.

Dread seeped into her mind. Her first thought was vandals had broken in; her second was to check it out before phoning the police. Dom had a hair-trigger temper. He didn't lose it often, but when he did his rages entailed throwing things around. Usually it didn't last long before he walked out and left her to clean up the mess. She didn't want to bring in the law only to find Dom had thrown a worse than usual tantrum.

Leaving her stuff on the floor, she walked to the bottom of the stairs and shouted up.

"Do--om?" The silence grew heavy. The hall and stair carpets were a mess, like he'd walked through the soup before going upstairs to his office. With her heart pounding, she climbed the stairs and approached his door.

"Dom?" No reply. Dom considered this room his inner sanctum, a place where he did his own dusting. Entry came by way of invitation. One look inside showed her the room had suffered the same fate as the kitchen. Sweat prickled under her arms.

The continuing silence sounded unnatural. Where was Ratz? With the shock of seeing all the mess, she hadn't given the dog a thought. The exuberant Jack Russell usually barked a greeting when she arrived home, hurling himself at her like a black and white football.

With both Dom and Ratz missing, it was logical to think they were together. Had Dom taken a walk down the back, along the riverside to cool off after his show of temper?

Whose was the car in her garage? She looked at the papers strewn around the floor. On one letter, the familiar logo of their bank caught her eye. She crouched, picked it up and straightened it enough to read. Although addressed to her as well as Dom, she had not seen it before. She took a sharp intake of breath.

11

The letter was to inform them that as they had ignored repeated requests to reduce their overdraft, the bank would be forced to take action. Unless they replied within seven days, the bank's solicitors would apply to the courts to initiate foreclosure proceedings. She checked the date on her watch. This was the seventh day.

Oh, God! Why didn't he tell her? She placed the letter flat on his desk. Things were going to have to change around here.

Now that she thought she'd found the cause of Dom's temper, she felt some of the tension leave her. The problem was fixable, wasn't it? Meet up with the bank manager, agree to sell the house and buy something cheaper. Dom wouldn't like giving up his Lamborghini – but if it got them out of trouble that's what he'd have to do.

Plans for instant fixes tumbled through her mind as she headed for their bedroom. She needed a hot shower, a change of clothing and time to adjust to the crisis before Dom returned. Even so, she opened the door cautiously.

With the evening drawing in, the light inside the room was dim. But she saw enough to stop her. Underneath the scarlet and black king-size duvet lay two people-sized humps.

At first, she thought she'd caught him at it. Unsure what to do next she did nothing but gape. Then the stillness registered. No sound of breathing.

The stultifying atmosphere of the room got to her, an unpleasant sweetish smell. She stood rock still, while her mind continued to assimilate the scene. Her eyes followed a trail from the duvet to the shadowy white, leather-covered bed-head now daubed in patterns of red. Involuntarily, her hands came up and slapped her mouth to prevent the scream from tearing out.

As the moments passed, she gained control of herself, understanding the reality of the scene. But was she staring at death, or injury? She had to know.

Forcing her feet to move, she stumbled towards Dom's side of the bed. She stood beside it willing her lungs to work. The duvet's rich hue had absorbed the shocking colour of blood. It appeared darker than normal, its pattern obliterated. One corner of the duvet, hanging down by the side of the bed looked free of bloodstains. She used it to lift the cover and peered underneath.

She recognised the back of his neck, the mole on his shoulder and his black curly hair, now sticky with matter. He lay naked and face down. A purple wound gaped on the right side of his neck; his scarlet pillow soaked in blood. She replaced the duvet as she'd found it, took a step back and squeezed her face between her hands to control the urge to retch.

Before calling for help, she needed to check the second hump. She could walk out now. No one would blame her. But, if any shadow of life lingered in whoever was there, perhaps she'd learn who did this. And besides, a morbid streak of curiosity demanded to know who was in bed with her husband. She edged around the king-size frame to the other side and lifted the cover.

Beneath it, a woman lay on her back; clouded eyes wide with terror, her short blond hair matted in blood. Multiple wounds to face, neck, chest and stomach released the vile smell of death. Clenching her emotions tightly within her, Pug stumbled towards the door. Had to get out – going to be sick. A small sound paralysed her. Whirling around, she searched for the source of the noise. Was the killer still here? Run or freeze?

It came again – from behind the closed door of the en-suite. She listened, breath suspended. The noise sounded like scratching. Relief flooded her system. She opened the door and Ratz burst out, his tail between his legs, his body quivering in fear. She bent to pick him up, but with the whites of his eyes showing, he fled from the room. He must have been there when it happened. What did he hear, what did he see? She ran back into the en-suite, leaned over and vomited into the toilet bowl. Her legs gave way and she sank to the floor, waiting for the convulsions to cease.

Phone police now, the words drummed in her head. There was a telephone by the bed on Dom's side, another in his study. She knew about not contaminating evidence, and so didn't want to touch anything more in this house. She climbed to her feet and without knowing quite why, tiptoed out of the room.

Once outside, barely controlling her panic, she ran down the stairs back to the kitchen where she found Ratz huddled under the table. She grabbed him and wrapped a towel around him. She collected her bag, jacket and briefcase and fled the same way she'd come in. Back inside her car, she dropped Ratz on the front passenger seat and locked the doors and windows. Then she pulled out her mobile and made her call. The police would be here in minutes.

She looked at the extra car in her garage. The image of its owner brought a fresh wave of nausea to her throat. How many times had that woman used her bed? She swallowed her bile and started the Volvo.

13

She backed out of the drive and into the circular space of the cul-de-sac ready to flee if the killer should return – looking for her.

* * *

4

As dusk fell, Sergeant Kathryn Sinclair sat in the patrol car listening to the distraught woman stumble through her story. Kathryn's car had been the second to arrive on the scene. The uniformed officer already there had placed Ms Germaine in her care, while he made a start on securing the area with tape.

Constable Jodie Bligh sat next to the trembling woman, occasionally putting a hand out to stroke her equally shaky dog. More blue lights flashing in the gloom had brought a few of the neighbours out rubbernecking.

The Scene of Crime Officers arrived and parked their van in the driveway of the up-market home, followed shortly by the doctor's Ford. White-suited personnel filed in through the front door. Lights blazed from every window in the house. More headlights turned into the cul-de-sac.

A car pulled up behind them. "This could be the DI," Kathryn said. She turned back to the young woman. "Wait here a moment."

She opened the door and stepped out to greet Detective Inspector Ed Buchanan as he climbed out of his car. At five foot ten, his was one of the few whose level gaze looked her straight in the eye.

"Sergeant Sinclair." He took a quick glance around then ran a hand through his prematurely white hair. "Looks quite a party. What have we got here?"

"Two dead upstairs, sir, Dr Denny is with them now. Victims: one Dominic Spencer, and a woman not yet ID'd. We have the wife in the car, if you want to talk to her. She's badly shaken."

"Who found the bodies?"

"She did – says she doesn't know the woman in bed with her husband."

"She found them cuddled up together, did she?"

Kathryn watched her supervisor as he pursed his lips, looking thoughtful. Although the incident had the hallmarks of a violent domestic, from what she'd heard of Ed Buchanan's thoroughness, he wasn't given to snap judgements.

"Where're Truscott and Jodie?" he asked.

Kathryn pointed towards the house. "Louis Truscott's on the door and Jodie's in the car keeping the wife company. By the way, the wife goes by the surname of Germaine, not Spencer. She has a dog with her, says it's traumatised. She won't go anywhere without it, reckons it witnessed the attack."

"So, what are we supposed to do – take a statement from the dog?" He turned away and walked towards the SOCO's van, leaving her standing there. She folded her arms and watched him go, wondering whether she should accompany him, or go back to the woman in the car. She'd only arrived at the station the month before. So far, the DI had given her no real responsibility, and seemed to regard her as wet behind the ears. She'd come as Matt's replacement and believed that was the reason for Ed Buchanan's chilly acceptance of her. That slight gleam of disappointment in his eyes whenever he dealt with her was not her imagination. She resented that – Matt's death was not her fault.

He stopped and looked back. "What are you waiting for? This is your first homicide isn't it? Let's see what you're made of – get geared up and follow me. I want a word with Bruce Denny."

She caught up with him as he headed towards the back of the van. Not that they could do anything until forensics had finished their work, but they needed to look at the death scene. Attired in paper suits they approached the house where they stopped to slip on plastic overshoes.

DC Louis Truscott's solid frame blocked the light from the front door. He stood to one side to let them enter. The duckboards were already in place as Kathryn stepped cautiously into the hallway.

"Dr Denny is up there, if you want him, sir," Truscott said, and dipped his ginger flattop to acknowledge Kathryn.

"Thanks Louis. You and Jodie take Ms Germaine back to the station. Give her a cup of tea. If she's up to it, get prints and blood. I'll be back to question her shortly. I'll see if I can get a time line off the doc first."

Truscott nodded and headed back to the patrol car. Ed turned to Kathryn and handed her a large plastic bag.

"What's this for, sir?"

"No barfing on my crime scene. If you feel the need, use that." She took the bag without a word, stuffed it up her sleeve and prayed she wouldn't need it, not in front of him, anyway. She followed him up a narrow cordoned-off section of the stairs.

16

Kathryn could smell the carnage before she reached the open bedroom door. Her stomach lurched. She tried concentrating on something else – the camera flashes that reflected back from the walls as the forensic photographer worked. Ed hesitated in the doorway, then moved on into the room. Kathryn fell into place beside him. Like he'd said, this was her first major crime scene; she was determined not to put a foot wrong.

Bruce Denny, forensic pathologist, a big bear of a man, stood beside the bed. He raised a hand in greeting. "Evening Ed."

"Looks messy. What have we got here, Bruce?" Ed asked.

Denny wagged a teasing finger at him. "Before you start, I know nothing for certain except that the victims are deceased. Who's your friend?"

Kathryn nodded as Ed introduced her. Bruce Denny gave her a warm smile. "Take no notice of our banter. It's a friendly battle we wage on every case, with Ed trying to gain any small advantage to start his investigation, and me, unwilling to pass on anything yet unproven by my laboratory." Denny turned back to Ed, "Messy is right," he said, "though, most of the blood has been absorbed by the mattress."

Kathryn looked down at the naked, blood-covered bodies, their hands already encased in plastic bags. The man lay face down, partially on his left side, left arm jutting out behind him. The woman lay face up; the bloodstained duvet was folded back for the doctor's examination and the photographer's benefit.

"Looks like stab wounds – any sign of the weapon?" Ed queried.

Denny shook his head. "Haven't found it yet – probably a knife. I'll know more later." He moved his hand quickly, gesturing to various points. "Wounds to the neck; severed artery; blood on the headboard; expiratory spatters ... arterial ..."

"Is that how the witness found them?" Ed asked.

Kathryn stood, hands behind her back, staring at the bed. No wonder the wife was in such a state. Ed glanced at her as though to check she was taking it all in, or maybe to see if she had weakened and resorted to the sick bag.

"When I arrived they were fully covered by the duvet, not even their heads showed," Denny said. "Someone covered them post mortem. You'll see the photos."

"The widow, do you think?"

17

"Not unless she was the killer or here very shortly after the killing. Some of the blood had dried between the bodies and the duvet, causing it to stick in places, so they were covered while the blood was still wet."

"And the dead woman?"

"Multiple stab wounds. Frenzied attack. He really went to work on her."

"Definitely a 'he'? Could a woman have done it?"

Denny shrugged. "I used the term generically. If she'd taken them by surprise, there's no reason why a woman couldn't have done this. She'd need to be quick and strong. Anyway, we'll know more after the autopsy, eh?" With the hint of a smile, he raised an eyebrow and winked at Kathryn.

"Timing?" Ed asked.

"Can't tell you much yet. It's a warm room – duvet to insulate them, so cooling would be slower. The bodies have reached ambient temperature, which doesn't help."

"Rigour?"

"Almost complete. At a rough guess, you're looking at eight to twelve hours."

"Right, that's a start." Ed checked his watch. "I wonder what the wife was doing between seven and eleven o'clock this morning. Have you identified the female victim?"

"We have her bag containing a full set of ID, including a standard British passport in the name of Chantelle Kohl. She had enough paperwork on her to leave the country."

"Right, thanks. Let me know as soon as you have something I can use. Are you ready, Sergeant? Seen all you need?"

Kathryn had seen more than she needed. Dead bodies were the downside of her job. The challenge started now. In working out who did this deed, she hoped to make her mark. Not trusting her voice, she nodded and preceded him out of the room.

*

Back at the station Kathryn followed Ed into the squad room where they found Louis Truscott preparing a report.

"Where is she?" Ed asked. "It's time we had a talk."

"Ms Germaine? She's had a cup of tea, didn't want to eat anything. Right now Jodie's taking fingerprints." Truscott looked at Kathryn, "Do you really think she's a suspect?"

Kathryn hesitated, but the DI waited for her to answer the question.

"She is a person of interest on two counts. She's a betrayed spouse, and she found the bodies. At this stage we have nothing else on her."

Ed nodded. "But it's early days yet. She wouldn't be the first to kill her husband and his mistress in a rage. We need to get something to either put her in the frame, or clear her entirely." He turned back to Louis. "How far have you got?"

"We have the swabs. She understood and was co-operative." Truscott said. "She turned down an offer to see the doctor, but did take a couple of headache pills. The lab's looking at her clothing. She doesn't appear to have a speck of blood on her."

"She could have showered and changed before calling us. She's had plenty of time. Put her in Room Two and let me know when she's ready. Meantime," he looked at Kathryn, "I suggest a quick coffee before we settle in. It could be a long night."

Relieved to have something normal to do, Kathryn fetched the coffees and took them to Ed's office. She told him the story the wife had already gone through in the car as he prepared the questions he wanted answered. Truscott knocked on the door to say the witness was ready.

Ms Germaine looked pale and vulnerable as she sat at the table fingering her hair. Temporarily dressed in a white jump suit she somehow looked lost without that dog in her arms. Kathryn smiled, trying to reassure her, then sat beside Ed and waited for him to begin.

In the full light the widow looked younger than Kathryn had realised. Early thirties, she gauged. The dark shadows under her eyes contrasted with the pallor of her face. She didn't seem to know where to put her hands. In turn she scooped her hair back behind her ears, folded her arms, unfolded them and clasped her hands in her lap.

"Ms Germaine, I am sorry for your loss," Ed began. "Remember, you are here on a voluntary basis, and free to go at any time. But, if you can stick it out, I'd like to ask you a few questions. The sooner we collect information, the sooner we are likely to find your husband's murderer."

She nodded and folded her arms again. "Okay."

"Right. When you opened the bedroom door, you saw two figures in the bed – what position were they lying in?"

She put her hand to her head. "I only saw two humps under the duvet. They were covered up."

"Did you uncover them?"

"I only lifted a corner of the duvet. I did put it back like it was."

"Why didn't you call us when you first saw the house had been ransacked?"

"I only saw the kitchen and Dom's office. At first, I thought Dom had messed the place up. I only realised how serious it was when I saw him ... dead."

"Did your husband often ransack the house?"

She gave him a wan smile. "Not really, but when he's in a temper and starts chucking things about, you never know how it's going to end. I didn't know what to think."

"Was your husband a violent man?"

"Oh, not towards me, only for things that didn't fight back."

Kathryn noticed the wan smile was back again. There was history there somewhere.   "Right. Since it's your home, your prints are obviously there, but did you touch anything belonging to the woman?" Ed continued.

"Oh, God, no. All I wanted to do was run. It was awful. You've no idea. Then I heard this noise. I thought the killer was still there. But, it was Ratz. Someone had shut him in the ensuite. He was terrified."

Ed's eyes met Kathryn's, his message clear. Was the widow more bothered about her dog than her dead husband?

He turned back. "When was the last time you saw your husband alive?"

"At breakfast ... was that only this morning?"

"And what was his demeanour then? For instance, did he act like he was expecting someone to call?"

She looked to one side and pursed her lips before replying. "Irritable – he's not a morning person, Inspector. After his coffee, he said he was going up to his study to work. I didn't get the impression that he was expecting anyone. I left shortly after."

"What time?"

"Around eight, don't know exactly."

"Around eight," Ed repeated it, emphasising the interesting time scale, bang inside the doc's window of seven to eleven.

"Can anyone verify the time you arrived at work?" he asked.

She looked at him and frowned. "I didn't do it, if that is what you're thinking. Okay, there have been times when I've said I could cheerfully have killed him. But, everyone gets moments like that. Doesn't mean you're really going to do it, does it?" She shuddered.

"We have no suspects yet." Kathryn didn't see the point of rattling the witness at this stage. "But it would be good to eliminate you from our enquiries, wouldn't it? Like the samples they took from you earlier, it's all part of the elimination process. Can anyone confirm the time you arrived at your business premises?"

"The shops either side of me open at nine, so I would have been in half an hour before either of them. I don't suppose anyone else would have noticed."

No substantial alibi before 9.00 a.m. The unspoken words hung in the air.

Ed resumed the questioning. "Did you leave the shop at any time during the day?"

"No – and Celeste will back me up on that. She runs the New Age shop next door. We're friends as well as neighbours."

"What does the name Chantelle Kohl mean to you?" he asked. No reaction reached her eyes. She shook her head.

"Do you know her?" he insisted.

"No, I don't. I know a bloke called Viktor Kohl, spelt with a K."

"Okay, tell me about him."

"He's Dom's friend, not mine. He sells antiques and second-hand stuff. His shop is not far from mine, bit nearer the market."

"How did he and your husband become friends?"

"Through Dom's work, I think. Originally, Viktor was a client who insured his business with the company Dom worked for. They became friends and he called around the house sometimes. They'd have a couple of beers up in Dom's study and put the world to rights, you know the sort of thing."

"Did you know his wife?"

"I never met her. Chantelle could have been her name, I suppose. Though, he usually called her Charlie."

"We believe Chantelle Kohl was the woman in your bed," Ed said.

As Kathryn noted the desolation in Pug Germaine's eyes, a sense of *deja-vu* washed over her as her own bitter history rustled.

* * *

21

5

Bone weary, Pug picked up her briefcase and preceded the detectives out of the interview room. They'd kept her until midnight answering questions. Finally, with the return of her clothes the sergeant said they'd finished for the night, and asked if she had anywhere to go. Her first thought was to call her mum. But, she'd packed her mother off on a round-the-world trip with a friend from the Over Sixties Club, on Sunday. Again, was that only yesterday – time had lost all meaning. She brought her mind back to the problems in hand. Where to go? She could stay at Mum's home, she had the key, but her car was still back at the house.

She wouldn't let the police call Celeste – not at that time of night. The problem with working all day in a shop was that most of your friends were people you met through the business, rather than socially. She'd never been home long enough to get on intimate terms with the neighbours. Dom had been her friend. Dom ... was dead.

She settled on spending the night in a bed and breakfast place near the police station. They fixed it for her.

"What about my car?" she asked Kathryn. "I'll need it tomorrow to get myself sorted. I have to go to the bank. And what do I do about the shop? When do I get Ratz back?" Her tired mind choked on unresolved problems.

"Constable Bligh took your dog home to feed him, don't worry, she'll look after him. She's nuts about dogs. He'll be here in the morning. If you give me the key, I'll get your car brought to the station for you. We'll get the formal identification of your husband's body over first thing and then you'll have time to catch your breath."

DS Sinclair apologised to the landlady for their lateness, the woman gave Pug a toothbrush, still in its wrapper, towel, soap and flannel and showed her to a room.

Alone at last, Pug sat on a bed in a stranger's room, rubbing her eyes and scrubbing her face with her hands. She drew up her feet and hugged her knees, her head pounding. Their constant probing had laid her bare. Nothing was sacred. They'd emptied her briefcase, and examined the contents. The pictures and booklets of the Blood Opal caused a stir, until she explained what she was working on, when their interest waned.

And that reminded her. What was she going to do about the TV program? She'd have to cancel. The thought of appearing before cameras in the circumstance appalled her.

With shaking hands, she opened the case and tipped the contents out on the bed. The photograph of the pendant lay face up. The beauty of the red and black stone hammered at her mind. The colour pulsated behind her eyes – the colour of blood.

She saw again the blood soaked duvet; the scarlet pillows, Dom's matted hair, the terror on that woman's face. She gazed around the unfamiliar room. Everything coloured red stood out as though it were fluorescent. The pattern on the curtains, a picture on the wall, the lampshade, and the fire regulations pinned on the back of the door. She closed her eyes. The colour remained behind her eyelids. She pushed the heels of her hands into her eye sockets and ground them until the colour turned to star-studded black. Celeste's voice came back to her. *Leave strictly alone.*

Abruptly, she left the bed, walked to the hand-basin in the corner and bathed her face in cold water. Thank God she was not the superstitious type; she had enough problems to deal with. More than anything, she needed sleep if she was to cope with everything that awaited her the next day. She laid her jacket and skirt over the bedside chair with care, as it occurred to her she had nothing else to wear until she could collect the clothes from her wardrobe.

The thought of returning to that death house filled her with dread. The sergeant told her every room had been ransacked. They needed her to go back to the house as soon as they had the all-clear from the crime scene investigators. The police wanted to know what, if anything was missing and she was the only one who would know.

In time, she turned off the lamp and lay beneath the bedcovers, staring into the darkness. Sleep wouldn't come. Sorrow at Dom's death hardened into anger at its manner. Who could have done that? The police implied that as a betrayed wife, she had a motive, but what about the woman's husband, didn't he also have motive? What were they doing about him? The image of Viktor Kohl came to mind, nothing very startling, slim build with dark hair and a prominent beaky nose. What would he have done if he'd discovered his wife's affair with Dom?

Eventually the sky paled. As daylight seeped in through the window she lay still awake and watched the details of the room emerge through the greying light. Today, she'd say her final goodbyes to Dom.

How was she going to climb out of the mire he'd left her in?

*

Kathryn finally crashed around one in the morning and slept like the dead until the alarm went off. The excitement of starting her first murder case was somewhat dimmed by the horror of the death scene. At least she hadn't weakened in front of the DI and hadn't needed his wretched sick bag.

In deciding her choice of clothes for the day, she aimed for the dress code of Ed's group, smart casual. She selected her mocha trouser suit with a paler matching shirt. Tall and barely sixty-five kilos, she looked gangly in anything less than a full cover-up. Her short fair hair posed no problem; it had a permanent laid-back style of its own.

Her home, a ground floor flat at the back of a large townhouse, had been part of a gentleman's residence in its former life. Kathryn liked the high ceiling and generous size of its rooms. She locked up and dashed out to her car, housed in a lean-to carport. Starting out this early in the morning, she escaped the worst of the rush-hour traffic. As she drove into the yard at the back of South Side Police Station, she was pleased to see Pug Germaine's Volvo there awaiting collection. Her first task would be to escort the widow to the mortuary to formally identify her husband's body.

Kathryn pushed the inner door open. Her shoes clacked on the lino as she marched down the short corridor. While the station looked nearly as old as her flat, it bore none of its charm. An attempt at modern paintwork had its walls a two-tone colour of dark blue and old corn. She followed the line of glassed-in offices to the incident room.

A constable handed her a large envelope. "This came a few minutes ago, Sarge."

Kathryn opened the packet and laid the selection of photographs taken of the two slain bodies. She read the information written on the white board and affixed the photos in the order the photographer had numbered them.

The office phone rang. Ms Germaine had arrived.

"Did you get any sleep?" Kathryn asked when they met.

"Not a lot. Kept seeing him, you know." Pug Germaine looked pale, but otherwise in control of her emotions.

"Okay, let's get the official stuff over. I can't say you'll feel any better, but at least it will be one thing out of the way."

"It's like I'm on auto pilot."

Kathryn nodded, she knew that feeling. But she didn't want to go there today. "I can understand that. When we come back, you can collect your car from the rear of the station. Your dog will be back by then, too."

She led the way outside. The unmarked police car she was using for the day was ready in the car yard. They drove in silence to the hospital. The double ring of their steps echoed as they walked down the corridor to the mortuary.

"Will you stay with me?" Pug asked.

"If you want." Kathryn remained beside Pug as she approached the observation window. On the other side of the glass, the pathologist wheeled a steel trolley into position. A sheet covered the body. She saw Pug's eyes widen in anticipation of what she was about to see. The pathologist looked through the glass and raised his eyebrows, querying whether the widow was ready.

"In your own time," Kathryn said.

Pug nodded and Denny lifted the sheet. He folded it back into the neck, carefully hiding the terrible wound, leaving only a grey colourless face exposed. Someone had cleaned the blood from the black curly hair and combed it. Bruce Denny had a sensitive side when it came to presenting bodies to loved ones, so the DI had told her.

Kathryn waited. Pug stood, wide eyes, both hands covering her mouth as she gazed at the face of her husband. It was obvious that even though she had seen him the evening before, in a worse state than this, the shock of seeing him dead all over again, jolted her anew.

She turned her head towards Kathryn, her voice breaking as she said formally, "Yes, that's my husband, Dominic Spencer." She looked back at the corpse. "Why?" she whispered.

Why what, Kathryn wondered. *Why* did he die, *why* was he unfaithful, *why* my bed?

Denny covered the face again and moved the trolley away. Kathryn took Pug out of the room. "Come on. Let's get you into the fresh air."

Once back in the car, Pug sat with shaking hands covering her face, hiding the tears. After a few moments, she turned to Kathryn. "What about the woman, what have they done with her?"

"Mrs Kohl's body is also in there. No one has yet come forward to identify her. We're still trying to track down her next of kin. You say Viktor Kohl used to come to your house to see your husband socially. Do you know where we might find him? He's not at home and not in his place of work."

"He could be away. I think Dom mentioned about him being off somewhere over the weekend. His son, by his first marriage, runs the shop when he's out. You could ask him. Viktor's an antique dealer, so he goes to auctions, sales and things."

Back at the station, Kathryn handed Pug the key to her Volvo and took her to the car yard. As they drew near, they could hear a steady lonesome bark coming from the wire compound kept for lost dogs.

"It's Ratz." Pug quickened her pace. As soon as the dog saw her, he went berserk jumping at the fence trying to get out. Kathryn set him free. He ignored her and ran to Pug. She picked him up and cuddled him, tears wetting her cheeks. Eventually, Pug put him inside her car and closed the door. She got into the driver's seat and looked at Kathryn through the open window.

"What happens now? When can I go and collect my belongings from the house? Short of going out to buy more clothes, I have nothing to change into," she said.

"I'll let you know. It should be sometime today. Where are you staying tonight?"

"At my mother's home for a while, I can't even think of living in that place again."

"Okay." Kathryn made a note of the address and contact numbers. "I'll let you know as soon as it's cleared. Stay handy in case we need to talk to you again."

She watched Pug drive out of the station wondering at the woman's self-control. Perhaps it hadn't hit her yet. Pug had caught her husband in bed with another woman, and Kathryn knew the pain of that particular humiliation. The image of her husband entwined with her best friend in the marital bed reared again. They too were still – so still that for a fleeting instant she thought she had walked in on a crime scene. When her husband's breathing erupted into a snore, her fury almost boiled over. Could she have taken a knife to him at that moment? Oh yes, and she'd have gone for the balls! But, the point was

26

– she didn't. She had turned her back and walked out of her marriage. Was that the difference between her and Pug?

She checked her watch – only ten minutes to the DI's briefing. She turned back into the building and saw Ed, striding through the front office and up the stairs. No doubt to parley with their boss DCI Hawke. He moved well – his white hair belied his forty-seven years.

She'd learned a fair bit about him from other members of the staff, Jodie in particular. Most people got on well with Ed, and no one else seemed to have come in for his cold shoulder treatment like she had.

Kathryn pushed through the swing doors into the hum of the workroom, the rattle of fax, the ringing of phones, her daily background music. If she and Ed Buchanan were going to work together on this case, she must try to break down whatever barrier he had set up between them

* * *

6

Pug parked the car in a metered space outside the bank. She checked her face in the mirror. Her eyes were still red, but otherwise she wasn't too blotchy.

It had been years since she'd come here. There had been no need. She conducted her stamp business at a different branch nearer her shop. Although they had a joint account, Dom saw to their finances. She pushed the door open and walked inside. At the enquiry counter, she asked to see the manager. The girl behind the counter looked at her sideways and asked if she had an appointment.

"No, but if you tell him it's Ms Germaine about the Spencer-Germaine account, I'm sure he'll want to see me."

The girl indicated the waiting section, and said she would be right back. Pug crossed the marble tiled floor to an area furnished with soft comfortable chairs and a low table. She picked up a magazine and idly flicked through it. It was worse than sitting in the dentist's waiting room. What was she going to say to the manager? Selling the house was the obvious move, that and Dom's car should be more than enough to get her back on the level again.

Eventually, the girl from the counter came and invited Pug to follow her. Mr Jeffery Curtis, the bank manager, remained seated and greeted her with a curt good morning. He pointed to one of the two chairs in front of his desk. She sat down, too suddenly as her knees gave out. Her hands began to shake again – she folded them under her arms. His sour expression didn't auger well for their discussion. Mr Curtis took up a lot of space, his chair was surely larger than most. His pink, round face supported dark framed glasses; eyes glinting behind the lenses watched her carefully.

"I had expected your husband to accompany you," he said, brusquely. "We have much to discuss."

Pug felt her mouth dropping open. Didn't he know? Then she realised that it was only last night she knew about it. Maybe the news of the murders hadn't made headlines before he'd left home this morning.

"My husband died yesterday." She gave him a brief account.

His mood softened a touch. He asked if she would like a cup of tea while they discussed business. She declined, wanting to get things sorted and get out of there.

"I want to know where I stand financially. How much do we owe the bank, Mr Curtis? My husband dealt with our money matters, and I wasn't aware there was any trouble until I saw your letter, last night."

The look in his eye made her feel foolish and incompetent that she should have been so cavalier with her money.

"I understand your position," he said, "But, you too must understand I have the interests of the bank to protect. Now, this is the situation." He tapped the keyboard and read out the information appearing on the screen.

Apart from the loans taken out to purchase the cars, computers, the plasma TV and a host of electronic equipment, Dom's credit cards had maxed out and the interest was galloping away into impossible figures. The house mortgage was three months in arrears.

Almost speechless with anger, she blurted out. "Why did you lend him so much?"

He told her it was a policy of the bank to be as helpful as possible to its trusted clients. It was only in recent times that the repayments failed to come in on time. But now things were spiralling out of control and it was time to rein them in.

"I suggest you talk to one of our financial advisors and see if we can come to an agreement on how to repay the debt. In the circumstances, if we can work together rather than through the courts, it would be preferable. Don't you agree? If you'd like to talk it over with Mr Pertwee, he's available now."

She didn't have a choice. The idea of having it dragged out through the courts appalled her. Curtis called in his assistant and asked her to take Ms Germaine to Colin Pertwee's office. With a sense of travelling a conveyor belt from one disaster to another, Pug followed the woman out of the room and down a corridor to another door.

Colin Pertwee was the antithesis of the bank manager. Small, slight and wearing frameless glasses, he looked smart and efficient in a charcoal business suit, striped shirt with a blue and silver tie. He sprang to his feet as she approached his desk and held out his hand. He shook hers with a light but firm touch. Thankfully, someone had already apprised him of Dom's death. When he offered his condolences, tears flooded her eyes.

Straight down to business, he asked if she had any ideas of her own to put forward.

"I can sell the house, the boat, Dom's car and all his computers, for starters. And then, if we still need more, well, I run a business. If I were to pay a regular monthly sum, can we meet it that way?"

Colin Pertwee gave her a slight, mirthless smile. "Let's put all the cards on the table first, shall we? Can you give me a detailed list of all the joint assets you and your husband hold, including any life insurance policies?"

He picked up a fountain pen and twiddled with its cap, while he waited for her answer. She noted his fingers were long and agile, his nails manicured, he looked a tidy sort of man. She'd bet he didn't write "fuck" in the dust. Or, maybe he had the sort of wife that never allowed dust to accumulate.

"Yes, he had life insurance, though I don't know what it amounts to. I don't think we ever discussed it. He works – worked for The Steadfast Insurance Company. They call it TeeSic for short," she elaborated as he wrote it down.

The way things were going, she wondered if Dom had borrowed against his life insurance as well as everything else.

Pertwee nodded thoughtfully. "Then, of course, there is the marital home, in joint names. We'll get an assessor in to give us an evaluation, and the same goes for the two cars, Volvo C70, the Lamborghini, and the yacht. What about jewellery, or any works of art?"

"I don't think we have anything of value up on the walls, but you might want to check that. I have some jewellery. I'm not sure of the value." She thought of the gifts Dom had given her over the years. The last was a pink Argyle diamond pendant he presented to her on their seventh wedding anniversary. She'd wondered at the time how he could afford such a lavish gift – now she knew. It was on over-borrowed money. "He had an expensive watch, a gold chain he wore around his neck sometimes." Did he really want her to dot the 'I's and cross the 'Ts'?

Colin Pertwee wrote the information down in neat columns. He paused – looked once more at the screen. "And then we come to your business. There is the stamp shop, and the commercial property next door, which you currently lease out. You used both these premises as collateral for the original mortgage. We can sell one with a sitting tenant, but the real value would be the premises known as Germaine's

World of Stamps. Sold as a going concern, it would bring in a substantial amount."

"Sell my business?" Her voice came out as a squeak.

"To answer your earlier question Ms Germaine, as it stands today, you would need to hand over your entire income to the bank just to cover the interest on the loans. I'm afraid your business will have to go."

*

Kathryn's next task was to visit the New Age shop next door to Pug Germaine's business. In her mind it was a loose end waiting to be tied.

The shop doorbell rang as she opened it. She threaded her way through the fairies, witches and dragons in towards the main counter. It was not her type of shop, too cluttered, too full of make believe and nonsense. The cobwebs on the ceiling appeared less than authentic, but the spiders were much too lifelike for comfort.

The scent of sandalwood in the air brought her to a standstill. She closed her eyes momentarily and breathed it in. At first she thought no one was around, then she spotted the young woman, dressed in a silk caftan of rainbow colours, at the back of the shop lighting scented oil lamps on a display table.

"Celeste Berryman?" she asked.

The woman looked up smiled. "That's me. Can I help you?"

Kathryn showed her ID. "I'm making a few routine enquiries. I'd like to talk to you about your movement yesterday morning," she said.

"Oh, alright, what do you want to know?" She blew the match out.

"What time did you arrive to open the shop?"

"Yesterday ... Monday... As it happens I was in earlier than usual. I got here about half-eight, I suppose. Had to put up another display," she said. "But I opened the shop at the usual time, nine o'clock. Oh, this is about next door, isn't it?"

"What do you know about that?"

"Pug phoned me this morning to say why she wouldn't be in. Awful. That poor woman."

"Did you see what time Ms Germaine arrived here yesterday?"

"I saw her car go up to the car park. I had only just got in myself and was too busy to stop and say hello until later. So that would've been around eight-thirty."

"What about during the day, did Ms Germaine leave the shop for any length of time?"

Celeste looked straight at her, a frown on her face. "Oh, I get it. You think Pug left her shop to go home, murder that crappy husband of hers and then come back here as though nothing had happened? You are joking!" she said, scorn in her voice.

Kathryn was satisfied Pug's alibi had been confirmed. But, against the melancholy tones of whale-song in the background, Celeste continued her diatribe.

"Look, I *know* she spent the full day here in her shop. I took the rent over at one time, some printouts of the Blood Opal another, saw people going in and out all day. No way had she left her shop that day. You're not hounding that poor woman are you?"

Kathryn smiled. "No, we're not. We're looking for answers. The Blood Opal, you mentioned. Why was Ms Germaine so interested in that?"

Celeste told her about the TV program. Again, it confirmed what Pug had told them.

"I wish she'd leave the subject alone," Celeste added. "I've told her."

"Told her what?"

"The Blood Opal carries a curse … It's all right, you can laugh, and Pug's just the same, a non-believer. Take a look into the history behind it. They say of the Blood Opal, '*Those who harm it – die.*' Its history bears that out. It's now out there on the loose, and already one man has died handling it – did anyone warn that courier?"

Kathryn's smile had not been directed at the Blood Opal, but had been more to do with a memory of her mother who had also been leery of opals. Fanatically so, in her case, she judged them all to be unlucky, without a shred of evidence.

Now that Kathryn had what she had come for, confirmation of Ms Germaine's alibi indicating Pug had nothing to do with the double murders, she didn't need any more crack-pot ideas going around her head. She thanked the woman and took her leave.

* * *

7

DC Louis Truscott drummed his fingers on the steering wheel waiting for the red light to change. Kathryn glanced sideways at him. A good solid bloke who spent time working out in the gym. In spite of his plague of freckles, he wasn't bad looking even when his complexion had him colouring up at the most inopportune moments. He was a good cop and he did things by the book, so she'd heard.

Everyone on the station knew he had the hots for Jodie. He couldn't keep his eyes off her. Perhaps with Jodie's youth and sense of fun, it was not surprising. Although, to Kathryn's ear Jodie's jokes and teasing ways sometimes bordered on the ridicule. Not that Truscott seem to notice – he lapped it up like a lovelorn puppy.

"How long have you worked with Ed?" she asked, as they drew away on the green light, on their way to Viktor Kohl's shop.

"Four months. I came in shortly after Sergeant Matt copped it," he said.

She'd been earning her sergeant's stripes in Truro at that time and remembered the case. It was enough to give any patrolman the heebie-jeebies. When officers pull over a speeding car, they don't expect a shotgun in their faces.

"At least they got the pair," she said with relish.

"And with a boot full of amphetamines, but that doesn't bring Matt back, does it?"

Kathryn shook her head.

Louis slowed the car. "There's Kohl's place, and it's open." The shop window had the words, "Antiques and Collectables," painted across it in gold copperplate. With every metered space in front of it occupied, Truscott turned into an alleyway at the side of the shop and parked in the rear yard. "Found this when I was checking up on the shop last night."

Kathryn glanced around the yard. "Looks like the back way in – it might prove useful. Let's approach from the front first, though."

Once inside the shop, Kathryn led the way, weaving between items of mellowed furniture, reminiscent of years gone by. On every flat surface stood china ornaments or other knick-knacks, most of which, she wouldn't give houseroom to.

An assistant, who looked barely old enough to shave, sat behind the counter, eyes intent on the computer screen set into a back shelf. As they approached, he stood and hit a button that silenced his PlayStation game. His gelled hair, dark at the sides, stood up in a blond tuft on the top of his head.

"Yeah?" he asked. A diamante glinted from his right earlobe.

"Victor Kohl about?" Kathryn asked.

"Who's askin'?" His eyes shifted from one to the other warily.

"DS Kathryn Sinclair and DC Louis Truscott," Kathryn said, holding out her ID, as Louis reached for his. "And you are?"

"Elvis Kohl. I work here with me dad. I run the place when he's away."

Kathryn heard the small hint of pride in his voice. Elvis Kohl fancied himself as an up and coming antique dealer, perhaps. "Okay, Elvis, and how old are you?"

"Eighteen. Whatcha want to know that for?"

"We need to speak to your father, urgently. Can you tell us where to find him?"

"Dunno. He should've been in today. In fact, he should've come in, like, yesterday. He's been around. He'd dealt with the bank and stuff before I got in yesterday. They been away for the weekend, took a van load of stuff to sell."

"Victor and who else?" Kathryn asked.

"Uncle Derrick, he's me Dad's brother. What do you want to see him for?"

"Okay, Elvis," she said, getting out her notebook. "Let's have addresses, first yours then your uncle's." She noted the information as he mumbled through it.

Louis checked his notebook and frowned. "Chantelle Kohl is your stepmother, I believe? You don't live with her and your dad?"

"Nah, I live with me own mother. She don't have nothin' to do with Dad's bit of stuff," he said, amusement scribbled on his face.

"When was the last time you saw your father?" Kathryn asked.

He screwed up his face trying to remember. "Must've been, like, Friday night when they loaded the van. Far as I knew, they were coming back Monday lunchtime. Derrick's back, so Dad's probably sleeping in. Try his home."

"I checked last night. He wasn't there then," Louis said.

"Where did they go at the weekend?" asked Kathryn.

"Up to Exeter for the weekend market – markets is good for business. Why d'you want to know all this stuff?"

"Where's your Uncle Derrick now?" Louis asked.

"You looking for me?" A man appeared from the curtained doorway behind Elvis. He came in wiping his hands on a towel, a big man, thickset, with thinning black hair. Kathryn put him around the late forties and wondered how long he had been standing there listening.

Elvis appeared startled at his abrupt entry. "They're looking for Dad."

Louis did the introductions this time and added. "We need to see Viktor urgently. It's about his wife."

"Charlie," Derrick groaned, "What's she been up to now? Had her car towed away, again?"

Louis exchanged looks with Kathryn. "It's a bit more serious than that, Mr Kohl," he said. "A woman carrying Chantelle Kohl's identity papers was found dead last night. We need to contact Viktor. See if he can identify the body. Now, do you know where he is?"

For a moment Derrick was speechless. Then, he turned away and slapped a fist into his towelled hand. "Oh, shit, not Charlie – he idolized that woman."

The boy stood open-mouthed, staring at Louis.

Derrick recovered his composure. "How'd it happen?"

"She was murdered. So, you see, we need to get hold of Viktor quickly," Kathryn said.

"Jeez man. I don't bloody know where he is." He jerked his thumb in the boy's direction. "He's got a key to Viktor's place – you want him to take you there? It's all right, Elvis, I'll manage the shop."

Outside Viktor's house, Kathryn told Elvis to stay in the car. As there was no reply to their door knocking, they used the key. While Louis swept through the ground floor, Kathryn called Viktor's name and mounted the stairs. Nothing looked out of place. She reached the main bedroom. One cupboard door was open. A very few items of female apparel hung lopsidedly from hangers. On the floor, a long-haired chestnut coloured wig lay curled like a sleeping ginger cat. Kathryn opened the second cupboard.

"Shit! The bastard!" She glared at its emptiness. "He's done a bloody runner! Louis, gettup here."

35

Louis' feet pounded the stairs. She pointed at the empty wardrobes. "Look! He's gone. Taken his clothes and buggered off."

"Shit! He could have twenty-four hours on us."

"Pity you didn't break in last night."

He looked at her as though searching for criticism. "Last night I didn't have reasonable cause to break in. You don't break down the door to tell a man his wife is dead."

"It's okay, Louis – hindsight is a wonderful thing." She phoned in to report their find and asked for a search-team to examine both home and shop premises. She turned back to Louis, who was still looking mildly hurt. "Back to the antique shop. We'll get the brother to identify Mrs Kohl."

They found Elvis sitting outside the car on a low wall waiting for them. The sullen look on his face suggested he was prepared to argue his right to get out of the car.

Kathryn patted his shoulder and opened the back door for him. "It looks like your dad's taken off somewhere in a hurry. Any idea where?"

Elvis shook his head violently. "He didn't say anything to me."

Louis drove into the walled-in backyard as before, and parked alongside a lean-to shed filled with, what appeared to Kathryn to be piles of junk furniture, or maybe they were antique items waiting for their makeovers. Louis climbed out of the car and inclined his head indicating he was going to look around.

Kathryn followed Elvis in through the back door. He took her through a storage room, an office with a kettle and drink-making equipment, and on to the curtained doorway that led into the shop. She looked around the place where Derrick had stood and eavesdropped on their earlier conversation. This time the tables were turned. Kathryn was in time to hear part of a heated conversation. Derrick Kohl's voice sharp, angry – his fist thumping the counter.

". . . told you, I gottit in hand. Just bloody tighten it up, mate ..." He turned his head and saw Kathryn approaching and wheeled around, his back to her. "Gotta go." He snapped his mobile shut and turned to face Kathryn.

"What's your problem?" he asked.

"The problem is we can't find your brother," Kathryn said. "It appears he has left home and taken all his clothes. I ask you again, Mr Kohl, do you know where your brother is? We do need to contact him."

"Don't you think I would've told you if I did, what with his missus dead, an' all?"

"Was that him on the phone?"

"No – a customer bellyaching about a late delivery."

"We need someone who can formally identify the body of Chantelle Kohl. I understand you knew your sister-in-law well. Would you be able to do that for us?"

"Jeez man, that's Viktor's job. Can't you wait until he turns up?"

"No, Mr Kohl, we'd rather get on with it. And we need to ask you a few questions, too. So, if you would get your coat, our car is out the back."

"I'll be right with you. I need to discuss business with Elvis before I go." He called Elvis over and Kathryn stepped aside to let them talk.

Louis popped his head around the curtained door. "Here," he said, beckoning her.

She followed him out to the yard. "What have you got?"

"Might be nothing, but the incinerator in the yard has recently been used. It's cold, but not cold enough. Feel it, what do you think?" he asked.

She opened the shutter. Inside the fire was out, the ash grey. It was still much warmer than the air outside. Not everything had burned out. She took a poker and drew some of the solid pieces towards the front. She picked out one piece. It was warm to her fingers. Although black and burnt, it was recognisable as a metal button, the sort you see on jeans or overalls. Other metal pieces of different shapes lay among small bones.

"So, who had the time to spend burning this lot, considering they're short handed with Viktor absent," she said. "Well spotted, Louis."

"That's been done in the last twelve hours, I'd guess," he said.

"Stay here. Keep an eye on it. Don't let Elvis near it. We don't want anyone shovelling this lot out. Phone in and get forensic down here to check it."

Derrick came striding towards them, a scowl on his face. "What do you think you're doing?" he asked. "Shouldn't you have a warrant if you're going to poke around the place like this?"

"Why, have you got something to hide, Mr Kohl?" Kathryn said. "Do you object to us having a quick look around?"

"It's not my bloody business, is it?"

"Precisely. But you are here, so perhaps you'll be good enough to tell us what it was you last burnt in there." Kathryn pointed to the incinerator.

"Nothing. It's not me. Maybe Viktor burnt some of the rubbish we brought back, stuff that wouldn't sell. That's what it's for, burning rubbish."

Kathryn opened the rear car door for Derrick to enter. "Yeah. C'mon, let's go."

* * *

8

Derrick Kohl's manner was a little more subdued than it had been earlier. Having come face-to-face with his dead sister-in-law and her horrific injuries may have had something to do with that, Kathryn surmised, as she showed him into an interview room. All they knew about Kohl so far was that he'd left the army last year, was a bouncer at the Laughing Parrot, and odd job man to his brother, Viktor.

Ed followed them in, put a file on the table and sat down. He leant back in his chair, hands clasped together behind his halo of white hair, relaxed and chatty.

"Odd jobbing, a bit of a come down from the army, isn't it?" he said.

"I'm having time out. Get the discipline of the army out of my system."

Ed leant forward. "Right, Derrick. Let's get down to business. When did you last see your brother?"

"Around seven o'clock on Monday morning when I left him."

"Left him – where?"

"At the shop. We'd just got back from Exeter, from the Antiques market."

"Wait ... let's backtrack. You went to Exeter, when? Start there."

Derrick let out a sigh as though he found it all too much trouble. "We started out late Friday afternoon, drove to Exeter to the bloody Indoor Market Place and set up our stall. We opened Saturday first thing. Come Sunday afternoon we'd sold a fair bit, and Viktor was happy enough with that. The plan had been to get back home by lunchtime Monday, only Viktor changed his mind, said he wanted to get back earlier."

"Did he say why?"

"He doesn't like leaving the boy on his own for too long. We loaded what was left Sunday night and set off around dawn Monday, arrived back around seven that morning. We unloaded the stuff, and I left him to it."

Ed paused and looked at something in his file.

"Did you go straight home?" Kathryn asked.

Derrick turned to look at her, his dark eyes unfathomable, a hint of amusement hovered around his lips. "No, I called in to see Janine on the way."

"Who is Janine, and where does she live?" Ed asked.

"She's my ex-sister-in-law, Janine Kohl." He paused, looking from one to the other. "She's Viktor's first wife, Elvis's mother."

"What's your relationship with Janine?" Kathryn asked.

The smile disappeared. "She's my girlfriend. Not that it's any of your bloody business."

"Does Viktor know about this relationship?" she asked.

"'Course he knows. Why should he care? He's happy with what he's got."

Ed resumed the questioning. "Okay. How long were you at Janine's?"

"Three or four hours, I suppose. When I arrived, Elvis was getting ready for work, he left and I stayed on till eleven then went back to my place."

"When did you last see Chantelle alive?"

Derrick shifted his position and paused to think. Kathryn studied him. At six feet two with the build of a heavyweight boxer, he had surprisingly small hands and stubby fingers.

"Must've been last Friday, before we left the shop."

"Did you know she was having an affair with Dominic Spencer?"

"No." He gave a mocking laugh. "It doesn't surprise me. Never could see what a sexy little number like her saw in Viktor, poor cow."

"Over the weekend, did you notice anything odd about Viktor's behaviour?"

"Nah, same as ever."

"Who else was at this market who might remember seeing you and Viktor there?"

"I can give you a list if you like." He smirked. "Dozens, I should think."

"Someone lit the incinerator on Monday. Was that you, or Viktor?"

"I wasn't there. Must've been Viktor, Elvis said he hadn't touched it."

"From the shop, would Elvis be aware of who came into the back yard?"

"Not unless he came out the back door to look. You can't see the yard from the shop."

"Okay. Thank you Mr Kohl. That's it for now. Perhaps you would write out that list of who saw you at this market place and, in particular, who made contact with Viktor." Ed turned to look at Kathryn and raised his eyebrows.

Her glance flickered back to Kohl. "That's a nasty graze you have on your hand, how did you come by it?" she asked.

Derrick held out his right hand, looking at it. "Oh, yeah, that. Got it unloading stuff from the van, scraped me hand along the edge of the door. Bloody hurt at the time, too."

* * *

9

S ell her business! Pug left the bank, reeling from the news. She climbed inside her car and closed the door before giving way to a wail of despair.

Ratz, waiting for her in the back, leapt over the front seat, his tail whacking the air in his efforts to console her. He wriggled onto her lap, making grunty noises, his cold nose probing her neck. She hugged his black and white body, tears stinging her eyes at the touch of familiarity in this new, alien world of hers.

Eventually, she moved him to the passenger seat. "Stay. We're okay; we're going to manage. You hear me?" Her voice came out a lot firmer than she could believe. If talking to the dog gave her confidence, she'd be doing it all day.

She started the car and without any clear destination in mind, concentrated on simply manoeuvring through the traffic. In time she realised she was back on familiar roads heading towards her shop. Where else? Dom was dead. Life as she'd known it was over. A taste of bitterness exacerbated her grief.

She parked at the back of the shop and took Ratz with her. Police sirens sounded in the distance. They were coming from the other side of the market. Kohl's antique shop was over there. The nagging questions at the back of her mind asked, had Dom and that woman been murdered due to a burglary-gone-wrong, or had Viktor Kohl unwittingly visited Dom and caught the pair of them out. Whichever, both Dom and that woman paid a high price for their extra-maritals.

Pain hit her behind the eyes as she saw a note stuck on her door. "Sorry, closed due to family bereavement," it read. Celeste's work no doubt. Pug had phoned her early this morning to tell her what had happened and why she wouldn't be in the shop today.

She took the notice off, unlocked the door and walked into the familiar atmosphere, determined not to break down. Working by rote, she followed her usual routine, put her briefcase under the counter, hung up her coat, put the kettle on and opened the safe.

There was the valuation she was working on only yesterday. How could so much have happened in so little time?

She telephoned the customer; he said he'd be in within the hour. Next, she rang the TV station. Joan, her producer, had been waiting to hear from her. She'd heard the news and was not surprised when Pug said she couldn't make the program this week. Pug offered to send the information she'd already compiled on the Blood Opal, complete with scanned photographs of the relevant stamps, if they still wanted it.

It wasn't a comforting thought that Joan already had someone in mind to take her place for that night. Pug put the phone down, instinctively knowing that was the end of another era. She dealt with a few minor enquiries and actually sold some first-day covers, but it was not a market day, and business was always slow on a Tuesday. Once the customer collected his albums, she stuck the notice back on the front door and told the dog to stay. "I'm just going next door, won't be long."

Entering Celeste's shop was like walking into a magical cavern. Glittering fairies gathered around rocky grottos, silky spider webs decorated the ceiling corners whilst collectable witches on broomsticks hung from a starlit painted ceiling. Pug breathed in the scented air of the aromatherapy section. Burning candles, warming oil and incense sticks thickened the atmosphere with their essence.

"Hi Honey, won't be a moment," Celeste called, from beside a customer examining a display case of amethyst, tiger's eye, and other colourful gemstones. Pug waited until the shopper had completed her purchase.

As the customer walked out of the door, Celeste came from behind the counter. "I am so sorry to hear about Dom; you must be devastated." She took Pug by the arms, and pressed her down onto a wooden barstool in front of the counter. "Want to talk about it?"

"I don't want to – but I've got to. There's something you need to know," Pug said. Before she got on to business, she told Celeste of her arrival home yesterday and filled in the details she had omitted on the phone. Occasionally, the entry of customers interrupted her account and she fell silent until they'd gone. She'd never realised how popular Celeste's line of business was.

"So, what it boils down to is I'm going to have to sell up. That means Germaine's, and I'm sorry to say, this property."

Celeste's eyes widened, her mouth dropped as she realised what Pug was saying.

"It's all right," Pug added hastily. "Don't worry about your business. It shouldn't make any difference to you. Nobody can evict you; you have five years to run on your lease. All it means is a change of landlord. You'll be giving your rent cheque to someone else in future."

"And you'll be left with nothing?" she asked. "How can they do that?"

"Easily, apparently. I could object, take it to court and hope for a better deal. But with so much owing the chances are I'd still lose the lot. Then I'd have legal costs to pay on top. And it will drag on for months. I don't care about the big house, Dom's stupid car, or all the fancy jewellery, but the stamp business is different. That was *mine*. And the boat – we used to have a lot of fun in that. We were supposed to be taking time off and sailing to Spain in August."

"But you could still fight them. How can you give up so easily?"

"I'm not giving up. I'm doing what's best for me. I don't want to fight. I don't want anything more to do with it. Whatever I do, I'm going to lose the business. After that, nothing else matters. One day I may want to go back into business. I don't want the bankrupt label hanging around my neck. Right now, I want out, cleanly, ASAP."

"Where are you going to live? What will you do?"

"I suppose, like anyone else, I'll get a job somewhere. I want to cut the dead wood away and start afresh. They're working everything out on paper first and getting the assessments in. The longer we leave it the more the interest mounts. If I cooperate, it'll be quicker and there might even be some left over for me."

Celeste leaned on her counter and looked into her eyes. "You know, there could be something in it. What they say about the Blood Opal bringing bad luck," she said softly.

Pug was feeling too miserable even to raise a smile at the suggestion. "It has nothing to do with it. All I have is pictures, posters and stamps. I've never even seen the wretched stone. And I don't believe in that sort of mumbo-jumbo, anyway. No offence."

"There are many things in this world we do not understand." Celeste put her hand out, and touched Pug's arm. "Don't mock it, okay? I've a spare room, if you want until you get sorted. You'd be very welcome to stay."

Pug squeezed her lips together and turned her head away. She concentrated on the face of a dragon breathing pretend fire outside a papier-mâché castle. Celeste's offer pierced the shell she'd begun pasting around herself.

"Thanks, I really appreciate that. But I've decided to move back into Mum's house until she gets back from her holiday. I was going to keep an eye on the place anyway."

"What did your mum have to say about the news?"

"I haven't told her yet. She's been in transit. But I have the number of the hotel she's staying in." She checked her watch. "She should be there by now."

"You can ring her from here if you like."

"Thanks. I'm dreading it. If I know my mum, I'll have to go through it with her in detail. It's best if I do it from my place."

Pug's mobile rang and it made them both jump. They exchanged looks – was she too late, had Mum already heard?

It was Sergeant Kathryn Sinclair. "We have clearance from SOCO to go back in the house. Can I meet you there around 4:30, today?"

That was only an hour away. "I'll be there," she heard herself say.

"Gotta go," Pug said as Celeste's doorbell jingled and a customer entered. She gave Celeste a wave and returned to her own premises. Ratz greeted her as thought he'd thought she'd abandoned him for the day. It was time to make the dreaded call.

The sound of her mother's cheery voice brought a lump to Pug's throat that threatened to choke her as she tried to pass on her message.

"Hey, hey, slow down. What are you saying? Dom's dead? Murdered! How, when?" Pug gave her the salient facts without mentioning the financial side of things.

"Oh God, darling I am so sorry. You must be distraught. Look, I'll cancel the holiday and get the first flight back. I'll be with you in no time. You need people around you."

"No Mum, please don't." Mum's fussing, however well intentioned, was the last thing she needed. Eventually, she persuaded Mum not to cancel her trip.

"One thing, though. Could I stay at your house until I've sorted things out? I don't want to go back to mine."

"Of course you can, love. And listen, ring Peter, he'll help you sort things out, right?" Peter Arbeleiter was Mum's solicitor. He would be a good man to have on side.

By the end of the call – her mother finally shocked into silence. Pug's knees buckled and she sank to the floor.

*

45

Ed's impatience drove him back to the mortuary. He'd attended the autopsy earlier, but had to wait for serology results to come through from the lab. He needed answers.

Bruce Denny looked up from his paperwork. "You again, why don't you move in?" the pathologist joked.

"Not my scene, too cold." Ed scraped a hand through his frost-white hair. "What've you got for me?"

"Weapon is confirmed as a knife. Come."

Denny took him back to the examination room. He pulled the sheet down, revealing part of the stitched "Y" cut on Dominic Spencer's body.

"It wasn't a traditional slitting of the throat, but more a stab at a vulnerable spot. Your killer started out on the left side of the bed, with the victim lying face down. He thrust the blade into the exposed right side of his neck, cutting the windpipe and severing the main artery. Not a pretty way to die."

"Size of knife?" Ed asked.

"Minimum length: twenty centimetres, probably more, as there's no handle compression. Width: three centimetres at it's widest. Blunt one side and sharp the other, narrow pointed tip. No bits of blade left behind."

"Could a woman do this?" He pointed at the blue and purple wound.

"Still gunning for the wife, eh? Possible."

"In this scenario, could one person tackle two people at the same time?"

"Possibly. Both victims were asleep when the first blow fell."

Ed knew Denny better than to think this was speculation, but he wanted it spelled out. "Okay, talk me through it."

"The male was struck first, whilst asleep. No defence wounds. The female was on her back, but only one of her wounds was inflicted from *her* right. Inside that wound were two different types of blood. So, the male victim's blood had come in on the blade."

"You're saying the attacker struck the man first, then leant across him and stabbed the woman?" Ed repeated, to get it clear in his mind.

"That first blow to the woman's abdomen would have incapacitated her long enough for the killer to move around the bed to her side to finish her off. Defence lacerations on arms and hands. Cause of death, stab to the heart."

"What can you tell me about the assailant?"

"Average height, a small person wouldn't have had such an effective reach. Fibres and hairs are currently being analysed. We might get lucky."

"The killer would have been covered in blood. How the hell did he get away in daylight without anyone seeing him?"

"Fortunately, my friend, that's your problem – not mine." Denny said, with a smile.

* * *

10

Stomach churning, a head fit to bust, anyone would think he'd been on a bloody bender. He gently kneaded his temples trying to rub the pain away and swallowed a couple of pills. He needed to think.

It should have been a perfect job – they'd got clean getaway. Then the whole thing had blown up in their faces. Their plans ruined in the gory aftermath. And for what, a piece of arse, a quick screw? Why the hell couldn't they have waited just long enough to get the business done? Now, if he couldn't come up with the merchandise, he'd be in dead shit. Problem was he didn't know where to look. Was he wasting his time here?

He kept his eye on the parked Volvo. He may have to wait until she closed the shop, but she was his last hope. Then he spotted her crossing the car park. He checked his watch, nearly four. This could be the break he needed. He started his motor and leaving plenty of room between them, he followed her car.

It soon became obvious she was going home to Mullion Road. He overtook the Volvo and went on ahead. He left his transport by the riverside car park and jogged to the end of the cul-de-sac. The road ended in a semi-circle of green lawn, planted with a weeping willow tree. Good cover once he was under its umbrella, and from there he could see right into her drive.

He nearly shit himself when the first car arrived. It was not the widow, but the tall female cop in an unmarked car. He hadn't been expecting that. Within minutes the Volvo turned in. He'd been working on the assumption that if the widow had become involved, then sooner or later her actions would give the game away.

But the cop there was a worry. Did the widow intend to front up to her? He let out a string of oaths at the turn of events. He couldn't go in, fists flying and force them to hand over the merchandise – he could be on the wrong horse altogether. Never had a job gone so bloody wrong. The two women disappeared into the house. He could do no more than stay put and see what developed.

*

The thought of going back into the murder house made Pug feel panicky. It had gone beyond butterflies; the grinding sensation inside her belly felt more like a cement mixer at work. Ratz whimpered as she turned into their road.

"It's all right; you won't have to go inside. I'll leave you in the car. Okay?" Kathryn's unmarked police car stood in the driveway. Pug pulled up beside it. On reflex, she touched the remote. The garage door swung up; her space was empty.

The sergeant approached her. "I hope you've prepared yourself for the mess," she said. "It'll look even worse than when you last saw it."

Pug knew that. They'd already explained that it would negate the exercise if they cleaned up before she'd checked it for anything missing.

"I'm okay." There couldn't be much left to faze her. She straightened her shoulders and willed her shell to grow thicker. She walked ahead of Kathryn, through the garage towards the door leading to the laundry, her usual route into the house. In the passageway, between the house and garage, she saw zip-up canvas bags lying on the ground, women's clothing scattered about.

"Well, for a start, that lot wasn't there when I left home Monday morning," she said, with steel in her voice.

The large kitbag Dom used when they went on sailing holidays lay on the floor in the laundry. It was also empty. His clothes scattered haphazardly around. Her basket of ironing stood on top of the washing machine, no longer in its neat folded pile.

When she'd arrived home the previous night, she'd entered through the front door, and had gone out the same way, so she hadn't seen this mess before. It hit her with sickening reality once again that Dom had been in the process of leaving her. A wispy notion touched on the edges of her mind. Something else in the laundry room was not right, but as she tried to grasp its evasive image, the thought disappeared.

The soup puddle on the kitchen floor had congealed into a red pancake. Dark fingerprint dust created shadows where normally there were none. A marker pen had circled things on walls, floors and cupboards. The place smelled foul.

Kathryn stood beside her. "I know this is distressing, but it really will help. If it gets too much for you, let me know and we'll take a break. Okay?"

Pug regretted her offer to help. She didn't need this and the sympathy in the sergeant's voice was getting to her. "What do you want me to do?"

"Start here," Kathryn said. "In particular, I want you to look at the cutlery and tell me if there's anything missing. It doesn't matter what you touch, SOCO's finished here. Don't worry about the cleaning – we have contract cleaners to do the job."

No matter what Kathryn said, it needed a bit of tidying up just to see things in the right perspective. Collecting the kitchen tools together, she looked around again.

"The carving knife is missing. It's normally kept in that knife block." They searched all the drawers. It was not in the kitchen.

"Oh God, is that what he used?" It brought it home to her, more than anything she'd seen so far. She knew that knife – she used it almost daily. Hot saliva washed her mouth as she recalled the sensation of the knife slicing into raw meat.

"Right, let's move on." Kathryn led her out of the kitchen.

As she visited each room, Pug shook her head. "The pictures are askew, but nothing's missing here. Look, even loose money is still lying about."

"Whoever did this didn't vandalize for the sake of it," Kathryn said. "And it wasn't petty thievery either. They were looking for something specific. What?"

"They? You think there was more than one?" Pug asked.

"It's possible."

The bedroom reeked. Pug unsuccessfully tried to avert her eyes from the bed as she felt the icy touch of déjà vu. With the pillows pulled down beneath the duvet it looked almost the same as when she'd first seen it, two humps in the bed. She looked around the rest of the room. It was dusty with more strange markings on walls and doors.

The dressing table drawer stood open. "Ah, look here, the jewellery's gone." Pug said. Finding a reason for this madness was almost a relief.

Kathryn quickly came to her side. "Where was it?"

"In here. Only my old stuff is still here." She picked up her gold cross and chain that her dad had given her, and a charm bracelet she'd had for her twenty-first and put them in her pocket. They had sentimental value and would not be included in the bank's haul. The gifts that Dom had given her over the years were missing.

"There should be a string of pearls, a sapphire ring and matching earrings. We kept them in here, except the Argyle diamond, which Dom kept in his safe," she said.

"Safe? You didn't mention a safe."

"I forgot." She'd heard the edge to the sergeant's voice. "I just forgot, that's all, I wasn't trying to hide it. It was Dom's. I never used it."

"Where is this safe?"

"Downstairs, in the lounge, I'll show you. Can I collect my personal stuff, now?"

"Let's finish the search first, and then I'll help you carry it out to the car. Okay?"

Pug looked through the open door to Dom's office. A mess of scattered papers, the same as she'd last seen it, only the empty spaces on the desk were new.

"His computers have gone. I'm sure they were there when I last saw this room."

"The computers have been taken in for examination. Don't worry, they'll be returned. Anything else that's different about this room?"

"Not that I know of. This was Dom's lair."

"Let's go find this safe."

Back in the lounge, Pug pointed to the floor. "It's under there." She pushed a small table aside, lifted the rug beneath it and dragged it away. She put her finger in a knothole in the parquet flooring and lifted a section out to reveal the metal face of an under-floor safe. "I've never liked it. It was too much of a hassle getting into it."

"Do you know the combination?" Kathryn asked.

It was a mixture of their birthdays. Pug tapped in the set of numbers and the lid clicked. The safe underneath held a leather document case. She went to lift it out.

Kathryn raised her hand. "Wait. This hasn't been fingerprinted." She took a pair of latex gloves from her pocket and snapped them on, then lifted the case out and laid it on the floor in front of her.

"So, what's in here, do you know?" she asked.

Pug shrugged. "Papers, I suppose."

Kathryn inserted her ballpoint pen into the zip tag and without touching anything, unzipped the case around three sides, and then opened it out like a book. Pug leaned over to look. One of the pockets held Dom's passport, in the others, she saw personal papers, credit cards and a wad of banknotes. Lying loose in the centre, between the two leather sides of the case was a soft black velvet bag. Kathryn opened it enough to show its contents. She whistled softly as a diamond pendant necklace slid forward, then the rest of the jewellery that Pug had told her about.

"Looks like he'd packed all the valuables ready to leave the country," Kathryn said. "And, you had no idea?"

Pug closed her eyes, as she understood the completeness of Dom's betrayal. Not only was he leaving her for another woman, and leaving her to clear up his financial mess, but in taking away the gifts he had given her, he was thumbing his nose at everything they'd ever meant to each other. She tried to control her anger in front of this policewoman. But the bitter words spilled out. "No, I bloody didn't. What kind of a shit does that?"

Kathryn zipped the case. "I assure you there are plenty of them about." She shoved the case into an evidence bag, her face grim. "I'll give you a receipt for this, and get it down to the lab for them to check out. Do you think this is what the searcher was looking for?"

"Who knew we had it? He only let me wear that diamond outside the house once, and that was to a private party with friends of his. He said it was for security reasons."

Kathryn gave her a speculative look. "Odd. Didn't he want you to show it off?"

Pug looked away. There were other times she'd worn it. The sergeant didn't need to know about those. Dom had a yen for the pretty, pink rock, as he referred to it. Upstairs on their scarlet bed, he liked to see her dressed in nothing but the Argyle diamond, brilliant under a spotlight. It turned him on. He'd take her through the whole gamut of his sexual repertoire. She knew he was getting off on the glitter, not her, but so what – if that was what he liked – it was harmless. Had he done that with his new woman? Why should she care? He was dead.

"Did Viktor Kohl ever see this diamond?" Kathryn interrupted her musing.

"Oh, yes. It came from his shop. As well as antiques, he deals in second hand jewellery. I think Dom brokered some deal with him. Dom would give him good rates on his insurance business and Viktor would let him know when something special was coming on the market. It was a business arrangement. I don't know the details. But Viktor didn't know about the safe. Dom said only he and I knew that."

"Okay." Kathryn took her mobile from her waistband. "You go and collect whatever belongings you're taking. I have a call to make."

Pug collected the contents of her wardrobe, the dog's bed and food. She could hear Ratz barking in the distance. No doubt he was fed up with being in the car.

He continued to bark as she went to and from the house with her belongings. Kathryn helped her load her laptop, files and backup. There was no point in taking anything else of value; it would all have to be written off against the debts anyway. On her way out through the laundry for the last time, it came to her. She stopped abruptly.

"What?" Kathryn asked

"That!" She pointed to the laundry basket on top of the washing machine. "Dom's sweater is missing. It was on top of that, and his grey cords, they've gone too."

Kathryn raised her eyebrows. "You sure about this?"

"The sweater – it was dark red. I had to hand-wash the wretched thing, or it turned everything pink." She looked down at the mess of clothes around the floor, they were not there. "Why would anyone take *them*?"

"Because they were clean," Kathryn said.

Pug looked her in the eye. "Oh, not bloodstained, you mean."

"Yes, that's how he got away. Good. We can use that in his description. Now, are you finished here?" Kathryn locked the house as they left. "You'll get the keys back after the cleaners have done. You aren't planning on going away in the next few days, are you?"

"Only to my mother's place."

"Good. Stay around we might want to talk to you again."

Ratz continued his barking. "Shut up, Ratz. We're going right now."

"You all right?" Kathryn looked concerned.

Pug nodded and climbed into the driver's seat. She silenced Ratz with a soothing hand. With one last look at the house she'd shared with Dom, and hoped never to see again, she engaged the gear and followed Kathryn's car out. She drove to her mother's home, stopping only to pick up a take-away – she still needed to eat.

She arrived as dusk was falling, weary beyond measure. Opening the front door and crossing the threshold brought her a sense of security – like entering a secret hidey-hole. She'd grown up here, gone to the grammar school down the road, attended business school at the tech and got married from this house. Nothing could harm her here.

*

When the dog started barking, he slid deeper into the foliage of the willow tree. The barking slowed, but didn't stop. The bloody dog knew he was there.

The women returned, they appeared friendly enough – it wasn't an arrest job, then. He watched them load the widow's car. Something odd was going down. The cow was moving out, just when he needed to keep track of her. The next time they disappeared inside, he emerged from his hiding place, ignored the dog's renewed barking and jogged back to his car.

He waited until the Volvo appeared from the cul-de-sac, then he pulled out and followed her to her next bolthole. In a moment of self-congratulation, he conceded his time had not been wasted.

* * *

11

In her mother's old semi-detached house, in the same bed she'd used as a child, Pug slept well. It made a change from her usual restlessness, with Dom snoring beside her. Today, she woke to the sound of songbirds outside her window. That was before the weight of recollection dropped like a shroud over her shoulders. Dom was dead.

She lay staring at the moving shadow of a tree sweeping the ceiling. When the telephone rang, it jolted her into the new day. She ran down the stairs to answer it, thinking it was Mum checking up on her yet again.

"Ms Germaine? It's Colin Pertwee."

She recognised the name, the financial advisor from the bank. She recalled the neat dapper man with the deft movements and quick mathematical mind. "Yes?"

"I want to arrange a time for the auditors to do a stock-take and general audit at Germaine's World of Stamps. Would some time today be convenient?"

She closed her eyes and monitored her breathing. It had begun.

"Are you there?" His voice, sharp and businesslike sounded in her ear.

"Yes, I heard you," she said, her voice suddenly losing power as ordered thought evaporated from her mind.

Although she didn't want the break-up of her finances to drag on, she dreaded its inevitable progression. She fixed a time with Pertwee for later that afternoon. A quick call to her Mum's solicitor, Peter, confirmed he could see her this morning. The sun shone through the circular stained-glass window in the front door and lit the tiny hallway. Ratz sat on the bottom stair, head tipping from side to side, ears cocked, watching her.

She hung up and wandered from room to room picking up this or that of her mother's possessions and putting them back. In one silver photo frame, the coloured picture inside showed her with pigtails and a gap tooth, her smiling father in a dark-cherry-red jersey. Pain scythed through her head as she recalled Dom's similar red jersey, stolen by his killer. The sergeant had told her composite photos would be made of Victor, their prime suspect, wearing those clothes and circulated. He'd had a twenty-four hour head start. London to Paris in two-and-a-half hours on Eurostar – he could be anywhere in the world by now.

She dragged her thoughts back the framed photo. They were on the family's sailing dinghy, and she was holding the tiller. The memory was so poignant she could almost smell the sea.

Her dad taught her to sail. He'd made her a Mirror dinghy from a kit. She sailed with the junior club members and even won prizes. She'd loved her dad and over the years, he'd groomed her to take over his business when he retired. But the take-over happened earlier than either of them expected. When she was twenty-two, some hoon ran a red light and crashed his speeding car into her father's wagon. Her dad died before they could cut him out of the wreckage.

Another photograph showed her and Dom on their wedding day. She closed her eyes, overcome by a searing sense of loss. Not wishing to be reminded of that day, she placed it face down in the sideboard drawer.

In the kitchen, she put the kettle on for coffee before she remembered she had no milk. The fridge stood empty, turned off for the duration of Mum's holiday. She also needed bread, fruit and other food to eat. The corner shop was still in business, she could pick up some groceries there. "Come on Ratz; let's go get some people food."

His favourite "f" word had him dancing at her feet.

*

"Come, take a walk with me," Ed whispered in her ear. Kathryn looked up startled, she hadn't heard him approach. Why was he being so mysterious? Intrigued, she shut down her computer and followed him back to his office.

"What's up? Where are we going?" she asked.

"Back to the house."

She groaned at the thought of entering the crime scene yet again. She'd had her fill of the Spencer/Germaine residence. "I thought we'd given the keys to the cleaning contractors."

"Not until four-thirty. I want another look before it's too late."

He waved a rolled sheet of paper at her. "I called at the lab on the way in. There is something we need to take a closer look at. Let's go."

With no windows open, the atmosphere at the crime scene had not improved. It hit Kathryn in the face as she opened the front door once more.

"Phew! Smells like a bloody slaughterhouse," Ed commented, as he made his way down to the kitchen. He unrolled his chart onto a clear area on the counter. "Look at this."

She held down one corner of the curling paper. "Clue me in, what is it?"

"It's the floor plan. This is the pattern of footprints throughout the house. As we found it difficult to tell the red soup stains from the bloodstains, serology has charted the vegetable matter in yellow, to make it clearer."

Kathryn glanced at the dried up soup stains on the floor and the shoe prints left by someone who had walked through it, and compared them with the corresponding yellow daubs on the chart.

Ed continued. "According to their chart there are *no bloodstains* in the trashed rooms on the ground floor, apart from the route from the stairs to the laundry. I want to verify that by literally walking in their footsteps." Kathryn followed him though the downstairs rooms.

Serology had been right. Now the stains had dried out, it was easier to see the difference between the two types of stain. The soup stains still appeared red, whereas the bloodstains had gone brown with age.

"So, what does this mean? Are we looking at two perpetrators? One who did the killing and the other who searched the house?"

Ed shuffled the papers and found a separate sheet showing a pair of full-sized shoe prints. "This is the tread of the trainers found in an outhouse at Viktor's home. Note, in both cases, red and yellow, the shoe print looks identical. The left one, in particular, has a nick in the third tread down from the toe. *This one pair of men's trainers made two separate journeys through the house.*"

"Then, it does look like two perpetrators," she said.

"Except they couldn't both be wearing the same pair of shoes."

"Well, obviously not at the same time. What if the killer searched the place after he'd cleaned himself up?"

"Unlikely. The lab says that with the quantity of blood involved, the perp would have taken traces of it wherever he went. We know he hadn't rinsed his hair, showered, or used the bath – he only used the laundry sink. There were no bloodstains on the bags containing Spencer's clothes. If the killer had been the one to open them, there would have been residue. Secondly, some of the scattered clothes were lying on top of the bloodstains on the floor, so the evidence indicates the emptying of the bags came *after* the murders.

"Okay," Kathryn said, "What if that one perpetrator worked alone, went away, cleaned up more thoroughly elsewhere, changed his gear and then came back to search the house, still wearing the same shoes."

"Possible. Viktor Kohl was one of the few people to know they possessed the Argyle diamond. If we are to assume Viktor was our killer, then the search of the house makes sense. But ..."

Kathryn raised her eyebrows. "You doubt it?"

"The team found no blood traces in Viktor's house."

"So? He could have taken his bloodied clothes straight to the incinerator."

"Then, at what point did he empty his wardrobe? And, more to the point, how did his size eight shoes get home, and if he took them, why didn't he burn them along with his bloodied clothes? At this stage, we cannot be certain that Viktor was present at the crime scene – *only, that his shoes were.* "

* * *

12

When Pug arrived at the solicitor's office, she learned her mother had already phoned and put him in the picture. As Pug expected, he wanted to fight it out in the courts, but when he could not guarantee to save her business, she refused to let him go any further. All she wanted was someone to represent her and to ensure the bank gave her a fair hearing. That he promised to do.

While she was there, he'd called Colin Pertwee with a view to hammering out some sort of deal that would let her get on with her life. She left his office in a lighter mood. At least something was on the move.

Back at the shop she pulled up on a double yellow line outside the door. Scrawled across the front of her display window were the letters R.I.P. spray painted in red.

"Oh shit!" Her earlier moment of optimism plunged. This was an answer to Celeste's note on the door about the family bereavement, she assumed. Moron.

She unlocked and quickly moved inside to phone the graffiti removal service. Before the auditors arrived, she wanted to take out her personal possessions. Her British Commonwealth Stamp Collection for one. It had been her dad's, and after his death, she'd kept it up. Now, it was worth a lot of money. But it had nothing to do with Dom, and she wouldn't let them take it from her. She opened the safe and removed the albums into the boot of her car.

The Blood Opal stamps were still there in her safe, not yet returned to their drawer. She felt the pull of its beauty, its rich colouring. With its history and its present notoriety it would have made a terrific story for the TV program. The one Joan put on in its place was mundane in comparison. Maybe one day she could still do that story. She collected the remaining opal stamps into a large glassine envelope and dropped it into her briefcase, to join the booklet and printouts Celeste had given her already there.

While she was loading the last of her personal belongings into the car, the graffiti man arrived. He got out of his van and surveyed the message on the window.

"That's real nice of somebody. Kinda makes your day, doesn't it?" he said.

"I've known better starts to a day, but they're thin on the ground just lately." She left him to it, took her car to the parking area and walked back to the shop.

The auditors arrived dead on time. A man and a woman, wearing grey business suits and calculating looks. Pug showed them where everything was and relinquished the keys for them to open the safe.

"It's all right Ms Germaine; you can leave us to get on with it. It'll take a few hours, if there is something else you'd rather be doing," the man said diplomatically to her. What he meant was they were in charge and would Pug kindly bugger off out of their way.

She could twiddle her thumbs, take Ratz for a walk, or talk to the graffiti man who was still working on her window. There was no reason for her to stay. Once they had done the audit, she could sell nothing, anyway. For a few minutes she watched the two of them at work, their calculators clicking away her time and money. With a lump in her throat, she turned the notice from Open to Closed for the last time.

"If you want me, I'm in next door," she said to no one in particular. She put Ratz's lead on and took him with her.

Celeste, tall and willowy, looked lovely. Today's caftan was dark blue with silver sequins. She looked as though she'd wrapped herself in the night sky. She smiled as Pug walked in, then returned her attention to her customer.

"Can I make you a cup of tea?" Pug asked Celeste as she finally bagged the order.

"Mm, love one, make it chamomile."

Pug brought the two cups out from the shop's tiny back room when she heard the customer leave.

"How's it going?" Celeste asked. "Are you still carrying pictures of that opal around with you?"

Pug did have a purpose in taking the remainder of the opal stamps. One day she would put together another stamp story, but in the meantime she had a personal stake in them and that had nothing to do with good or bad luck.

60

"Can we agree to differ?" she asked, tired of Celeste's insistence that they were the cause of all her troubles. "They are only stamps, pieces of paper. They can't hold a curse."

Celeste shook her head. "Let's hope you're right."

Pug pressed her lips together, let out a deep sigh and changed the subject. "Dom's funeral is on Saturday. It's going to be awful."

*

As funerals went, it was one of the worst Pug had endured. Her dad's had certainly been the most heart-breaking. She and her mum were emotional basket cases by the end of it, crying into each other's shoulders heedless of people around them. In contrast, this one had no pretence of being a celebration of Dominic's life. It was a raw service of necessity prior to cremation. She mourned the loss of the love and trust they had originally shared in their early days. Her sense of betrayal remained painfully present.

Dominic's parents travelled from London. They booked into a hotel for the night. Pug did not attempt to offer them accommodation at her mother's place. Even Dom had never got on with them and hadn't made contact with them for years. She'd met them only a couple of times. They did condescend to attend the wedding, but the memory of his mother's plaintive voice echoed through the years.

"A shop girl, Dominic? Is that the best you could do?"

They'd brought friends with them and they huddled together, casting embittered looks in her direction. Pug knew exactly who they believed responsible for their son's death.

Representatives from Dom's insurance company attended and said nice perfunctory things about him. Friends of Dom's, who she knew only vaguely, turned up to stand around looking like spare parts.

With her mum still away, if it hadn't been for Celeste turning up to support her, Pug would have been alone. The detectives were there to watch and wonder, but Viktor Kohl, Dominic's closest male friend, was a no-show.

*

His car moved at a funereal pace, partially hidden by a hedge of climbing roses which divided the public from the private roadway. He

61

pulled into a parking space, stopped, and killed the motor. He watched the family groups gather outside the chapel of rest.

He didn't give a shit that Dominic Spencer's body would be going up in flames any minute, all he wanted to know was where had he put the damn thing? He must have been the last to get his maulers on it. Did his missus find it, or not?

He raised his binoculars and spotted the widow. A small woman in a drab loose dress, face grey, expression grim. Silly cow, no wonder Spencer filled his bed with something tastier. She was acting the grieving widow all right, but giving nothing away. How much of the plot did she know?

For all he knew, Spencer may have clued her in. If so, the bitch could have found it and was keeping it under wraps until the ruckus was over. Or, was revenge on her mind? Get back at her cheating husband by handing it in and claiming the reward, and so drop the rest of them in the shit. But until he was sure he couldn't show his hand.

He swung the binoculars around checking out the rest of the group – didn't know any of them. He was getting nowhere. He turned his glasses to the shapely blonde beside the widow and followed her every curve. She was more his style.

His phone rang, rattling him. He looked down at his mobile flashing on the passenger seat and licked his lips. The last time *they* called, it was to threaten him with a nut-crusher if he failed to deliver.

The message ran out. His eyes lit on the last line "... unless you'd rather a bullet in the brain..."

* * *

13

Sunday morning: Ed was on the receiving end of a very early call. Forensics had made some interesting finds amongst the wood-ash in Viktor Kohl's incinerator. He looked across the bed to his dozing wife. "I'll be right there," he said to his caller.

Helen waved her fingers at him and cuddled further under the duvet. All right for her, she didn't have to get up. He called Kathryn and arranged to meet her back at the station. Then he slid down under the covers, spooned around his wife's back, nuzzled into her neck and slid his hands up her sleepy-warm body. She let out a tiny squeal as he nibbled her earlobe.

"Mm, that good, eh?" he murmured.

"Your hands – they're freezing."

"Only the phone hand. Anyway, can't stop for any more." He stumbled naked from the bed and into the shower. There'd be no nooky this morning.

John Daly, the forensic investigator was in his twenties. Short, slim and dark haired, his pasty face swamped by oversized spectacles. "Here's the report," he said. "I've separated the different items we found and labelled them as far as we can identify them."

"Right. What have you got?" asked Ed. Bemused, he watched the various plastic bags come out of Daly's case. Kathryn picked up one and studied its contents.

Daly peered at it. "That one's metal buttons – the kind you see on boiler suits, or overalls. I found fifteen of them, some more burnt than others. Also, metal clasps like you find on trousers, and a couple of zips. Whoever did the burning didn't wait around for everything to burn out."

"But he obviously did burn clothing," Kathryn said.

"If you count up the metal remains I'd say probably two, maybe three sets of men's clothing," Daly said.

Ed raised his eyebrows. "Anything else useful?"

"There's this." He pointed to a larger plastic bag containing a few pieces of hard black material. "It's animal hide. It could be part of a leather satchel, briefcase or something similar, but not the right shape for shoes. We also found a medallion."

Daly checked through the bags until he found one containing a small round metal disc with the remains of a light chain. "It looks like it had been attached to something."

"Whereabouts in the incinerator did you find the leather and chain?"

"Near the top, along with the buttons, among the last burnings, I'd say."

Ed studied the medallion through the plastic. "It has something embossed on it."

Daly referred to his notes. "Yes, there're a couple of letters on it, could be a code number, initials, or a fancy zip tag. It reads G.D. Might prove useful for identification purposes, but I wouldn't hold my breath." He grinned at them, pushed his spectacles further up his nose. "Anything else you need to know?"

"I'll be in touch if there is." Ed said, as Daly turned to go.

Ed looked at Kathryn. "Three sets of clothes?"

"For three different men – or perhaps three sets for the same man, do you think?"

*

The following morning, Kathryn drove the unmarked car along the A38 on the way to Exeter. In the passenger seat, Ed was absorbed in the list Derrick Kohl had given them of the contacts he and Viktor had made in the two days preceding the murder.

Ed's silence allowed Kathryn's early memories to creep in. Exeter was home turf – she'd completed her initial training in the police headquarters there some ten years earlier.

Back then, her boyfriend of the day had objected to her working night shifts with male partners. Objections had escalated into tirades, then threats. But until the day he'd actually hit her, she'd been reluctant to acknowledge that the relationship was abusive.

She'd finally given the bastard his marching orders, furious with herself for being in denial for so long. How ironic, when the reason she had joined the police force in the first place was to stop domestic violence. She'd seen the way the black eyes and broken ribs had turned her best friend's mother into a cringing shadow. Back then, she'd had no inkling of how a man's charisma could hold a woman tighter than any chain – but she did now.

Hurt and confused, she'd married one of his friends on the rebound. He hadn't had a jealous bone in his body, and she'd thought she'd been saved, until she'd discovered that total lack of jealousy arose from a total disregard for marriage vows. The divorce had left her questioning her own judgement when it came to men. How could an intelligent woman like her make such foolish choices?

She smiled to herself as another thought struck her. Pug Germaine's friend, Celeste, would lay the blame on fate, crystals and the stars. All Kathryn would have to do was get rid of the opal ring her grandmother had given her and Mr. Right would saunter through the door. As a child Kathryn had loved the shimmering stone, with its vibrant blues and greens. Her mother had been so leery of opals that Gran had willed it to Kathryn instead. She still treasured it and wore it for special occasions.

As for Ed's marital status, she'd learned he was firmly hitched to Helen, a former cop. His was a long-lasting, solid relationship that few dared violate. Any who tried, and there had been some, were stonewalled until they learned better manners.

Ed snapped his sheaf of papers as though coming to a decision. The market manager had faxed the stall plan and the names of the participating vendors. He tapped a finger on a section of the top paper.

"Our first job is to locate the stall holders on either side of the Kohl brothers."

Kathryn turned her face to look at him. "What makes you so sure someone got to Viktor at the market?" she asked.

He cleared his throat. "Viktor's family had seen no change in his behaviour recently. Yet, the day he returns from this market, he *allegedly* kills his wife and her lover. So, did he get to hear of his wife's affair *before* that Monday morning? We need to find out. If he did, that's his motive. He could have turned up unexpectedly to have it out with Spencer, found them together and lashed out in fury."

"A crime of passion." She paused, "I see it as rage, and rage has to be triggered."

"And you think that's a good excuse?"

"No, I don't!" She looked at him sharply, saw the smile play around his lips and decided he wasn't taking the piss.

"It makes you wonder why the lovers left it to the last day that Viktor was away. Why not go Saturday, or Sunday?" he mused.

"Because ... Dom's wife was at home over the weekend, but on the Monday she would be back at work. It gave them a longer time before anyone discovered their absence."

"Viktor insisted on going home earlier than planned. Why? I don't buy his excuse about seeing the boy was okay in the shop. Viktor supposedly dealt with the banking before Elvis opened the shop, but never even made contact with the boy. And, why does the bank say they received nothing from Kohl that day? Where did their weekend takings go?"

"In his pocket? He took it with him – extra cash for his getaway," she suggested.

The traffic increased as they reached the outskirts of the city and conversation petered out. Kathryn pulled into the car park of the police station where they were due to pay their courtesy visit.

"We shouldn't be too long in here," Ed said, opening his door.

Sergeant Wilson was behind the front desk and had been expecting them, but he didn't look too happy at their arrival.

"Sorry sir, I can't send an officer with you," he said to Ed. "I've no one spare right now. We're being run ragged with our own problems." He jerked his thumb towards a poster on the wall behind his shoulder. It was a reward for information leading to the safe return of the missing Blood Opal. "You've come at a busy time."

Kathryn noticed it the moment she walked in. It was a copy of the photo she'd seen in Pug's briefcase. She recalled Celeste's comment, *Those who harm it – die.* A little shiver danced along her spine. Of all the police stations they could have come to – it had to be this one.

Ed raised his eyebrows. "That robbery, on your patch, was it?"

"Centurion House, five minutes down the road. You'll pass it as you go," Wilson said and gave them direction to the Indoor Market Place, eager to send them on their way. Once back in the car, Ed made a call to the market manager to let him know of their imminent arrival.

"Perhaps now we will learn more about our missing suspect," he said. "Keep your eyes and ears open. No matter how minor, if anything sounds out of kilter – sing out."

* * *

14

Pug couldn't believe a whole week had gone by since Dom's death.
It still felt strange not going into the shop, yet it was not like
being on holiday either. She slumped into a chair. What was she going
to do with herself all day? At least she didn't feel as bad as she had
yesterday. Sunday had been awful. Sunday, it had finally hit home.
She'd woken in a morass of depression and couldn't drag herself out
of bed. Scenes from the funeral replayed in her mind. Other scenes of
happier times, thoughts of carefree sailing holidays, sun, fun and
laughter taunted her as she lay under the duvet, hiding from the world.

Tears had soaked her pillow, as she indulged in an orgy of what-
went-wrongs, what-ifs and similar negative thoughts. No one was here
to see her, she could cry as much as she liked. Perversely, the tears
dried, as though that very admission was enough for them to say, okay
we've done our bit. Now get up and get on with it. The bedside clock
had read nearly eleven, and the dog was desperate to go out. That was
yesterday.

So, what was she going to do with today? She got up, showered
and ate some cereal. When the telephone call from her solicitor came,
it provided relief and gave her a purpose. Peter needed her to sign
some papers. Could she come in today? Would ten o'clock suit? Pug
returned to the kitchen to fix the coffee.

On the way to Peter's office, she wondered about the papers he
wanted executed. When would she have to relinquish the car? What if
he asked for it today, how would she get home? She glanced across the
front passenger seat at Ratz, with his head out of the window, ears
flapping in the wind Dumbo style. She hadn't travelled on public
transport since she was married. Did they even take dogs on buses
these days?

Peter Arbeleiter invited her into his office with a benevolent smile.
He asked how she was and if she'd heard from her mother lately. The
niceties taken care of, he offered her a chair and sat behind his desk,
waiting for her to settle.

"We have some good news," he said, jerking his wrists out of the cuffs of his Armani suit jacket. "I've completed the property search, there are no caveats outstanding. This means that nobody apart from the bank will be expecting to receive anything from the sale of your properties."

"That makes a change," Pug couldn't resist saying. He looked at her over the top of his rimless glasses, a sparkle in his eyes, a smile hovering around his lips.

"And, the Argyle diamond currently being held by the police is being returned. All the figures are now in, everything has been taken into account and on paper there appears to be a surplus." He beamed.

Hope quickened. "The stamp business?"

Peter inclined his head to one side. He looked crestfallen, as though his good news had fallen flat. "Ah, I'm sorry, not to the extent of your business. In fact, the bank already has a prospective buyer for that. You're lucky it's located in the trendy part of town. Those commercial properties are highly sought after. The quicker the property goes the better for you." He tapped his desk softly with his pen.

"So, what is left for me?" A lump lodged in her throat, heavy as a brick.

"An approximate surplus of thirty-thousand pounds, the bank has calculated the figures on the lowest acceptable price in each instance. They suggest that you accept that sum, or the equivalent in kind, immediately. That will let you get on with your life. Then when everything has been sold and the bank's loans fulfilled, there may even be an additional surplus, depending, of course, on the proceedings going as projected."

Thirty-thousand pounds. The cash wouldn't be enough to buy a home no matter how modest, and there was no way she would get a mortgage now, even with that as down payment. If taken in kind, she could keep her car. It was a last year's model Volvo C70 with low mileage. Today's market price would be around that figure. But, what was the use of driving a prestige car if she couldn't afford to insure it, or even buy the petrol to go in it? "Do I have to decide right now?"

Peter sat back, a frown on his face. "It's a good deal. I thought you'd jump at it. You could invest the amount and bring in some interest to tide you over until you find gainful employment. But you don't have to decide now. Go home and sleep on it. Give me a call in the next day or two."

Gainful employment. Ten days ago, she had gainful employment. She drove home to her mother's place thinking about how to apply for a job. With her place in her father's business assured, she'd never had to do that before. Perhaps she'd look online and see what opportunities were available. By the time she pulled into her mother's drive, her mind was busy formatting her CV.

*

Trevor Gardiner, a tall, lanky man in an overlarge brown suit waited for them at the main door. He introduced himself as manager of the Indoor Market Place, and asked what they wanted to see. Ed told him, then asked if he'd been there at the weekend and if everything had gone as normal.

The man dropped his cigarette stub and flattened it with his heel. "Yeah, no problems, other than the usual."

"What's the usual?" Ed asked.

"Oh, you know a kid gets lost, a mother panics. Someone tries to nick off with stuff they haven't paid for, cops come flying in. Someone has too much to drink and starts a fight. Nothing worth writing home about, but it all has to be sorted."

"What about Kohl's stand, any disturbance noted?"

He shook his head. "Nothing reported."

They followed Trevor into a vast open hall where a mild odour of stale coffee and curry hung in the air. A layer of scuffed dust covered the floor; discarded papers littered the corners, chairs and tables stacked in piles. Their footsteps echoed on the wooden floor as Trevor led them to a far corner. He checked Ed's diagram and pointed to an empty space.

"That's where Kohl's Antiques and Collectables stall would've been. Next door that way, was Jimmy the rocking horse man, kid's toys he does, all hand-made, you know, in wood. Nice stuff if you like that sort of thing."

"And on the other side?" asked Ed.

"He was the wood-turning bloke. Make your own furniture. He demonstrates how to do it with his machines, sandpaper and tins of stain. Both of them regulars, they have their own permanent stalls in the outdoor market if you want to catch up with them." He grinned, showing a mouthful of brown teeth.

Kathryn looked around, trying to imagine working in here on a stall for two days. Where were the loos, for instance? How did they manage about leaving their stand? At least in the Kohl's case there were two of them.

"Where did they eat?" she asked Trevor.

"There's the hot-dog stalls, Indian take-away, Chinese, you name it, they're all here at the weekend. Or they could go up to the canteen." He pointed to an upstairs area at the far end of the hall, now unlit and empty. "They'd take it in turns, or get someone to keep an eye on their stall while they go and eat. A lot of them do that, being neighbourly like."

Ed walked towards an exit sign on the wall not far from the back of the Kohl's stand. "Where does that door lead?"

"Out to the car park. It's an emergency exit, never locked in trading hours."

Ed tried the door. It was locked. He looked at Trevor.

"Ah well, see, it's not trading hours today." He took a bunch of keys that were hanging from his belt and opened the door.

Ed pushed his way through and found himself outside the building not far from where they had parked the car. "Is it used as a short cut? Can people come in through here behind the stall holders?"

"You can't come in that way. It's an emergency exit only. Well, not unless you've fixed the door first, but that's against the rules. Not that the rules stop anyone, you understand." He treated them to another mahogany smile. "You didn't get that from me!"

Ed pointed to a CCTV camera fixed on a high point on the edge of the building. "Do you have the footage of that weekend still available, should we need it?"

"Nah, the cops came and took it. After that opal robbery, they took the footage from every camera surrounding Centurion House. Anyway, what's all this got to do with the Indoor Market Place?"

"Probably nothing, Trevor, thanks for showing us around. Right now, where will we find the Kohl's two neighbours?"

*

The outdoor market was on the other side of the car park. Stands of every kind, grouped together in a large courtyard. Some, not much more than a large table under a plastic roof, others like an open fronted canvas tent selling everything from cheap souvenirs to blown glass

70

ornaments. Under an overcast sky, traders with open barrows of fruit and vegetables called out their prices and joked with their customers.

The wood turner displayed his finished articles for sale. He remembered the Kohl brothers, but he hadn't had much to do with them. As far as he was concerned, nothing out of the ordinary happened the whole weekend.

"Let's go and get a coffee," Ed pointed to a small café with outdoor tables nearby. Kathryn heard the frustration in his voice. They took their coffees to a table, sat and watched people go by. Ed's phone broke his reverie.

"Louis Truscott," he told her afterwards. "He has the latest info on Spencer's jewellery. The Argyle diamond isn't hot but still a 'bit iffy,' his words."

"What does he mean by that?"

"They've traced its provenance. It used to belong to the wife of some wealthy TV guru. She'd got herself in over her head with a gambling debt and pawned the diamond to pay it off. Because she needed to keep it quiet from her husband, she didn't get the funds back in time to reclaim it. The pawnbroker sold it for way below its actual value. Guess who picked it up."

"Viktor Kohl's Antiques and Collectables," Kathryn said.

"And, he sold it to Spencer. The transaction was legal."

"So, Spencer gets it at bargain price. What about the rest of the jewellery?"

"That also came through Kohl's business. Kohl could have obtained them the same way, but until we're sure, we're hanging on to them. The diamond will be returned to Spencer's estate."

"So, what does Kohl get out of it?" she asked.

"Makes you wonder, doesn't it? Especially, as Spencer was shafting his wife." Ed said, getting up. He waited pointedly while she downed the last of her coffee. "Let's go and find the rocking horse man."

Jimmy sat at the back of his tent, chipping a wooden block that had the recognisable shape of a sailing boat. Carved wooden artefacts covered his display counter, a solitary rocking horse hung from the framework. Jimmy rose and stepped forward to meet them, giving their badges a cursory glance. Tall, slim with long hair, a wispy grey beard and John Lennon glasses, he was casually dressed in jeans and sweatshirt.

"Yeah?" he asked. Chisel in hand he listened to their opening spiel. "Yeah, I know the Kohls. What do you wanna know?"

"We're primarily interested in Viktor Kohl," Ed said. "Did you notice if there were any signs of arguments, or bad mouthing going on at his stall?"

Jimmy looked blank. "I dunno. I didn't notice anything like that."

"Okay," Kathryn said, "let's break it down a bit. We're interested in how Viktor Kohl spent his time here. For instance, did he stay on his stall all day on both days?"

"Had his breaks. Had to eat, take a slash, if you know what I mean."

"And who looked after the stall when he had these breaks?"

"He and his brother took it in turns. A couple of times they went off together, then I'd keep an eye on their stall. And they did the same for me."

"When were these absences?" Ed asked.

Jimmy frowned a moment. "Breakfast the first day. We hadn't really got started. They'd set up the stall early, then hiked off for breakfast up at the canteen, it was quiet then, no one around. I kept an eye out for him. Then teatime Saturday, around four I suppose, he and Derrick said they were going up to the caff for a cuppa."

"How long were they away that time?" Ed asked.

"About thirty, forty minutes I suppose. I didn't actually see the time they got back – they were just there." He sniffed.

Ed cocked his head. "Could they have come in the back way?"

"Well, they said they were going up to the canteen. If they were going out, they should have said. As it happens, I wasn't too busy at the time, so it didn't matter."

"Right, Jimmy. So, you can recollect nothing that might have upset Viktor over the weekend." Ed tried one final time.

Jimmy smiled. "Nah. Quite the opposite, specially, when he came back from his tea break, him and his brother slapped each other on the back and joked around like they'd won the lottery."

* * *

15

Kathryn sensed Ed thought something was 'out of kilter' as he'd put it earlier. He looked pensive as they left Jimmy the rocking horse man and walked back to the car.

"Right. Let's get back to Sergeant Wilson," he said. "I need to see that footage."

"I think I know where you are going with this," Kathryn said, starting the car. "If the Kohl brothers were supposed to have been upstairs in the café having a tea break, why would they return through the back door? If they needed to go out, why pretend to Jimmy they were going to the café? What was the point of lying?"

"Exactly. First we need to confirm they did return through the exit door," Ed said. "If they didn't, then the point is moot. Don't mention this to anyone yet. Right?"

Sergeant Wilson was still behind the counter when they walked in. He leaned forward, his heavy eyebrows raised. "Did you find what you wanted at the market, sir?"

"Not yet. What's the name of the officer in charge of the opal robbery case?"

The sergeant looked at him. "That'd be DI Theo Pappas. Did you want to see him?" He picked up a phone at Ed's nod.

They waited a few minutes then the internal office door slammed open and a fast moving officer strode in heading for the sergeant's counter. Tall, built like an athlete, he talked rapidly into his phone, his free hand waving erratically and a look of frustration on his face. Abruptly, he closed his phone and tilted his head at the duty sergeant.

"What now, Wilson?"

The sergeant nodded in their direction. He repeated their names. On hearing their ranks, the shadow slipped away from the officer's face, as though he was pleased to see colleagues rather than more members of the public. Ed, who had been perusing the notices on the wall turned and put his hand out.

"Theo Pappas," the officer said, shaking Ed's hand, then Kathryn's, his dark eyes seeking hers. "You guys are far from home, what can I do for you?" He looked from one to the other.

Ed answered. "Can we talk in private?"

"Sure, come this way." Late thirties and, Kathryn noticed, taller than both her and Ed, Theo Pappas led them to a small interview room.

"Take a seat. The sergeant thought it was to do with the opal robbery. If you have anything that makes sense, I'd welcome it. We're under a lot of pressure to make an arrest. But you can't arrest thin air, can you?"

Ed pulled a face. "Sorry about that, but it's not about the robbery itself. We're hoping you might have something for us." Ed told him about their search for the suspect in their double murder case. "I understand you have the CCTV footage from the back wall of the Indoor Market Place. Our man was working there that same weekend, and we're trying to track his movements."

Theo's sigh marked his disappointment. "We should have everything within a one-kilometre radius of Centurion House for that Saturday. What time is your interest?"

"From three until five p.m. should do it."

Theo cocked his head. "Interesting time frame, it's the same as ours. Do you want to do it now? You can't take the tape away with you. But if it'll help, you're welcome to look at it here, or I can get someone to make a copy, if you're in a rush."

"Rather look at it here, right now, if that's convenient."

They followed him down a corridor through the workroom to a side office.

"We're hellish busy here. The Blood Opal's insurance company has put up a large reward for its return undamaged. Every man and his dog believe they saw something suspicious that day. It's not making my job any easier with people muscling into the enquiry hoping to get rich. Right, there're a couple of monitors in here." He indicated the small room.

Inside, an officer sat in front of one screen watching it with glazed eyes. He raised his head and nodded, then turned back to watch time drag by in monochrome.

"You must have hundreds to get through." Kathryn said, watching shadowy figures cross the officer's screen.

"We're still sorting them," Theo said. "We haven't reached the market tapes yet."

A young woman, in uniform, carrying a cardboard box came into the room. Loose strands of dark hair fluttered around her harassed face.

She gave Theo a tired smile. "Last box."

"Gina, perhaps you'd help our visitors," Theo introduced them then turned to Ed, a look of relief on his face. "I'll leave you in Constable Gina Mattock's hands. Use that monitor, she'll get you the tapes you want. I'll come back and see how you're getting on later. Okay with you, Gina?"

*

An hour later Ed sat at the table, his eyes fixed on the monitor. He occasionally looked away and rubbed his face with his hands, to stop his skin turning into parchment. Of all the jobs in the station, this surely must be the dullest. Back home he would have delegated this to a junior, but here only he and Kathryn were available. She had gone out seeking Gina, and hopefully a cup of tea for them both.

The officer on the other monitor had changed shift half an hour ago. A young constable now watched the screen with care. Like Ed, she was waiting for that little shift that might indicate something interesting. He looked back at his screen. Whoa, what was that? He backtracked and tried again. The grainy black and white picture still showed a portion of the car park, a side wall of the market building, and the outside of the fire exit door behind Kohl's stand.

He'd observed the comings and goings of anonymous traffic over the last hour. Now, as he watched, a large white van, with no logo on the sides, crept into the scene and stopped near the door. The distance was too great to get any fine detail.

Kathryn came into the room with a tray, two mugs of tea and a plate. "Got some. Also, got a couple of blueberry muffins, if you're interested," she said, putting the tray down on the table beside the monitor.

"Sounds good," he beckoned her towards the screen. "Take a look, we might have something here." He rewound a couple of minutes. He felt the air move as she came to stand behind him.

On the screen, the large, white van appeared again and stopped. Two men got out, one from the front passenger seat, the other from the rear. Both men wore dark clothes, one man a full head taller than the other. They walked away from the camera's eye, pushed the fire exit

75

door open and disappeared inside. The white van continued into the car park and pulled into a bay. The time on the digital clock read 16:35.

Ed bit his lip, straining forward trying to make sense of the grainy detail. "Can you see who's behind the wheel?"

Kathryn leaned over his shoulder, her mouth open, watching. "Not yet."

The driver's door opened. A woman in a black business suit climbed out. For a moment, her face was straight on to the camera. She slid back the rear door of the van, reached inside and pulled out a large, bulky shopping bag. She locked the van and walked away, but only to the next row of parked cars, to a light coloured sedan. She placed the bag inside on the back seat and climbed in the driver's side. Within seconds, the car backed out, she turned and drove steadily out of the car park.

Chantelle Kohl drove a silver Sonata and Viktor, a white van with no logo.

"Recognise her?" If he was right, the last time he had seen this woman she was laid out, a bloodied mess on an autopsy table.

Kathryn stepped back; her eyes had taken on a gleam of excitement. "It's gotta be. Let's get the techies to enlarge the pictures, see if we can confirm the registration numbers. If that *is* Chantelle Kohl, why did Derrick claim not to have seen her since Friday?"

"And, if those two are the Kohl brothers, where have they been in that thirty to forty minutes they were away from their stall?"

Their eyes met. The timing was perfect.

* * *

16

Pug didn't need to sleep on it. Long before bedtime, she'd made up her mind. It was too late to call Peter. He would probably try to talk her out of it, but once the idea took hold there was no stopping it. Come the morning she anxiously watched the clock until it reached the time her solicitor's office opened.

"Peter? I've decided what to do about the bank's offer." She firmed her voice to show him she was brooking no argument. "I want the boat."

There was a strained silence on the other end. "The boat?"

"Yes, the boat. She's a sailing cruiser, with a 25 horsepower motor. She's fibreglass and in good nick. Second hand boats of her class are currently fetching around the thirty thousand pound mark. There should be no problem if, as you said, I could take it in kind."

"I know its value – I have it written here. I'm surprised you'd want it, that's all. What will you do with a boat?"

"Live on it. It will provide a home and mobility, well, around the coast, anyway."

"Are you sure you won't reconsider the lump sum? You could invest it and watch it grow. How can you afford to run a yacht like that?"

"What's it going to cost me? It doesn't need anything doing to it this season; it has mooring fees paid up to next year. Sails are good; the wind is free. All I need is the diesel for the occasional use of the motor and that will be minimal. Later on, if I'm desperate, I can always charter my yacht to sailing holiday-makers, so it can even make money for me." That should satisfy his need to see her obtain some financial security. She could hear the tap of his pen on the desk as he thought about it.

"Alright, I'll put it to the bank and we'll see how quickly we can get it organised. I'll give you a call when I hear back from them. Are you sure you wouldn't like more time to think it over?"

"Peter, I do know what I'm doing – with boats anyway. I'll be fine."

*

Ed leaned forward in his chair. His eyes only inches from the screen as he rewound the short section of tape.

"Play it again," Kathryn said.

The constable on the other monitor sensed their excitement and glanced curiously across at them. "Found something?"

"Could be. Not sure, yet." Ed hit the play button.

"A pity we can't see the men's faces a bit better," Kathryn said, as the sedan drove out of the car park one more time. She picked up a mug of tea. "Sugar?" she asked.

"Two please." She handed him a mug and two sachets.

Kathryn heard footsteps as someone came in behind her. She turned to look. It was the tall, handsome Greek.

"Are you getting anywhere?" Theo Pappas asked, standing behind Ed and looking at the screen. Ed ran the tape again from the time the van first entered the picture.

"We think our suspect is one of these two men, the shorter of the two. Their stall is on the other side of that door. At the time this was taken, they should have been in the canteen, or so their neighbour who was looking after their stall said. So, we're wondering what they're doing outside the building, and where have they been?"

Theo pointed to the digital clock. "How long have they been out, do you know?"

"Their neighbour, Jimmy, the rocking horse man, said they'd been gone thirty to forty minutes."

"Who's the woman?"

"We think she's our suspect's wife. If so, she was one of the murder victims. Can you get this section of the tape blown up? See if we can identify the vehicles."

Theo walked to the office door and bellowed for Gina. She came at a run. "Sir?"

"Get this over to the lab, and tell them I want answers back ASAP." He explained what time segment and particular details they wanted. "And, we need it like yesterday."

Gina rolled her eyes, in a so-what's-new gesture. Kathryn smiled and wondered what Theo Pappas was like to work with. From the little she'd seen so far, he appeared to run his staff into the ground. His pale blue open-necked shirt set off his tanned complexion, and she found

78

herself wondering how far his tan extended. It didn't look the bottled kind.

Theo turned back to Ed. "Perhaps you'd both like to come to my office. I think we need to talk. Can you fill me in with some background information about your line of enquiry? What brought you here in the first place?" They followed him through the workroom to his office. He closed the door and pointed to a couple of chairs.

Ed gave him a brief background to their crime scene and the disappearance of Viktor Kohl, their prime suspect. "We're putting in a bit of leg work tracing our suspect's movements, getting to know what makes him tick and finding out what he was doing in the hours before he allegedly killed his wife."

"You don't associate him with the opal robbery, then?"

"We've no evidence to suggest that," Ed countered.

Yet! Kathryn wanted to add. She watched Theo weighing them up. He was a good looking guy, but like most good looking guys she'd met she'd lay odds that he knew it and traded on it.

"Take a look at this." Theo switched on the monitor beside him and fast-forwarded through grey matter, backtracked then stopped. The camera watched a door at the far end of a corridor. As they watched, two bulky figures entered the foreground scene. Side by side they walked, at a moderate pace away from the camera back towards the far door, the taller one hefting a tool bag. "Although we can only see their backs," Theo said. "Your two characters reminded me of these two."

"These are bigger and are dressed differently." Ed pointed out.

"They could be wearing their normal day clothes underneath those overalls," Kathryn suggested. "They look bulky enough. Their woollen beanies disguise the shape of their heads. These look even more anonymous than our two. Who are they?"

"We don't know. We haven't tracked them down yet. But this tells us they were in the building around the time of the robbery." He paused the tape. "The overalls you see look similar to the work clothes worn by the carpet fitters employed by the development. But they say they had no one on the premises on Saturday."

"Is there a camera outside that door?" Ed asked.

Theo snorted. "Somebody covered it with a black plastic bag."

"Oh, clever stuff. So, is this the only take you have?" Ed pointed to the flickering images.

"The renovating is not finished yet, so there are places where the cameras are either not fixed, or just not working yet."

Kathryn studied the lumbering men and thought of the metal buttons found in Viktor's incinerator. The time on the screen read 16:27 – if they were picked up outside by the white van that would give them time enough to get to the market door by 16:35. "What time was the robbery?" she asked.

"Between four and five p.m. The new owner of the opal had been expecting delivery around four-thirty p.m. At five o'clock, he became anxious and sent his valet down to check. Something different about the position of an office door struck the man. He went to look and found the courier's body."

"How was the courier killed?" Ed asked.

"Blunt force trauma to the back of his head. A clean kill. Doc said it looked professional. The assailant knew where to strike him. He was dead before he hit the ground."

Derrick Kohl was ex-army. He'd know how to kill a man quickly, silently. The combined footage of the two tapes compromised his alibi for the time of the robbery. Derrick had lied about the last time he'd seen Chantelle. What else had he lied about? She looked at Ed – wasn't it time to come clean? Ed frowned back, reluctant to show his hand.

Too late, Theo had already caught the vibes. He looked from one to the other and spoke in a low-pitched voice. "Okay, guys, what's going on?" He sat erect in his chair, alternating eye contact between them. "If you've got something to say, let's hear it."

"We have no evidence to support our theories," Ed said with reluctance. "But, maybe if we lay all the cards on the table, we may find we're each holding some missing pieces of the other's case."

"This had better be good. I haven't time to waste. I've had it up to here with crazies in this case," Theo said, slashing his throat with a finger. "Tell me what you've got."

"Ever since we heard about the door behind the Kohl's stand, we've had suspicions that our two were running a second agenda." He gave Theo more details about the connection between the Kohl brothers, the murdered victims, the similarity of the vehicles, and the burnt remains in the incinerator.

"Those overalls would account for the metal buttons," Kathryn said, pointing to the monitor. They'd caught Theo's interest. He leaned forward listening intently.

"What happened to the courier's attaché case?" Ed asked.

"We haven't found it. Presumably, the perps took it. They used a bolt cutter to get the chain off his wrist."

"And, the courier's name?" Kathryn asked Theo.

"Gordon Drysdale. Poor bastard, he leaves a widow and a couple of young kids."

Kathryn jerked her head around to look at Ed. "G. D?"

Ed's mouth curved into a winning smile. "That's more like it," he said in a soft voice.

Theo looked from one to the other. "What the hell has G.D. got to do with anything?"

* * *

17

Ed turned his attention away from Kathryn and back to Theo, feeling more confident of his ground. "We found the letters G.D. embossed on a medallion among the burnt remains of a leather case in Viktor Kohl's incinerator," he said. "Did the courier's case have such an item on it somewhere?"

Theo's face creased into a disbelieving smile. "You are kidding me!" Ed made no reply. "Alright. I'll get it checked out. His widow would probably know." Theo took up his mobile phone and spoke briefly to a colleague.

"I'm not making any promises," Ed said. "But it's one hell of a coincidence. How did the robbers *know* the destination of the opal? Have you started looking for a weak link in the organisation, yet?"

"We've checked the auctioneer's office. They're clean. The robbers couldn't have had more than forty-eight hours notice of the courier's delivery point."

"What chance of a leak coming from the insurance company? I see they're offering twenty thousand pounds for its return, that's big bikkies for some little office clerk." Ed had read the notice and could well imagine the effect it would have on the public.

"The opal's insurance company is TSIC, they're based in London. I can't see that ploy working, myself. It's not like it was a spontaneous snatch-and-grab; this took thorough planning. The villains knew precisely where and when to attack. Their getaway so smooth, it ruffled no feathers."

"Who would have known the route and timing of the delivery?" Kathryn asked.

"The auctioneers, the insurers and those who dealt with the paperwork, would have known. The courier and whoever he may have told. We're still investigating that line. And, yes we are looking for a possible mole on the inside of the insurance company, someone taking backhanders to give out classified information, or another possibility – computer hacking."

"An opal of that value wouldn't be easy to sell on the open market," Kathryn said.

"It's most likely gone underground to a private collector. It's a steal to order job, with their customer already lined up," Theo said.

Another thought occurred to Ed. "Viktor Kohl's business could have connections to people who'd pay over the odds for something like this."

Theo dipped his head. "Viktor's the one you say has disappeared?"

"A few hours after the Kohl brothers arrived home, both Viktor's wife and her lover were murdered. It wasn't a planned killing. If your two robbers and our two brothers are one and the same pair, then it looks like the plan to steal the opal was interrupted when one of them deviated from the plan to take revenge on a cheating wife," Ed said.

"On the other hand, your suspect's disappearance lends credence to the idea he is currently delivering the opal to their pre-ordained customer."

"Or, he's gone to ground with it until the heat is off," Kathryn said.

"Possibly," Theo nodded. "TSIC have a private investigator trying to track the opal down. But, if we're making no headway, I can't see he stands a chance."

"TSIC?" Kathryn said. She turned to Ed. "That's the firm Spencer worked for."

"Who's Spencer?" Theo asked.

"Dominic Spencer was the other victim, Chantelle's lover," Ed said. "He worked in their Plymouth branch not the London office."

"But, as an employee, couldn't he get information from the office computer, or even be the hacker himself?" Kathryn asked. "It's another link."

Ed sat back in his chair feeling worn; the day had been long and full and the adrenaline rush evoked by their initial discovery was wearing off. His mobile rang.

"Sorry about this, must take it." He took a few steps away and answered his call.

It was the boss, Hawke. He listened quietly while the DCI spoke. He maintained silence to the obvious frustration of Kathryn who frowned and canted her head, eager to know what it was all about. Taking pity on her, he mouthed the words "They've got Viktor."

"Where, when?" She gasped in glee as he continued to listen.

"There's been a development here, too," he told his boss. Without going into detail, he told him something of their discoveries. He ended the call and put the phone back in his jacket pocket.

"Good news?" Theo asked.

"It seems Viktor Kohl is in a hospital in Bristol, brought in overnight. He was found unconscious outside a pub. The DCI wants someone to check it out. As we're nearly half way there, we're the obvious choice."

Ed checked his watch, "It's nearly six, and by the time we've eaten it'll be too late to start out. I don't want to drive up the M5 dog-tired." He looked at Kathryn. "I suggest we stay over and get cracking first light. They've put a guard on him, so he's not likely to walk. You okay for a night away?"

"No problem. How do we know it isn't another hoax call, or mistaken ID?"

"The cops found him, called the ambulance and followed him to the hospital. He matched the description and was carrying Viktor Kohl's ID inside his jacket. We need to check it and if he's well enough, bring him home. Do you know of a suitable motel nearby, Theo?"

*

Refreshed after a shower, Kathryn put on a clean shirt and underwear from her emergency pack. She'd been caught out once before, now she carried spare necessities along with a toothbrush for such eventualities.

Theo had suggested she and Ed join him for dinner and continue their discussions over a bottle of wine. Ed declined, waved his phone and said he had to call his wife and he had someone to see, but there was no reason why she shouldn't go.

A knock on her motel door sent her skidding out of the ensuite. She grabbed her bag and opened the door and did a double-take. Theo had changed out of his work suit into something more casual. She stared at his dark red cashmere sweater.

"What's up? You look like you've seen a ghost," he said.

She looked into his face, smiled and experienced that little kick of pleasure that looking up to the eyes of a man taller than her usually evoked.

"It's alright. Someone just walked over my grave." Dark red sweaters were as common as pale blue shirts.

The lines in the corners of his eyes creased into a grin. "Your boss not changed his mind?" He looked over her shoulder as though expecting to see Ed in there somewhere.

"No, says he's busy. If you want him, he's in the room down the end there." She indicated a unit further down the passage.

"Where would you like to go?" he asked her. "If you're interested, there's a good place not far from here. It used to be a Presbyterian Chapel in the old days, but they've turned it into a pub and eatery. It's the 'in' place to go, so they say."

"That sounds good. Lead the way."

Theo parked his car a short way from the restaurant. Kathryn walked beside him to the three-hundred-year-old edifice, built of red brick with light-coloured tuck points. They mounted the steps and walked in through the pillared porch.

Inside, the vast space held a host of small tables each laden with cutlery and shining glassware. The hum of patrons' conversation and background music thickened the air. Lights around the walls and candles on the tables added to the warm, welcoming atmosphere. Hungry after a day of coffee and snacks, the appetising aromas of steaks and seafood emanating from the open grills, had Kathryn's mouth watering.

A polished carved pulpit stood between two stained glass windows, reminiscent of its earlier life. Pillars along the sides of three walls supported an oak panelled gallery, where she could see bobbing heads of people sitting at the tables. She touched Theo's arm. "Let's go up there." She pointed to the wooden steps.

He followed her and chose a table. "This do you?"

"Mm, lovely." She peered down over the carved railing to a congregation of diners.

In spite of his idea to discuss business over a bottle of wine, so far Theo hadn't mentioned work. She picked up the menu and looked at it, wondering whether to bring the subject up herself.

After her marriage breakdown, she'd tried a dating agency for a while. Only the fear that someone from work might find out made her give that up – too embarrassing. She took a sly look at Theo over the top of her menu, and reminded herself this was not a date. He had invited her and Ed to dine with him as a courtesy.

He appeared relaxed and absorbed in his task of perusing the wine list. He turned a page, his hands strong and slim, his nails trimmed. There was no evidence of a wedding band. He raised his eyes and caught her watching him. He smiled. And the heat rushed to her face. God, at thirty-five she was no longer a kid to feel this awkward in front of a man.

"Seen anything you fancy?" he asked, nodding towards her menu. "Thought I'd have the salmon, and there's a nice Chardonnay that would go well with it. How about you?"

"Yep, I'll have mine char grilled – Chardonnay is fine with me."

With the meal on the way, and the wine poured, Theo lifted his glass. "What shall we drink to?"

"Satisfactory conclusions to our current cases?"

"I'll drink to that. Then, let's drop the subject and have a couple of hours off, yes?"

"I'll drink to that." She smiled and clinked her glass against his.

The talking became easier. Over dinner, she quizzed him on his background. Another thing she'd learned from agency dating, that you could fill in awkward moments by getting the man to talk about himself. Only, in that game, some went too far or spent the whole evening talking about their ex – so boring!

Theo Pappas was good company and she became drawn into the tales of his journey from schoolboy to detective. Born in London, he went to the local grammar school where the kids teased the life out of him for his funny name. But he grew so fast he soon towered over them and they dropped the jokes and called him Poppa.

She smiled at the image he created. The evening was starting to take on the feel of a real date. "What did you do when you left school, before you became a cop?"

He cast exaggerated glances all around him, then leaned forward towards her. "The washing-up," he whispered.

She laughed. "Huh? Tell me more."

"Bred from a family of Greek restaurateurs, I'm the son who escaped."

"Why? Didn't you want to follow the family business?"

"I hated kitchen work, loathed it with a passion."

She laughed. "That's something we have in common, then. You still see your family?"

"Occasionally, but I'm regarded as a bit of a renegade. Generations of Pappas have been in the restaurant business. Not for me. I have two brothers. They're happy enough to take it on. So, I got out of it." He pointed to the dessert trolley being wheeled around. "Do you want any gateaux to go with the coffee?"

She shook her head. "I couldn't eat another thing."

Theo's phone rang. He apologised, excused himself and left the table. Kathryn sat back, replete. She looked down at the level below to a kaleidoscope of colour, as people dined or moved around between the tables. Her roaming glance reversed suddenly as it recognised a familiar form on the far side of the room. She caught her breath. That shock of white hair was unmistakable.

Ed Buchanan leant across the edge of the table in earnest conversation with his partner, a pretty, young blonde. It didn't have the look of a business meeting. Was Ed playing away from home, or had she got it wrong? He'd been lauded as the ultimate faithful husband, was he no better than the rest? So much for the office gossip.

Theo returned to their table and sat down to his coffee. He didn't notice Ed and she said nothing. Theo paid the bill, refusing any input from her. She knew better than to create a fuss.

They left the restaurant and took a stroll down by the canal basin. They walked along its banks, past the quayside where the old TV series The Onedin Line filmed its Liverpool scenes. The night was cool but clear, the air fresh with the faint tang of river mud. They ambled across the bridges, looking at the quayside lights reflecting in the water, and back along the side of the River Exe in a wide circle returning to the car. It had been a great way to spend the evening and Kathryn was sorry when once in the car Theo resumed his mantle of colleague entertaining visiting colleague.

He repeated their arrangement made with Ed about contacting him as soon as they'd identified Viktor. He walked her to the motel door. She opened it and stepped inside.

"Thanks, Kathryn. It's been a lovely night; I enjoyed it." He raised a hand in farewell and backed away. "Maybe we'll do it again if I come down your way. You can take me somewhere." He smiled, then turned around and walked smartly back to the car.

Kathryn closed the door and leaned into it. The burning ache in the base of her belly was scary. She wanted him so much at that moment, while the scent of him was still with her. He hadn't put a foot wrong. But her raw sense of emptiness and the ache in her loins made her cry out his name and thump the door in frustration.

* * *

18

No news from her solicitor yet, but, Pug conceded, it was still early in the morning. She put the kettle on for tea and let Ratz into the rear garden. He raced away, barking furiously and the neighbour's cat leapt back over the fence.

She dusted and vacuumed the house through. Her mind filled with what she'd do once she'd got the okay to move onto the boat. She let the anticipation grow. Her rocky future was a challenge she intended to meet head-on.

Before Dom's death, her life had been organised, predictable. She had dug herself a rut and had willingly fallen into it. That was the past. Painful memories of Dom, their life together and his truly dreadful death waited for her back there. Think only of the future. She pushed the vacuum's plug into the hall socket and cast a lingering look at the telephone. Come on Peter, where are you? The bank had offered her the *in kind* clause, so they couldn't object now, could they?

Almost on cue, the telephone rang. She snatched it up. It was Peter to say the bank had agreed to the deal. He asked her to call in his office at midday if she wanted to fast track the paperwork.

Taking on the boat would give her a total change in lifestyle. No more luxury ensuites, she'd be showering in the public facilities along the quays of the ports she visited. With money she already had, the boat to live in and move around on, she would have time to sort herself out, away from the pressures of people. So many confusing thoughts, tumbling around her head made her giddy.

It was time to stop her wild fantasies and plan properly. She put the vacuum cleaner away and found a notebook. She needed to make lists of the gear she would need to take with her. Where had Dom kept it all? He usually did the packing for the boat, while she organised the domestic bits and pieces like food, clothes and bedding. Some of it they left on the boat for the season.

Ratz lay curled on an armchair. "Oi! How about some help here? Don't you fancy life on the ocean wave?" She danced a jig around him. He opened an eye and followed her movements with a patient air. "Peter's settled the question of what we're going to do today," she told him. "After we've signed his papers we're going to check the boat and find out what's already on it, okay?" The tone of her voice perked him up.

There was plenty of time before Mum was due back, so she didn't have to rush things. She picked up her set of boat keys, made sure the doors and windows were locked before leaving. Then she swung the car out of the drive heading towards town, Peter's office and ultimately, freedom. The knowledge that Dom's killer was still out there on the loose, had her checking her mirror frequently. But, she never spotted anyone deliberately following her.

*

Pug walked past the clubhouse out to the shoreline. Scores of boats, all different shapes and sizes were tied to the floating pontoons. She looked across the water to where her boat had its permanent mooring. The white mooring buoy, numbered 265, bobbed around in the water, but of her boat, there was no sign.

"What the heck?" She slapped a hand to her mouth. Had the bank already claimed it? In an instant, her newly revised future crumbled before her eyes.

"You lookin' for *Cazutt*?"

She spun around. Nobby Clark, the odd job man, ambled towards her, a pot of paint in one hand and clutch of brushes in the other.

"Hi Nobby, yes, where is she? Why isn't she on her mooring?"

He nodded towards a group of similar sized boats on the far side of the pontoon.

"She's over there, middle o' that lot. Been there nigh on a coupla weeks. Mr Spencer didn't say he wanted her put back. I coulda done it for him if he wanted, he only had to say." He looked at the ground and shuffled his feet. "I'm sorry to hear what happened to him, I s'pose that's why no one's been here to put 'er back."

"Thanks for that Nobby. I'll go and check her." She walked out along the pontoon, puzzled as to why Dom would bring the boat in. They usually only did that when they loaded up at the beginning of the season, or when they went on holiday. It was easier to bring the boat in than ferry all their extra stuff out in the dinghy.

She worked back Nobby's *'coupla* weeks.' Couldn't have been the Saturday, that day she'd gone to the salon and had these stupid stripes put in her hair, but she wasn't gone that long. There simply wouldn't have been enough time. But she'd spent the Sunday morning taking her mum to the airport and hadn't got home until lunchtime. Dom was out then and he didn't return for another couple of hours. He would have had plenty of time that day. He'd not mentioned going to the sailing club, nor did he volunteer any information. The mood he was in at the time did not encourage her to question him.

Cazutt was easy enough to identify even amongst other boats of her size. Her dark blue hull shone amongst the mainly white boats, and her name painted in white lettering stood one-foot high along her bows. Pug pulled the mooring line in until the fenders touched the pontoon, then stepped aboard over the safety rails. Ratz had other things on his mind; he was off chasing seagulls.

The first thing that struck Pug was that the rubber dinghy was already aboard, deflated and tied into its voyage position. One thing crossed off her list. She turned to open up the main hatch, and discovered the padlock had been prised open, leaving the boat unlocked. What was Dom thinking about? Had he forgotten to bring the key and simply forced it open? Or, had someone else been aboard?

With a sense of unease, she slid out the washboards and descended the steps into the cabin. The next thing to strike her was the musty, closed in smell that got worse the further in she went. She walked through to the fore-cabin and opened its hatch to let it blow through. On the bunk sat two sleeping bags, a pile of pillows and towels she did not recognise. She hadn't brought them. They hadn't even had a weekend away yet this season.

The smell was at its worst in the main cabin. She opened the food locker expecting it to be empty. Instead, it was jam-packed. Black mould grew inside the plastic wrapper of a loaf of bread. One by one, she opened the other lockers. Every inch of cupboard space was full to capacity, ready for departure.

Anxiety fluttered in her belly. She lifted the bunk cushions to get to the lockers under the seats. Tinned foods, enough to last for weeks, were carefully stacked, so as not to move around in rough waters. The lowest locker, the coolest, contained food boxes of cheese, butter, well-packed eggs and bacon, steaks, sausages, a carton of milk. The milk looked more like butter, and the meat was gross. No wonder the boat stank. She bundled the noisome plastic bags into a large bin-bag ready for dumping.

Everywhere she looked equipment was in place ready to sail, the fuel tank full, the freshwater container beneath the floorboards topped up. Navigation equipment all present. New charts she'd not seen before lay on the quarter berth. One she noticed was for Jersey the other the northern Spanish coast. She and Dom had planned a holiday in Spain next August, but that was three months away. Dom hadn't packed the boat for that trip. Yet, the day before he died he had prepared the boat, packed his money, his passport and their joint valuables, ready to leave with his new woman on the Monday morning.

Her eyes closed, a groan forced its way out as the realisation struck. She would have to report this to the cops. If Jersey or Spain had been Dom's destination, they would need to know that. Another delay while they examined the boat themselves.

The traumas of the past two weeks had hardened her, now fresh out of rage the shock was not as great as it might have been. In fact, she could even see the irony. Perhaps, if they hadn't delayed their departure for a quickie, they would have got away with it. Now, as it stood, Dom had unwittingly prepared the boat for her. She pulled out her mobile and tapped in the now familiar set of numbers.

*

Ed concentrated on his driving, his sergeant sat quietly beside him. Memory surged into his mind of the night when he and Matt had been returning from a job in the unmarked car on a road such as this, when some speeding motorist overtook them driving erratically.

"Gettem," he'd ordered and Matt put his foot down. Ed had stuck the blue light onto the car roof and prepared for a chase. The speeding car slowed. They followed it onto the hard shoulder. Matt got out and approached the driver, while Ed rang in a trace on the number plate. He'd heard the shotgun blast, saw his sergeant collapse and heard the squeal of tyres as the car raced away. With a head full of pellets and face blown away, Matt died in the ambulance on the way to hospital.

To get his mind off Matt, Ed turned his thoughts to his present case, to the man currently in the hospital bed in Bristol, and if he was up to answering questions. He glanced sideways at Kathryn. She hadn't said much at all since they started out. He preferred that to a partner who felt it necessary to chat all the time. He hadn't debriefed her after her meeting with the DI last night. He cleared his throat.

"Did you learn any more from Theo Pappas last night?" he asked.

She turned her head sharply, as though the sound of his voice had startled her after such a long silence. "No, we didn't discuss work."

He absorbed this in a few more moments of silence. Then spoke again. "Interesting development that the opal's insurance company is the same one Spencer worked for. Can't be a coincidence, can it?"

"Looks like Dom Spencer and Viktor Kohl had more in common than a hankering after the same woman," she said.

"We know they had a business relationship. Viktor sold valuable gems to Spencer at a cut price. But what did Spencer do for Viktor to earn that? Could he have relayed private information he'd discovered through his workplace?"

"That's something we can ask Viktor." She hesitated. "Assuming the man we're going to see is capable of speaking, and really is Viktor Kohl."

Ed took a sidelong glance at her. "What makes you doubt it?"

"Getting beaten up in a pub brawl doesn't sound like the man who has just committed the biggest robbery in God knows how long, then murdered his wife and his business colleague. I like Theo's idea that Viktor's disappearance has more to do with him delivering the gem to his customer and collecting his money. It sounds far more likely."

They lapsed into silence while Ed negotiated a large roundabout. It wasn't long before their turn off onto the A38. He kept an eye on the exit signs.

"Did you enjoy your evening?" he asked.

"It was good." She paused long enough for him to wonder what was coming next. "We went to The Meeting House for dinner."

He turned to smile at her. "So did we! Whenever I get to Exeter, my daughter insists we go there. She loves the place. Funny, I didn't see you. Where did you sit?"

"Your daughter?"

"Penny, from my first marriage, she's reading law at the university."

"I didn't know you had a daughter."

He paused. He'd heard the inflections in her voice. "No reason why you should." His retort was sharper than he'd intended. He shook his head. "So, who did you think she was, eh, Kathryn? A pretty girl half my age, and you thought I was dating her? Is that why you didn't come and say hello? You need to watch that, Sergeant. Jumping to conclusions won't do your career any good whatsoever."

*

Kathryn, still feeling chastened by Ed's words, took the photos she had of Viktor out of her bag. At the hospital, she followed Ed through reception and into the lift up to Viktor's ward. The constable watching Viktor's room was expecting them. He rose to his feet.

"PC Ian Taylor," he said and shook their hands as they introduced themselves. "First thing, he's not long out of his coma and the doctor says he's not up to questioning yet." He indicated the room a few metres away. They walked over to peer in through the glass-panelled wall. The patient lay in bed, motionless, eyes closed.

"His hands are bandaged," Kathryn said.

"He'd been in a fight and damaged his knuckles."

"So, you haven't taken his prints yet?" Ed asked.

The constable shook his head. "There is one thing, though. Is your man a diabetic?"

Kathryn jerked her head and looked at Ed. Nobody had mentioned that fact before.

"Don't know," Ed said. "You telling us this bloke *is*?"

"When they brought him in, the medics said it was a diabetic coma. They reckon he was mugged and left unconscious in the alleyway. People passed by thinking he was drunk sleeping it off, when in fact he'd been there long enough to miss his insulin dose. Our cops on night patrol found him eventually and got him hospitalised just in time."

"Right. I'm going in to take a better look. Bring the photo," Ed said to Kathryn.

Kathryn stood on one side of the bed and studied the face of the man lying there. He looked the right size, olive complexion and dark hair. He had cuts and bruises. Both eyes shut, one badly swollen. She studied his features and compared them with the photograph.   She shook her head. "Look at the mole on his cheek. This photo was taken recently and it doesn't show any moles on Viktor's face, and look at the difference between their noses. This bloke's is much smaller."

"All this way for bugger all!" Ed stomped away. He turned back and thrust his hand out. "Why didn't the locals pick that up? We faxed the photo to them."

The constable came into the room. "Any luck, sir?"

"I was told you'd found identification in his jacket pocket," Ed said, irritably. "What happened to that?"

"His jacket's here." Taylor opened a narrow closet and reach for the clothes hanging inside. "There was nothing *in* the pockets, sir. His money, ID and everything had been taken. But we do have this." He opened the jacket out. The tailor's label sewn on the face of an inside pocket showed the suit had been made by a firm in Hong Kong, and beneath that were the words, "Specially made for Mr. Viktor Kohl," followed by a number.

"And that's it? That's all you have?"

"It's not just anybody's name, sir. Viktor Kohl is a wanted man all over the country. It's not a common name. It was vital we let all interested parties know."

"Yes, yes of course. So, how did this man come by Viktor's suit?"

The door opened and a second officer appeared and beckoned to them. "We have a development," he said once they were outside. "There's a woman coming up in a few minutes. She posted a missing person's claim this morning. Her husband didn't come home last night, and she's worried because he's diabetic. Her description fits this guy."

"Right, let's see where this gets us," Ed said.

Kathryn moved away from the room and watched as the two police constables ushered in a middle-aged woman who stood beside the bed and looked down. She nodded and smiled, then bent over and kissed the patient on his forehead. The man opened his eyes and moved a hand. A few minutes into the reunion, DC Taylor spoke to the woman. She nodded as Taylor collected the suit from the closet and beckoned her to follow him.

Taylor introduced her to them as Mrs Trump, wife of the man in the bed. Relieved at finding her husband alive, the woman happily answered their questions. Ed pointed to the suit and asked her how her husband came to be wearing it.

"He bought it. He got it from the Sally Army shop down the road only a few days ago. Why, what's the matter with it?"

"Nothing's the matter with the suit," Ed assured her. "But it is part of our enquiries and we need to keep it for a while." He offered to buy it back for whatever she paid for it. She agreed, although reluctant to let it go. "For a second-hand suit, it still has a lot of wear, and it was good enough to go the dog tracks in. Never mind, the shop had plenty more where that one came from."

Kathryn strode alongside Ed back to the car. When they reached the address the woman had given them, the shop manager remembered the sale. "We'd practically run out of gents' clothing," she said, "but our Plymouth store said they'd had a glut. This suit was part of a consignment they sent up last week." She handed over a card with the address of their Plymouth branch into Kathryn's waiting hand.

"Right. Next stop the Sally Army in Plymouth," said Ed. "Let's go!"

* * *

19

Pug left the boat and walked back to the car park to wait for the patrol car. The interruption to her schedule was irritating, but she'd rather err on the side of caution than have the cops chasing after her later. The broken padlock was a mystery not yet solved, but no damage had been done to the boat and it was a simple matter to replace it.

She'd signed Peter's papers and agreed to hand over the car when she formally took possession of the boat. Peter hadn't been able to give her the date of transfer yet, though he expected it to be within the next couple of days. He said he'd phone her.

The police car pulled up. She'd met the two constables Jodie Bligh and Louis Truscott before. She approached them as they got out of the car.

"Okay, what's the problem?" Truscott asked as Jodie stopped to speak to Ratz.

"It's no real problem to me, but a while back Sergeant Sinclair asked if I knew where Dom was going before ... before he was murdered. I didn't know at the time, but now I think I've sussed it out, and thought you'd want to know."

They boarded the boat and Pug told them first about the broken padlock.

"Is anything missing?" Truscott asked.

"I don't think so. Quite the opposite, there is far more on the boat than I had expected. The radio, the bearing compass and other such equipment are all present. Dom could have just forgotten to bring his key."

She stood aside until they had gone down into the main cabin, then sat and watched them from the hatch, indicating the full cupboards, topped up fuel tank and water container. Jodie wrinkled her nose.

"And the smell comes from the meat and other fresh foods he'd packed in the cool cupboard. They must have been there for a couple of weeks. The stuff had gone off and was stinking, so I chucked it in the bin on the end of the pontoon. You don't want to see it, do you? I warn you, it's putrid."

"If we do, we can always send Jodie out for it." Truscott's teasing smile evoked an immediate reaction.

Jodie narrowed her eyes. "And if you do, I'll stuff that seedy pullover of yours right down inside with it."

"Nothing wrong with my pullover," he looked down to a blue and grey knobbly jumper. "My mum knitted it."

Jodie rolled her eyes. "Oh man, that is just so un-cool!"

Pug smiled at their banter but Truscott's face coloured slightly and she couldn't read his expression.

"Okay if we do a search of the boat, now?" he asked.

"Help yourself." Pug waved her hand. "What are you looking for?"

"Anything that might lead us to your husband's killer," Jodie said.

Truscott opened the lid of the chart desk. He picked out a chart. "What are these pencil lines?"

"They're my workings and position lines from last year's cruise," Pug told him. "The only new charts are those," she leaned inwards and pointed to the ones on the quarter berth. "There's one for the Channel Islands, mainly Jersey, and another for the coast of Spain."

"Any indication of which he was going to first?"

"No, but it would be logical for him to go over to Jersey first, then down to Spain, otherwise he'd be back tracking."

"What's in Jersey that might attract him?"

She shrugged. "Apart from fantastic sailing, I've no idea."

Jodie continued emptying each locker to check its contents. Pug was relieved to see her put everything back as she'd found it. In one locker containing towels, Jodie picked out a couple of items of female apparel.

She held them up. "Yours?" she asked.

Pug shook her head. The bikini was not hers. She took it and dropped it in the bag among the last remains of stale food ready for disposal. It was a reminder of the other woman in her husband's life. A feeling of nausea crept into her throat. She moved away from the officers and stepped out onto the pontoon. The sun had come out from behind a cloud and warmed her as she sat cross-legged on the boardwalk. Ratz came and wriggled onto her lap making low throaty noises that passed for his side of any conversation. She hugged him and murmured doggy-nothings into a black furry ear. Not content to sit still, he jumped off to stare cocked-eyed through the gaps in the planking to the movement of the water beneath them.

The bikini told her that the woman was already familiar with the boat. How often had they sailed together whilst their clueless spouses had been busy at work? How did Viktor learn about the affair? For one fleeting moment, she had a sympathetic thought for Viktor. Betrayal was something they shared. But never could she accept his way of dealing with it, if indeed he had been the murderer. She shuddered as the image of the blood-covered bodies seeped back into her mind.

Dom had timed his getaway for the day before the news of their financial straits was due to break. If his plan had worked, how long would it have taken her to check on the boat after Dom had walked out on her? It could have been days. They would've got clean away, and she would have been none the wiser about that woman. He'd bled their accounts dry and had packed everything of value that he could carry. Would it have been better not to have known? Maybe the pair of them would still be alive.

Finally, the officers came out of the cabin. They checked the cockpit lockers, and then satisfied they had covered everything, nodded to each other and stepped out onto the pontoon.

"Did you find anything worthwhile?" she asked.

Truscott smiled, "Only a bottle of Champagne in the wine locker."

Pug gave him a rueful grin. It was the only item brought by the *lovers* she had not thrown out. "Well, I couldn't really chuck that, could I?"

"One day you'll find a use for it," he said. "Thanks for letting us know about the charts. Your boat is not part of the crime scene. It's clean as far as we're concerned, so carry on doing whatever you were doing. You don't have any plans to leave the country any time soon, do you?"

"No plans in that direction. Once I've got the okay from my solicitor I intend to cruise locally for a while – get myself sorted. Don't suppose I'll go far. Why?"

"You're a witness. We need you to keep in touch."

She walked back to the car park with them. "Okay, I'll tell you when I'm ready to go."

"If you need to talk, or you remember something we should know, you've got my card, give us call," Truscott said.

As dusk set in, she whistled for Ratz and they headed home – well, Mum's home. Ratz became excited as they pulled into the driveway.

She let him out of the car. He raced around the top of the drive, sniffing the ground, then ran to the wooden fence separating the back garden from the front. He frantically dug at the concrete trying to get in under the back gate. He wrinkled his lips into a snarl. She got out of the car and locked it.

"Ratz, leave it. Come here." The neighbour's cat had been in again. Ratz took great exception to its presence and ignored all orders to leave it alone. She smiled at the dog's erratic behaviour. Then key in hand, she turned to the front door.

The dog raced after her, scrambled between her legs and was inside the house before she could get over the step. He alternately whined and growled as he raced from room to room, nose to the floor following a scent, even up the stairs. With growing unease, she stood and watched him. It was over the top, even for him. Standing still on the threshold, she pushed the lounge door open. Inside, every drawer and cupboard door hung open.

Her knees sagged. She could only whisper. "Not again. Please God, not again." Ratz ran down the stairs, panting, his sweep completed. He leaned against her legs, shivering like he did during thunderstorms. She waited no longer. With shaking hands, she called the number on Truscott's card. Reassured by Ratz's behaviour that the intruder was no longer in the house, she looked into the other rooms. No villain, no bodies, no blood – just chaos.

When the same two officers arrived, she led them to the lounge and told them, "It's like this everywhere."

"What's missing, do you know yet?" Jodie Bligh asked, taking out her notebook.

"I can't see anything missing, but they're not my things. I don't know exactly what was here. As you can see the valuables are okay." She pointed to her mother's silver coffee pot and tea service in the glass cabinet. "Is it the same person, who trashed my house, do you think?

Louis Truscott's light brown eyes held hers for a moment. "The MO looks the same, except nobody died this time."

She looked at him askance. "You mean, if I had been here …"

"No, I didn't mean that," he corrected himself hastily. "I meant that maybe he timed his break-in for when the house was empty."

"You mean he's watching me?" Involuntarily, her head swivelled towards the window. When Louis didn't reply, she continued more calmly. "I'll swear Ratz knew who had been here. He was there in the house when Dom was murdered. I think he recognised the scent." The very thought of that murderer walking through her mother's house turned her innards to water. If she wasn't safe here, where else could she hide?

"If it *was* the same person," Jodie said, "it means the intruder didn't find what he was looking for at your house, so he's trying here. What do you have that someone else wants real bad?"

Pug thought for a moment; she had nothing of value. Her father's stamp collection was still on the dining room table where she had unloaded it last week. "The diamond pendant is the most likely, but I don't have it any more. Your people took it in for examination."

"It was passed back to the solicitor dealing with your estate early this morning."

"Who else, other than the police and my solicitor knew that?"

"The executors, the bank – it's no secret." He shrugged. "Where did he break in?"

Pug led them to the kitchen and indicated a broken lock on the back door. Truscott pushed the door open and walked outside. The daylight was fading, but it was still light enough to see the fence at the far end of the garden. Ratz picked up a scent and raced across the lawn. One portion of the wooden planking leaned inwards with a gap large enough for a man to slip through. Ratz jumped through the opening into parkland on the other side, ran to a bare patch under a tree and stopped, baffled.

"He's lost the scent," Jodie said. "The intruder could have parked his vehicle there."

Pug called Ratz, intending to take him back to the house out of their way. He followed her back through the fence and along the path. At one point he stopped to sniff the paving around the base of a concrete birdbath. He pawed at ground and nibbled at something.

"Leave!" she yelled at him and darted back to see what he'd picked up. On the edge of the pathway between them lay a handful of blue pellets.

Pug screamed for Jodie and dropped to the ground. She straddled Ratz and held him between her knees. She got a headlock on him and prised his jaws apart as Jodie joined in the fray. Without a word the officer grabbed the upper jaw, while Pug pulled the lower one down. With her hand she scraped the blue crumbly substance from his tongue. Together, with tissues and water from the birdbath they cleaned the dog's mouth. He struggled but was no match for the pair of them, and yelped at the indignity.

Panting with exertion, Pug finally managed to calm him down.

"Not good to leave snail pellets around where dogs can get at them," Jodie said, scraping the remaining pellets into a plastic bag for disposal.

"I know that! They weren't there when I left the house this morning. I swear they weren't. Mum hasn't got any. *He* put them there on purpose. This man is sick!"

Ratz coughed again, retching from the treatment he had received.

"Think you got it all?" Jodie asked. "Maybe he should see the vet just to be on the safe side. Come on, I'll drive you."

Pug picked up Ratz and stumbled after Jodie.

Truscott waited in the house for SOCO to turn up and dust the rooms for fingerprints. "How'd you get on?" he asked when they returned.

"The vet thought we'd done a good job," Pug said. "But, he's keeping Ratz in overnight for observation." She'd thanked Jodie over and over. How would she have managed if they hadn't been here? Unknowingly, she would have let Ratz out the back before they went to bed and probably wouldn't even have seen him eat the pellets. Why poison the dog, for God's sake?

The finger print guys had taken over the lounge with angled lights, brushes and dusting powder. The whole house felt sullied.

One of the officers picked up her briefcase and dusted the outside. He looked at her and asked if she'd cleaned the case recently. Pug shook her head. "It's just as I brought it home from the shop. It should have my prints all over it."

"Nope, it's clean, both out and in." The officer opened the case and held it out to Pug to see. It was empty. All her research on the Blood Opal series was gone. She showed the empty case to Truscott.

His face brightened. "Well, if that is the only thing missing, it looks like he got what he came for. It's obviously not a random burglary."

"But why would anyone want this stuff? There was no value to it."

Truscott took out his notebook and extracted another card from it. "Here's the name of a repairman. If you give him a ring and explain it's a police matter, he'll come round and fix your kitchen door for you. We use him quite a lot. We've finished here. Will you stay here tonight, or have you somewhere else to go?"

"No, I can't leave my mother's house in this state." She watched the fingerprint officers pack up their gear and file out of the door. She looked up at Truscott. "You don't think he'll come back do you?"

"I doubt it. But you've got my card, give me a call anytime, okay?"

She so wanted out of this place. As soon as Peter could arrange it she'd slip off quietly in the boat, telling only those that needed to know. Maybe it was running away, but she needed a breather. Why would anyone steal her research into the Blood Opal? It was lunacy. The locksmith treated it as an emergency and said he'd be there within the hour.

She watched the two police officers drive down the road before she turned back into the silent, empty house. He might only be a small dog, but she felt more vulnerable without Ratz at her side. He, at least, would warn her if someone was about.

Feeling the need to talk to a friendly voice, she took out her mobile and keyed in Peter's home number to put him in the picture over the house break-in, and the attempt to poison Ratz. She asked if he could hurry the deal up.

"What do you mean by hurry the deal up? Didn't you get my message?" he asked.

"What message?"

"I left a message on your mother's phone. We can go ahead with the exchange, car for boat, as soon as you like. I knew you were in a hurry, so thought I'd let you know."

She hadn't checked the house phone for messages. "Oh, good, how about tomorrow?"

"Okay, what time of day would be good for you – at my office?"

"Erm, could we do it at the sailing club? Otherwise I have no transport to take my stuff down to the boat."

"Okay, it'll have to be evening, then." That was fine. It would give her time pick up Ratz, to clean the house, put it back the same way her mother had left it and arrange for the neighbour to water Mum's houseplants.

She checked her mother's answering machine. There were no messages although the machine appeared to be working properly. Had Peter forgotten to leave the message?

Or, had the intruder tampered with her phone? The skin on her arms prickled.

* * *

20

They rode the M5 back to their own turf. After a two and a half hour drive, Kathryn pulled the unmarked car up in front of the address they had been given. The charity shop was on a street corner in a run-down area of town. Dead-beat 1980s mannequins posed in the small dusty display window. Two large bins for donations stood on the pavement.

A hint of fried onions flavoured the air. The mobile lunch-van offering drinks and hot dogs stood on a pedestrian precinct ahead of them. Still in the driver's seat, Kathryn put a hand over her mouth to cover a yawn. She needed to stretch her legs.

She looked at Ed. "I'd kill for a coffee."

"Me too. Let's see what they're like. Hot, white and frothy, given the choice." He offered her a five-pound note.

Kathryn waved it away. "I'll get it, you got the last one." She approached the van and ordered a Kit-Kat and coffees-to-go. She handed the chocolate bar over to Ed and gave him a smile. "By way of an apology for my wayward thoughts," she said, looking up at him from her bowed head. Her faith in Ed restored. "I'm glad I got it wrong."

"When women jump to conclusions like that, there's usually a reason for it. But we're not all bastards, you know." He broke the bar in two and returned one half. "Apology accepted. We won't mention it again." They sat in the car to finish their drinks.

"You ready?" Ed took the plastic bag containing Viktor's suit from the back seat of the car and they entered the shop. Somewhere a plug-in floral air freshener did its best to battle the background musty smell of ancient building and old leather jackets.

The woman behind the counter, Lisa, according to the nametag on her red dust coat, gave them a smile and asked if she could help. They showed their IDs. Ed laid the suit on the counter and opened out the jacket so the label and Viktor's name were visible.

"Do you recognise this jacket, Lisa?"

She peered at it. Her finger traced the label. "Oh yes, I remember this one. It came in last week. It's a Hong Kong suit. I've seen a few of them in my time. They're hand-made-to-measure, for tourists in Hong Kong, cut and ready to wear in forty-eight hours, so they tell me."

"Did the clothing you sent to Bristol all come from the same donor?" Kathryn asked.

"Most of it. When it came in, I already had plenty for gents on my shelves, so I sent the bulk of it on."

"Can you remember who handed it in?"

"Yeah, she was an early bird. No sooner had I put the bins out than I saw this woman cramming plastic bags into one of them, so I went out to help her carry the stuff inside rather than fill the bin that early."

"This woman, did she give you a reason for having so many clothes to give away?" Kathryn asked.

"She said she was getting rid of a whole wardrobe for her friend, whose husband had recently passed on. We get a lot of that here."

"Can you describe her?" Ed asked.

Lisa turned her head to one side while she conjured up her memory. "Jeans, white T-shirt and a black leather jacket, tall, perhaps not quite as tall as you, though," she said, looking back at Kathryn. "Around 5'7, I'd say, slim build, in her forties, long dark hair, tied back. She looked a bit distracted, you know, like she couldn't get away quick enough."

Kathryn frowned; the description rang a bell. "Did she give a name?"

"I don't think so, I can't remember. But, I'd recognise her again if I saw her."

Kathryn opened her briefcase and fingered the file she had brought. Inside were copies of some of the photographs from the board back in the incident room. She selected three and placed them on the counter.

"Did she look like any of these women?"

Lisa's glance slid over the photos of Pug Germaine, Chantelle Kohl, and stopped on the third photo. "That's her. She's got that little gap between her two front teeth."

Kathryn gave Ed a knowing smile and held up the photograph of Viktor in a hug with Janine Kohl, his first wife, the mother of his son, Elvis.

Ed nodded. "Well, thank you very much Lisa, you've been a great help." While Kathryn put away the photos, Ed collected the Hong Kong suit, put it back in the plastic bag and headed for the door.

Once in the car, Ed called the boss and told him they were on their way home. He warned the DCI they had new information and would need to brief the whole team. When he disconnected, he looked across at Kathryn with a mildly surprised look.

"Well done, sergeant. I'm impressed."

"Just doing my job, guv." She smiled and slotted the key into the ignition. She'd taken the photographs of Viktor for identification purposes, should they have needed them at the Market Place, the others she'd included just in case they might prove useful. The one photo of Viktor that included Janine was pure luck. But she didn't need to admit that.

*

As the sun went down Pug pulled into the sailing club's car park and stopped. She tried to ignore the persistent feeling in her gut that she was running away. She thumped the steering wheel with both hands. Well, why not? What was there left to stay around for? If someone had it in for her, she wasn't going to wait around just to end up like Dom. Once inside the sailing club's ground she locked the gates behind her.

Ratz, fully recovered from his night away at the vet's, sensed her mood and dogged her footsteps as she unloaded the car. He stopped, raised his hackles and growled as someone moved out of the shadows and walked towards them. His grumbling stopped and he acknowledged the newcomer with a wag of his tail. Pug recognised the skinny frame and bow-legged walk of Nobby Clarke.

"Evenin' Missus, you alright? Do you need some help with that lot?"

"Hullo, Nobby. You're working late today."

"Had a job to finish. Makes no difference to me, never been a clock watcher."

Pug picked up her laptop and briefcase and slung a rucksack over her shoulder. Nobby hefted the remaining bags under his arms and led the way to the pontoons.

"The boat's still where Dom left her," she said, catching him up to walk beside him. "You say you were here when he brought her in."

"Yeah, I was repairing the end of the pontoon, you know, where someone bashed it a while back. He didn't bring her straight in. Went down to Zebedee's first."

Zebedee's boatyard was a short way down river. She and Dom hauled the boat out every winter to renew the anti-fouling and conduct any minor repairs. Zeb had a quay and a crane available for lifting masts, and his fuel tanks on a pontoon meant you didn't have to carry the stuff out to the boat in jerry cans.

"Was the woman with him that day?" she asked.

"Yeah, I s'pose she was." He hesitated as though not sure whether to go on. He stared straight ahead then continued. "After they finished at Zebedee's they came back here and tied up. Took things on and off the boat, like they was goin' somewhere. But then, like I said, they left her here instead of taking her back to her mooring, or movin' on."

She wanted to ask how often this woman had come with Dom, but didn't want to press Nobby who looked uncomfortable with the subject. She glanced back at the empty clubhouse. How many of their friends in the club knew about Dom's lady-friend? Had they gossiped about it behind her back?

"You headin' out then?" Nobby asked.

"For a while, get some new scenery, away from it all."

He nodded sympathetically. "Know what you mean. Do you want help gettin' off?"

"No, it's okay Nobby, thanks. I'm waiting for someone to come and collect my car." A quick glimpse at her watch told her he was due in half an hour.

Peter had called again this morning to arrange the time for his junior to pick up her Volvo C70 in exchange for the boat. She told him then where she intended cruising and gave him her mobile number.

After she'd boarded the boat and unlocked the new padlock to the cabin, Nobby passed the baggage over. He picked up Ratz and dropped him on the foredeck. "Okay, then, I'll be off. Take care of yourself, mind." He turned away and his swaying figure melted into the gloom. She watched as he disappeared and suddenly felt very much alone.

She and Ratz had eaten at Mum's place. But to make the boat feel more homely, she lit the Calor-gas stove and put the kettle on. The flames added warmth and the cabin lights gave a cheery look to her new home. She unpacked her bags and boxes and stowed away the essentials she had brought.

It would be okay once she was on the move. She tried to convince herself that she was doing the right thing. She wasn't being odd in wanting to get away. Her mother had done much the same thing after

Dad's death. She'd rented a cottage on the Scilly Islands for a fortnight – in mid-winter. She'd told Pug she needed to be alone. Now, for the first time, Pug really understood.

It gave her an idea. Perhaps she would sail on to the Scilly Islands. She had met a couple of friends her mother had made there. It would be a good opportunity to see them again. She had no charts for that area, but there was no rush, she'd sail down the coast, call in at Falmouth and buy her charts there. It would give her an objective, a reason to do what she was doing. And who knows, she might be able to get a summer holiday job for a couple of months. The small islands that stuck out into the Atlantic off the end of the Cornish peninsula were rocky and wild. And that just suited her mood. The kettle boiled and she made herself a cup of cocoa.

Before she had time to drink it, headlights flashed at the gate. She and Ratz jogged across the car park. She handed over the car key to the man she recognised from Peter's office. She watched with an unexpected pang, as he drove her beautiful Volvo out of the gates, and turned to follow the car whose driver had brought him. Then she locked up again, gave Ratz a walk around the bushy areas before making her way back to the boat.

In the clear night sky, stars gleamed through the navy canopy and a half-moon on the rise reflected in the quiet waters around the pontoon. *Cazutt's* twinkling cabin lights glowed like small beacons welcoming her aboard; even her cocoa was still warm enough to drink. Time belonged to her.

She planned to slip away quietly in the darkness, sail out of Plymouth Sound, to the River Yealm, to an anchorage she knew and loved. Not far as the crow flies, but in the morning at least she'd wake up in a different place somewhere she could start afresh. She knew the way as well as she knew the route from home to shop. In her previous life, going to the Yealm had been a favourite Sunday sail. Its very familiarity would help settle her into her lone sailing. Isolated on her boat, she felt safe. She glanced at her four-legged crewman. He might not be much good at pulling sails up, but at least he didn't shout and swear at her, as skippers were wont to do. He responded to her attention with eye contact and tail wag.

Nothing more to hold her back, she doused the cabin lights and prepared the sails by moonlight. The twenty-five horsepower motor started at the touch of a button. She untied the mooring lines and reversed out of the pontoon. Once in midstream, with a light wind behind her, she pulled the sails up and let the breeze take over before cutting the motor. In the ensuing silence, she heard the gentle swish of water from her bow wave, a call of a night bird on the riverbank and in the distance, the cough of a boat's engine starting.

By the time she was out of the river and into Plymouth Sound, the breeze became too light to make much headway. But now that she had made the first break, there was no way she would go back. Pug restarted the diesel motor and felt it throb beneath her feet. She looked back at the other boat travelling down river some way behind her. She'd been aware of its presence from the moment its engine fired.

Ratz stood on the bench beside her, his front paws on the raised sides of the cockpit. By the low compass light, she saw a smile on his face. He was accustomed to trotting around the deck, but tonight, she had him on a lead. If he fell overboard, she'd never be able to pick him up on her own.

Now and again, she checked on the boat behind her. Its navigation lights kept a steady parallel course and its speed matched hers. "It's just another sailor out enjoying a summer evening on the water, isn't it, Ratz?" She spoke aloud to convince herself. So much had happened recently that she was seeing bogey-men wherever she looked.

She lost track of the lone boat in the mass of lights, buoys and beacons in the Plymouth Sound and concentrated on rounding the breakwater. Keeping outside the buoys, she skirted the Mewstone Rocks, turned into Wembury Bay and into the mouth of the River Yealm. She followed the leading lights, dropped her speed right down and looked back into the darkness. No lights followed her in.

As the river broadened out in a curve to the left, she slipped into a small empty anchorage on the right. Sheltered from sight of anyone continuing up the river she dropped her anchor, turned the motor off and doused her lights. The moonlight was sufficient to pick out shapes on the black water and against the lighter sky. She only had to put up the anchor light then she'd be ready to go below.

She heard it before she saw it. A motor-launch glided up the river travelling at the same slow speed she'd used. But, more curiously, it ran without lights. It continued upriver, away from her. She stared after it, then sat cross-legged on the deck with Ratz in her lap and waited. It didn't turn back. Finally, satisfied the launch had gone she went below for her first night alone on her boat.

"Your turn to keep watch," she told Ratz. She had every confidence that he would let her know if anyone was about.

*

Kathryn sat at the top table with Ed and their boss, DCI Hawke. She watched the faces of her police colleagues while Ed brought them up to date with the latest developments. It was old ground to her and she found herself tuning out and planning her next course of action. She needed to meet up with Pug Germaine to find out how involved Viktor Kohl was in Dominic Spencer's affairs, but Pug was not answering her phone.

Ed dwelt on their visit to DI Theo Pappas, the investigator of the opal robbery and the murder of its courier. At the mention of Theo's name, her interest quickened and caused the heat to rise in her face. Embarrassed at her own reaction, she pulled herself out of her muse and stared across the room to the window. Concentrate on the job, woman. She looked back at Ed and listened to his voice.

"And we have two sets of CCTV footage, which when put together, indicate the strong possibility that our own murder suspect, Viktor Kohl, was one of the robbers of the Blood Opal, and therefore also implicated in the courier's murder."

Kathryn caught Truscott's eye. She could read his whispered "Shi-it," echoed by other officers as they shuffled on their chairs.

Ed raised his voice over the hubbub. "If we can prove a connection between the Kohl brothers and the opal robbery, then our investigation becomes the highest profile we've seen in a long time."

A new rash of murmurs broke out, and then a hand went up and waved urgently.

"Yes, Truscott?"

"What about the break-in at Ms Germaine's mother's house, sir?"

"Is that relevant?"

"It's a link, sir. Someone broke into the house and searched it the same as Mullion Road. No valuables stolen, but according to Ms Germaine, papers and a load of postage stamps showing the Blood Opal have gone missing."

Kathryn heard again Celeste's plaintive cry, *"Did anyone warn that courier?"* The curse of the opal was all nonsense, of course. But the nagging thought *what if* ... She dare not tell Ed, if he thought for one minute she was being influenced by stories of a curse, his opinion of her would drop through the floor.

Ed raised an eyebrow. "Right, thank you Truscott, see me afterwards with the report. Any more questions before I hand out more assignments?"

Briefing over, Kathryn tried Pug again.

Still no answer.

* * *

21

Kathryn stopped in the open doorway and looked into Ed's office. "We have Janine Kohl waiting to be interviewed," she said. "Shall I take Jodie in and carry on?"

Ed looked up. "No, I want to see that woman. I'll be with you in a minute."

Kathryn watched Viktor's ex-wife sitting at the table in the interview room. Her dark tinted hair scraped back and tied with a rubber band made her face look hard. Her blue shirt and crumpled jeans looked like she'd slept in them.

The DI came in and placed the plastic bag on the floor against the table leg, then sat beside Kathryn.

Janine looked him up and down. "Oh, bringing out the big guns – about time. I haven't got all day to waste, you know."

Kathryn switched on the tape recorder. Janine folded her arms across her chest, giving out heavy sighs and rolling her eyes.

"Right. I'm interested in the clothes you took to the Salvation Army shop on Banner Street, Tuesday, thirteenth of May." Ed stated without preamble. "I understand they were men's clothes. Who did they belong to? And why were you giving them away?"

"Cos' Elvis had grown out of them. Why do you wanna know that?"

"I want to know about Viktor's clothes."

"Yeah, some were Viktor's. They'd been stuck in my wardrobe for the past two years since we split. I wanted them out. Derrick's about to move in and I don't want the place cluttered with my ex-husband's clothes, do I?"

Ed picked up the bag that held Viktor's Hong Kong suit folded to show the label inside. He put it in front of her. "What about this one?"

"That's years old. We went there at least four years back. He left it at my place."

"According to your son, Viktor wore that suit less than a month ago. Elvis said he used it when attending house sales and auctions."

She sat forward. "What've you been doing questioning my son?"

"He's eighteen, Mrs Kohl. He's old enough to question without your say-so. So, how did you get hold of Viktor's suit?"

"I dunno. What's the big deal?"

"How much other stuff exactly did you get rid of?" Kathryn asked. She took out her notebook and flipped back a few pages. She held it up as though about to compare Janine's reply to her notes. Janine watched Kathryn carefully before turning back to Ed.

"Apart from the suit, there were a few old shirts, pullovers, slacks, jeans and jackets. He'd bought himself new gear to go with his new bit of stuff. Didn't walk around looking such a prat with her as he did with me, you can ask anyone."

"A full wardrobe of clothes, then?" Kathryn asked.

"Yeah – so what, it's not a crime is it?"

"It is if they belong to someone else and you don't have their permission to dispose of them." Ed patted the bag lightly. "I put it to you Mrs Kohl that you went to Viktor's house, on Monday twelfth of May, or very early on the Tuesday, stripped the wardrobe of his clothes. You took them to the charity shop, where you were found trying to dispose of them in the outside bins. Why did you do that?"

Ed was on a fishing trip but Kathryn had to give him credit for the way it came over, so assured that Janine was momentarily speechless.

"Mrs Kohl?"

"If you're going to accuse me of stealing his clothes, I want a lawyer. Now."

"So, you don't deny it."

"No comment. You'll get nothing more out of me. I want Derrick here, and a lawyer."

Ed looked sideways at Kathryn. They'd caught Janine out in a lie. If she told one, she could have told others. He'd wait for the brief. He terminated the interview, picked up the suit and left the room.

Kathryn showed Janine out and hurried back to Ed's office. Derrick had been pulled in for the second time but had gone the "no comment" route. They rescheduled his interview for later in the day when his solicitor could make it. They had a lot to get through before then.

Ed stood behind his desk with Truscott's report in his hand. He filled Kathryn in with the details on the ransacking of Mrs Germaine's house and Pug's boat.

"I still can't get her on the phone," she said.

"Why did Pug Germaine have information on the Blood Opal in her briefcase?"

"She's a stamp dealer, and was about to do an item for a TV show. That was her research," Kathryn said. "She'd picked the opal story because of its topicality. What we should be asking is why would anyone steal a handful of pamphlets and a bunch of stamps? It can't be for their value. Unlike the Argyle, it didn't amount to much more than a few quid."

"Forget the Argyle diamond. What if it's *the opal* our intruder is looking for?"

Kathryn's heart missed a beat. "You mean someone after the reward? How could such a person home in on Pug Germaine?"

"It wouldn't take much. Anyone at the market noticing the Kohls behaviour could have worked out the timing and put two and two together. Anyone connected to the Kohls is fair game. With Chantelle's body found in her bed, Pug Germaine's connection was public knowledge."

Kathryn frowned. "If we are widening the net to that extent, it could also be *the illegal buyer* looking for what he believes is his."

"Or, his *agent* – he wouldn't get paid until he delivered the goods."

"So, if the delivery has not yet been made, the buyers could be hounding the robbers."

"Exactly: Spencer and Chantelle could have died, not because they were lovers, but because they got in the way of the opal-fanatic.

Kathryn felt goose bumps break out over her arms. *Those who harm it – die.*

She shook her head – she wasn't prepared to take the husband off the hook yet. "Don't forget we have Viktor's shoes to account for. And the damage done to his wife was personal."

"So, what was the plan? Where did it go wrong?" Ed asked.

"And, was Spencer involved at that stage?" she added.

"According to Truscott," Ed continued. "Dom Spencer's was leaving the country by boat. His first port of call was Jersey and Chantelle Kohl was definitely going with him." Ed scattered his papers about his desk searching for something.

"Looks like the two lovers were working an agenda of their own," Kathryn said.

"Then, why wasn't the opal with Chantelle when she turned up at Spencer's place that Monday morning?"

"Security. Perhaps she'd hidden it away until they were ready to collect it, but died before that moment came."

Ed smiled. "And, their secret died with them? In falling out – the thieves lost their haul! If it wasn't so damn serious, it'd be funny."

Kathryn frowned. "Do we still have Pug Germaine under surveillance?"

"No, Truscott found nothing incriminating on the boat. But, if she *is* involved, she could be waiting for things to cool down before moving in to collect it."

"Then why would she draw attention to herself with the opal stamps business?"

"It shows she has more than a passing interest." Ed said with a shrug. "Not having the opal doesn't necessarily make her innocent."

"Or, safe, come to that," Kathryn retorted.

"Or, safe," he nodded.

Ed's telephone rang. He grabbed it and held up his hand to stop her leaving. She saw the grin spread across his face as he answered his caller in monosyllables.

"Where, when?" She felt his interest, but could only wait for him to explain.

"Viktor?" she asked, as he put the receiver down.

"Next best thing. They've found his white delivery van. It was in some dark corner in a multi-storey car park near the train station. So well hidden in the shadows no one had noticed it. One diligent copper spotted its muddied registration plates, scraped one clean enough to read. It's Victor's alright."

"How long before we get any answers?"

"Forensics are on their way. You know them – as long as it takes. In the meantime, you catch up on this." He'd found the paper he'd been searching for and waved it at her.

"It's the forensic report on Spencer's hard drive and a run down on his computer activities. Go and see Pug Germaine and find out all she knows about her husband's background. Check his employer TSIC, and go over his Internet dealings with the company. Dominic Spencer has left a footprint in places he had no business to go. He's also been using encryption and data wipers and that always gets our techies interest, they like a challenge."

* * *

114

22

Pug woke to the touch of the early morning sun percolating through the long cabin window. It had little warmth but the promise was there. She had a quick wash in the galley sink, pulled on her jeans and a warm sweater and took a mug of coffee out to the cockpit.

The air was fresh and the view magical. Anchored in a small bay she gazed at the tree-clad hills around her, their reflection echoing back from the clear emerald pool. Ratz stared across the water at the narrow ribbon of shore he recognised as his normal exercise spot. He whined, cocked his head and looked at Pug. She inflated the rubber dinghy with the foot-pump and rowed him ashore. He raced away to explore lumps of dried seaweed and jetsam washed up by the tide.

Pug walked barefoot along the shoreline to the point of land she had rounded on her way into the anchorage the previous night. She looked back at *Cazutt* alone in the semi-circular pool, her dark blue hull sharp against the clear green river, her gold anodised mast gleaming. Pug felt her heart swell. She hadn't lost everything. She had a home on the water, the ability to sail and her sturdy Jack Russell for company.

A motor-launch chugged down the river at a leisurely pace. The skipper, a shadowy shape inside the wheelhouse, would be able to see *Cazutt* plainly, but his course did not deviate as he passed the opening to her anchorage and continued downstream heading for the sea. She stood still to watch the red and black hull of the converted fishing boat disappear around the next bend. The same shape, the same sound, the same odd note in the thrum of its motor. For what reason would that boat enter a river at night without lights? The thought sat like a cloud of gnats around her head. Angry at feeling spooked, she kicked a bundle of seaweed.

"Ahh, shit!" She dropped to the ground nursing her bare foot while Ratz raced back to her. "You might have told me there was a bloody rock under it," she grumbled at him. She hobbled back to the rubber dinghy. "Come on, get in." She waded into the water, its cold, salty sting anaesthetising her wound. She pushed the boat out and climbed in behind Ratz, took up the oars and rowed. At least for now, with the launch gone, she didn't have to worry about its intentions. "We'll give him an hour or so to disappear before we leave, just to make sure, eh, Ratz?"

Back on *Cazutt*, Pug tied the inflatable dinghy astern. She'd tow it rather than deflate it. It was no easy job to pump it up every day, and in coastal sailing, it wasn't necessary. She made a cup of tea and spread a toasted croissant with butter and black cherry jam. Feeling safe down in the warmth of her cabin, she decided it would be feeding her paranoia to hang around in the River Yealm, waiting for the mystery launch to disappear over the horizon. She would get going as soon as she was ready.

It took time to secure everything below against the possibility of rough seas. She checked the chart and prepared her course to the River Fowey, a Cornish port some thirty miles down the coast. The shipping forecast had given her a southerly wind, force five, increasing to six later, which roughly translated into a four hour passage for *Cazutt*.

Once they were out in the Channel away from beach walks, Ratz settled into a cave locker in a corner of the cockpit, which she had emptied for the purpose. Attached to a safety line he curled up to wait it out. Pug, in yellow oilskins, her feet firmly laced into trainers to protect her sore toe, sat with both hands holding the tiller. Clouds scudding in from across the Channel covered the sun. The fresh breeze over her shoulders filled the sails. White caps dotted the dark sea as *Cazutt* sailed southwest to her next port of call.

Pug saw no sign of the red and black launch, although there was plenty of marine traffic plying to and from Plymouth. "See, he wasn't hiding behind the rocks waiting for us to come out. We've lost him already." Ratz, opened one eye at the sound of her voice, then went back to sleep. His trust in her was absolute.

*

Dominic Spencer's insurance company, TSIC, had its suite of offices in a high-rise building near the city centre. After Kathryn had parked the unmarked Ford Focus, she tried Pug's phone once more with no result.

She called Truscott. "The last time you saw Pug Germaine she was moving onto her boat, right? I can't get any response from her. Any idea where she is?"

"Not right at this minute. She was free to go," he said, defensively. "I checked she had no plans to leave the country. She said she'd be sailing between here and Falmouth and that she'd keep in touch. Do you want me to track her mobile?"

"Yeah, do that – call me if you get anywhere."

Kathryn left the car and walked into the TSIC office. At reception, a young woman in a smart black pin-stripe suit asked her to wait while she contacted Mr Skidley. She made the call then smiled as she put the phone down. "Come this way."

"Sergeant Kathryn Sinclair, sir." The receptionist introduced her as Kathryn entered Skidley's office, her warrant card ready. The atmosphere was one of quiet decorum with a plush carpet underfoot, original watercolours on the walls, and a huge window that overlooked the city.

Arthur Skidley stood behind his mahogany desk. Spencer's boss barely reached her shoulder. He looked at her ID, and then held his hand out to shake hers. His sharp grey eyes peered over half-moon glasses. She flexed her right hand as he released his grip. What was it with small men and big handshakes?

"It's about our Mr Dominic Spencer, I suppose. I've been expecting you to call. Have you found your suspect, yet?"

Kathryn put her ID away and studied his face but his expression gave nothing away. "We're working on it, Mr Skidley."

"Bad business that. After his death, I thought you people would be looking into his background. Do sit down." He indicated the chair in front of his desk. Once seated, they were more on a level. She extracted a file from her briefcase.

"First thing, Mr Skidley, I understand your company insured the Blood Opal. Did Dominic Spencer's job involve him with that particular gem?"

A shadow crossed Skidley's face. "No, Mr Spencer was in Claims and *officially* had nothing to do with the Blood Opal."

"And unofficially?"

He looked away, biting his lip, then turned back, anger in his eyes. "I'm sorry to say, the late Mr Spencer is currently the subject of an internal enquiry at head office. He's under suspicion of receiving unauthorised information from Security. His name has cropped up in an email from another employee also under investigation."

"Can you give me the name of that employee?" She wrote it down. Harry Norton was the same name the IT guys had come up with.

Skidley continued. "So far, we've found nothing suspicious on Spencer's computer in the office, but he did work at home regularly. We haven't yet had the opportunity to examine his home computer as your people took that away. Have you found anything I should know about?"

"Spencer received encrypted emails from this Harry Norton. This is what our people could decipher. Does it mean anything to you?" She placed the printout on the desk in front of him.

His glance darted from her to the paper and back. He spluttered and dabbed his mouth with a handkerchief. "This confirms information we already have. Unfortunately, the employee who sent this realised he'd been compromised and left the firm the day after Spencer's murder. His wife says he's gone abroad and she has no idea where he is."

And you didn't think to tell us that? Kathryn thought. Had the team known and connected the two crimes back then, how much further on would they be now? But, she had to concede that an employee going AWOL from the London office, and the death of a man in the Plymouth branch would mean nothing unless the investigators had already tied them together.

She pointed to the printed copy. "Can you tell me what these figures mean?"

"Dates and times and code numbers that refer to the items insured. This last one, for instance, refers to the Blood Opal. The last entry dated the day after the auction, gives its destination two days before its delivery. This is pure gold to anyone planning such a robbery." He slapped a hand on his forehead. "My God, imagine what this will do to our reputation if it gets out that the robbery was an inside job. These two should be shot!"

"One of them is already dead, Mr Skidley. I don't think we need any more bodies. Take a good look; is there anything else you can tell us about it?"

He sighed and went back to studying the printout. "It looks like they've done it twice before. I'll have to check on the code numbers to see what these items were. The dates go back a couple of years and the same type of information has been sent both times." He shook his head, his mouth hung open. "I can't believe that Spencer was stupid enough to leave this information on his computer."

"He thought he'd permanently wiped it. But our IT team can winkle out most things." She smiled at his grey stony face. "You say they've done it before. Can you tell me what went missing on those occasions?"

Skidley hesitated then tapped into his desk computer. "The first item was an original Van Gogh, auctioned in London, sold to a buyer in Manchester and stolen en route. The second was a rare and valuable piece of jade. That was twelve months ago, and neither of them have been seen since."

"That's two items insured by your company that have gone AWOL. Didn't you consider that a coincidence?"

He sat upright and looked her in the eye. "Sergeant, our company specialises in the rare and unique. The police investigated them both thoroughly. They didn't make any untoward connection with our company." His voice bordered on the indignant.

"And the dates these other two went missing?" Her pen hovered over her notebook as he turned back to the screen to read the information.

"Okay. Back to the opal," she said. "I understand it is likely that the Blood Opal was stolen for a specific buyer rather than a random theft. Who else would know before the auction that it was on the market?"

"Apart from us and the vendor, those dealing with the auction and the advertising data, and once they'd sent the catalogues out it would be open slather. Collectors, jewellers, investors, antique and collectable dealers, all would know the Blood Opal was coming up for auction. The robbers would have had weeks to plan."

"But only two days to learn of its destination," Kathryn said, "Which is why they needed inside information."

Skidley closed his eyes. He looked to be in pain.

"Thank you, Mr Skidley. I'm sure our colleagues in Exeter are doing their best to get the gem back for you." She wound up the interview and left him looking miserable. She, on the other hand, felt elated. Pay dirt! Spencer was involved right up to his eyeballs. It opened the avenue for a different motive for his killing, one other than domestic.

*

When Pug reached the quiet waters of the River Fowey, she motored to the sailing club's pontoon. Early June, and there were still places available where she could tie up. She planned to stay there for a couple of hours while she visited the harbour master to pay her dues for an overnight mooring buoy. Then she'd go on to the club for a shower and recharge the batteries on her phone.

Two hours later she discovered she'd missed a few calls. They were all from Kathryn. That was okay; she wanted to speak to her anyway. She returned the call.

"Hi, were you looking for me?" she greeted the sergeant.

"Hey, where have you been? I've been looking everywhere. Are you okay?"

"Yeah, I'm fine. I've been cruising that's all. What's the panic?"

"No panic. Where are you?"

"I'm moored in the River Fowey. Sorry you couldn't get me, phone was down. My charger doesn't fit anything on the boat, so I had to wait until I went ashore. Why, has something happened?"

"Can we meet? We need to talk."

"I'm in Cornwall, at least thirty miles away from you and have no car. What's the problem, can't you tell me on the phone?" The last thing she wanted to do was sail back to Plymouth.

"I'll come to you. Where can I find you?"

"In the village of Fowey, I'll meet you on the town quay. The road's very narrow, park at the top and walk down. There's a pub nearby. They do a good cappuccino."

"Okay, see you in an hour or so." Kathryn terminated the call.

Pug checked her watch; it was after three. She picked up Ratz's lead, locked the boat and went ashore. She could fill in the time walking around the village and do a bit of shopping – she needed fresh milk anyway.

The sun broke through and warmed her as she sat on the quay to wait. She gazed across the water to the opposite bank, to the village of Polruan and to a flotilla of boats moored there, her glance probing shadowed areas.

Gulls shrieked and swooped around a boat chugging into the river. A fisherman gutting his catch threw pieces into the air for them to grab, or plummet after. Although similar in size to the red and black launch this one's motor sounded sweet.

When Pug turned her gaze back inland, she recognised the tall figure in a brown trouser suit striding towards her. She envied the sergeant's slim figure. If only she could grow a few inches and lose a few pounds.

The sergeant spotted her and waved. "Hey, you're looking good," she said, "must be all this fresh air."

"You sound like my mother," Pug said. She indicated a redbrick building on the quay and Kathryn nodded.

They took their cups to a table on the sun terrace overlooking the river. Kathryn gazed out at the view. "What a lovely place – never been here before."

Pug spooned the grated chocolate, folding it into the froth of her cappuccino. "Yep, they call it an area of outstanding natural beauty, and that's official. You wouldn't think it, but it's also a commercial seaport for ships exporting china clay." She licked her spoon and pointed upriver with it. "They've hidden the commercial jetties behind a bend. You should see it when the ships are on the move; they look fantastic." A yacht in full sail swept upriver and Pug's glance followed its lines with pleasure. She looked back at the sergeant. "What's the problem? It must be something big for you to come all this way."

Kathryn put her cup down. "Look, I know we've been through some of this before, but I need to know more about your husband. Can you manage that?"

"What do you want to know?"

"Did Dominic mention anything about the Blood Opal to you, either in passing or to someone else in your hearing?"

Pug felt a chill on the back of her neck. "What are you suggesting?"

Kathryn gave her a brief update on her own suspicions. "If Dominic was involved in the planning of the robbery, we need to know who else he was involved with, if he had a local partner, for instance."

Pug's jaw dropped. "You're not joking, are you?" She shook her head. "Of course he wasn't involved. It had nothing to do with us. He was at home with me when it happened. He never even mentioned the name."

"Okay. Did he behave any differently in those last couple of weeks? I really do need to know. Take your time, there's no rush."

Pug hesitated. "I know he was stressed. I thought it was to do with me. We were going through a rough patch. It wasn't until I actually saw him in bed with that woman that I finally realised how bad …"

Kathryn gave her a smile, extended her hand and touched her lightly on the arm. "The wife is often the last to know, so they say." Her voice had a bitter edge to it and Pug wondered if she was speaking from experience.

"But, you're saying it's more than that. I don't know what else to say. I didn't know he was involved in anything dodgy."

"Okay. Let's break it down a bit. You said Viktor used to call at your house occasionally. Did he visit during those last few weeks?"

"He used to come around once a month or so. They stayed mainly in Dom's office upstairs. But more recently, it had been a couple of times a week. In fact I made a disparaging comment about it once, and asked Dom if Viktor was moving in, only joking of course, but he didn't like it."

"What did he say?"

"He said we '*owed*' Viktor. I asked him why, and that's when he told me that Viktor had given us a very special price on the Argyle diamond. I think the other two pieces of jewellery also came from Viktor at special prices."

"You didn't think that was odd?"

"Not really. I knew the jewellery wasn't new, that it was valuable and it came through Viktor's antiques business. I also knew they worked on a very high mark-up, so I assumed Viktor had simply lowered his mark-up to sell to Dom."

"You didn't wonder what Dom did for Viktor to earn this special price?"

Pug closed her eyes and felt the groan in the back of her throat. "I thought maybe he just gave him a discounted price on his insurance. I didn't really think about it."

"Okay. Can you tell me when those other two occasions were?" Kathryn took her notebook from her bag and flipped through the pages.

Pug stared, mesmerised by her movements. It was all happening again, questions, questions; would it never end? She told Kathryn of the occasions Dom had given her the sapphire ring, earrings set and the pearl necklace, tying it to a birthday and an anniversary.

"The silly part about it was I'm not really into jewellery. He didn't need to spend that sort of money on me. Stupid me, I treasured them not for their value, but because he bought them for me. Or, so I thought."

"And the Argyle diamond?"

"That was for our seventh wedding anniversary two months ago. I realise now that he was only buying this jewellery as investments for the future – his and that woman's." She looked away from Kathryn, feeling foolish that she'd been taken in so easily. "Why, what's going on?" she asked.

"We think Dominic traded information about *certain insured items* in exchange for peppercorn prices on expensive, clean jewellery."

Pug caught her breath. "And the Blood Opal is one of those insured items?"

Kathryn nodded. "Now, if Dominic had got his hands on the opal before he and Mrs Kohl were killed, where would he have hidden it?"

"The obvious place would have been his under-floor safe. But, we both know it wasn't there. Look, sorry, but I have no idea. What makes you think Viktor hasn't just disappeared with it?"

"We know it hasn't reached its illegal destination, because someone is still looking for it. When you phoned me earlier, was it just in reply to my calls, or did you want to tell me something?"

Pug had almost forgotten. "I was going to ask you if you had anyone tailing me."

Kathryn's eyes widened. "No, we haven't. Why do you ask?"

Pug told her about the launch following her up the River Yealm the night before. "It went out before me this morning and I haven't seen it since, so it's probably imagination."

"Don't be too quick to dismiss gut feelings. Anyway, let me know if it happens again. Maybe you should come back to Plymouth where we can keep an eye on you."

Pug shook her head violently. "Not unless I really have to. I don't want to go back. I want to start afresh. Besides, I feel safer on my boat than I did back in the city, and I can always radio the Coastguard in an emergency."

"Does Viktor have a boat?"

Pug looked at Kathryn, thinking furiously. Viktor pursuing her in the red and black launch was not a comforting thought.

"Don't know. Dom's never mentioned it."

* * *

23

Kathryn followed Ed down the steps, her shoes clacking along the stone-flagged corridor. A note, with a smiley face, stuck on the window of a pair of swing doors at the end announced they were entering "Daly's Domain." Located beneath the Southside police station, the cellars passed for a modest crime lab. Inside, the damp air had a faint chemical smell. John Daly sat hunched over his microscope.

"Morning, Daly, what've you got that's pulled us out of bed again so early?" Ed asked.

Daly's eyes, magnified by his overlarge spectacles, were bloodshot. It looked like he'd been working all night.

"Ah, I think you'll find it's worth the effort. Your suspect's van had a lot to tell us." He waved them over to a bench and pointed to the bags lying beside the microscope.

After her meeting with Pug the day before, Kathryn had arrived back at the station too late to brief Ed on the results of her interview with Arthur Skidley at TSIC. She'd intended doing it before the day's work got under way when this cropped up.

Daly's smile was too cheerful for this time of the morning. His spectacles slipped a notch down his nose.

"You should find something here you can get your teeth into." He picked up a clutch of papers and read out the investigators' findings. Ed leaned on the bench, one hand propping his elbow, the other his chin.

They had found hair from four different sources, three of which they'd identified as coming from Derrick, Viktor and Chantelle Kohl, and another long ginger coloured hair, human, but without skin tag, possibly from a wig.

Kathryn glanced at Ed. "That'll be Chantelle's. We found a wig that colour in her wardrobe." No surprises so far, they knew all three had been in the van the weekend prior to the murders.

Daly looked back at his report. "Next, we found dark red woollen fibres and short black hair containing traces of blood."

"Whose blood? Where?" Ed straightened and spoke out, suddenly alert.

"In the back of the van, down on the carpet – blood comes from three different sources, Spencer, Chantelle and Viktor Kohl."

Kathryn pursed her lips, understanding the point he was making. Along with the blood of the two victims, Daly had found their suspect's blood.

"How much blood are we looking at?"

"Traces found from Viktor's hair, plus a small patch no bigger than a 50p coin."

Kathryn tried to visualise the scene. Viktor's blood? Maybe one of the victims got in a blow before Viktor overpowered them. With the victims' blood on his hair, they could place him at the scene of the crime, but it didn't explain how his own blood got into the back of his van.

"Any of that blood on the driver's headrest?" she asked.

Daly shook his head.

"Sounds like he had a driver then," she suggested.

"From the positioning of the stains, we think Viktor lay flat on the floor, head up near the base of the driver's seat. We found a mat of loose, bloodstained cropped hairs in that one spot. The pattern is consistent with a head wound."

"So, whose prints were on the steering wheel?" she asked.

"It'd been wiped clean, same with the gear lever." He held up a finger. "Now lastly, we found a stray three-fingered print on the outside of the van just above the muddied number plate. It was different from the others. We've identified it as Janine Kohl's."

Janine! Kathryn thought of the charity shop and Viktor's Hong Kong suit. The ex-wife had disposed of Viktor's clothes, and now she had done the same with his van. Would a wounded Viktor have called on his ex-wife for help? Or, going one-step further was Viktor Kohl another victim, rather than the killer? Maybe they had it wrong and Viktor hadn't done a runner at all.

She darted a glance at Ed. "You keep saying that a woman could have done it. What do you think of Janine as our killer?"

"Motive?"

"There's no love lost between the two wives. You've heard the way Janine talks about Chantelle. The pathologist says a woman could have committed the crime. And then, there's the opal. Last we heard Chantelle was driving away after the robbery – most likely with the opal. What if Janine knew about it, through Derrick, and wanted a share?"

"Janine has an alibi. Her son Elvis was at home with her and Derrick until eight thirty. When Elvis went off to work, Derrick stayed on until eleven that morning. There's no forensic evidence to show Janine even entered the Mullion Road house. Unless I hear something to the contrary, she is pretty low on my list of suspects." He didn't say as much in front of Daly, but she noticed his eyes warning her about jumping to conclusions again.

But then, if Janine had been wearing gloves she wouldn't have left prints in the house. And Janine and Derrick could have collaborated on alibis. All she needed was time to work out how it related back to the opal robbery, and whether the victims died as the result of a crime of passion, or as a gang of robbers devouring each other to get to the prize.

She recalled the first time she'd seen Derrick in Viktor's antique shop. He'd come out from behind the curtain while she and Truscott spoke to Elvis. Derrick had been nursing a sore hand at the time.

She turned to Daly. "Did you find any trace of blood, or skin particles on the inside walls of the van?"

"No, if anything had been there, we would've found it. We spared not a square inch."

He shuffled through papers and selected one. "I sent samples of mud from the tyres and mudguards to our botanist. She says the earth came from a woodland area containing pine trees, in particular, *Pinus radiata,* and spores of rare fungi were present. She's included a diagram with a couple of likely areas. If that doesn't yield anything useful, she can go deeper into the analysis, but that will take time. Oh, and the mud on the number plates comes from the rose-bed around the car park where they'd found the van. And that is it." Daly beamed from one to the other.

"Right, thanks," Ed held his hand out for the report. "We'll get a search organised of those areas and see what, if anything, turns up. Anything else you want to ask, Sergeant?"

Kathryn shook her head. Not now, anyway, she had some thinking to do.

* * *

24

The warmth of the sun drew loamy scents out of hedgerows still damp from the morning showers. Ratz raced along the coastal footpaths, jumped through stiles and dashed off after different trails, while Pug strode along enjoying a newfound sense of freedom.

Inevitably, her mind turned to Kathryn's visit the day before and the momentous news she'd brought. In some way, the knowledge that Dom was involved in the Blood Opal robbery was liberating as well as scary. It was starting to look as though Dom's death was as much about thieves falling out as it was about extra-maritals. If so, that absolved her from the miniscule feeling of guilt in the back of her mind that she was somehow responsible for his actions.

For lunch, she and Ratz shared a bottle of water and an egg and cheese salad roll. She sat on a cliff-top bench and stared out over the sea to misty headlands in the distance. She would be sailing around them in a day or two. In time, she retraced her steps to the harbour.

Back on board *Cazutt*, she tied the inflatable to the stern cleat. Ratz bounced around her feet, his bright eyes and doggy grin, evidence to the quality of their day. She unlocked the cabin, slid inside and collapsed onto a bunk. "Phew! It's alright for you. I'm knackered. Not used to all this walking."

Eventually she got herself into gear, fed the dog and made a cup of tea. There was a leftover portion of a one-pot stew to finish. She heated that and ate it with a stick of crispy bread. As the evening grew dark, she switched on the cabin lamps and lay back on her bunk to read again the history of the Blood Opal. The booklet was the only piece of information she had left. It had not been in her briefcase with the stamps as she'd taken it out intending to read it through, but had never got around to it.

"Found in a dead man's hand." And the dead man was the miner Seamus Kelly, who had died extracting it from the ground. Black opals were not so popular in those early days, but the jeweller who'd cut it open knew he'd hit the jackpot. When, shortly after, he died a victim

of a wild bush fire, rumours of bad luck began to circulate. She recalled Celeste's ominous warnings. She understood that the run of bad luck hit some but not others, which only went to show there was nothing in the story of a curse. Otherwise, surely, it would affect everyone it touched.

On impulse, she picked up her phone. Celeste's silvery tones caused momentary tears to dampen her eyes. How she'd missed their daily chats, the cups of chamomile tea amongst the fairies and papier-mâché castles.

"Hey, Honey Pug! You must be psychic. I was just thinking about you! Where are you, what are you doing?" When Celeste paused long enough for Pug to get a word in, they talked of the past and the future – and the Blood Opal.

"This bad luck tag, can you tell me more about it?" Pug asked. "For instance why do only some people suffer death or disaster and not others?"

"Seems like the curse hits only those who harm the opal, like the miners and the jewellers who, *in the opal's eye,* caused it damage."

"Who else died, do you know?"

"Back in the sixties, a wealthy mining magnate bought the Blood Opal. He had it re-cut polished and turned into a pendant for his daughter. Then about a year later, his daughter died, the only victim of a light aeroplane crash. They say she was wearing the opal at the time and it survived undamaged. But mutterings about it bringing bad luck resurfaced. The mining magnate wanted nothing more to do with it. He sent it to the auction rooms. That's how it came to England. A British collector snapped it up."

"What happened to him?"

"Here's where the story changes. This collector was a lover of fine jewellery. He kept the opal in pristine condition, and didn't alter it in any way. Nothing bad happened to him and after another forty odd years, he died an old man of natural causes. His heirs sold off his collection piecemeal in this last auction. And, of course, you know what happened to it then."

If only she did, Pug thought. "So, was the courier's death coincidental?"

"If fate had decreed it was the courier's time," Celeste said, "nothing would have stopped it. As for you and the disasters that came your way, who knows, maybe it's because you're on the periphery, so you're getting a backwash of bad luck. You're not still carting those stamps around with you, are you?"

A cold draught whispered down her neck. Celeste didn't know the half of it. What about Dom and that woman? Was the Blood Opal responsible for their deaths? She couldn't believe she was even thinking like this.

She changed the subject and their conversation eventually dwindled until they said good night. With a history like that, why would anyone in their right mind want to steal the opal? It was all too airy-fairy for her. Surely, it had more to do with the greed of men, than any malevolent intervention.

Still fully dressed, she lay back on her bunk, closed her eyes and in the gentle rocking of the boat, drifted into an uneasy sleep.

Terror caused her legs to pound the earth as she ran. Red lights glowed from cavern walls; black sticky treacle embroiled her feet and slowed her escape. Arms flailing, she struck out as webs curled and tangled around her body. A huge black spider with shimmering red markings landed on her stomach. It clawed at her chest making fearsome grunty noises. She grasped the furry beast and flung it aside.

Jerked awake by her own scream, she saw Ratz fly across the cabin and land on the opposite berth. He looked at her with hurt-filled eyes. Too late she realised he'd been trying to wake her from the nightmare. She swung her legs off the bunk and went to him.   "I'm   so sorry, Ratzy," she hugged him, breathing in his warm doggie smell as the last threads of her dream dissipated. Apology came in the form of a biscuit – forgiveness, a lick and a tail-wag.

Not willing to go to bed yet, in case the dream recurred, she made a mug of hot chocolate and took it outside to the cockpit. The cool night air calmed her. Strains of music floated across the water from the harbour pubs, with shouts and laughter of people skylarking on the shore. Lights shone from villagers' houses and the occasional sweep of headlights flashed across the sky from the car park up the hill.

She missed Dom. That is the Dom of earlier years when they'd laughed and loved together, before he'd been bitten by the riches bug.

Above the distant night noises she heard another. She cocked her head and listened. It was the same motor, the same sound, its pitch higher than most. It was unmistakable. Leaning in through the hatch she grabbed her anorak, switched off the cabin lights and waited.

First she spotted its navigation lights. The launch appeared out of the gloom, making its way slowly up river. Huddled in her dark anorak, which she hoped rendered her invisible, she watched as it passed her by. The engine cut out and the boat glided forward. A shadowy figure leaned over the side and picked up a mooring buoy. She heard the clunk as he hauled the chain aboard. It was too dark to read the boat's name.

There appeared to be only one person on board. He was the right height, but there was no telling if he was Viktor Kohl; his oilskins disguised the shape beneath. She waited and watched. Nothing happened.

After half an hour or so, his interior lights went off. He didn't leave the boat, so she assumed he'd retired for the night. Ratz made little whiny noises as though he'd caught her sense of unease. A gentle pat hushed him; noises travel over water. She moved back into the cabin and lay on her bunk in the dark, unwilling to draw attention to herself by putting the cabin lights on. Another hour went by and no change in the launch's dark, silent form. She didn't want to see that boat when she woke up in the morning.

What were her options? To start the engine would be a dead give away. But with the tide going out and the wind offshore, *Cazutt* could glide away with just her foresail up. It was a tempting proposition.

Using only the tiny chart light, she checked out the true course she'd need to take her past Gribbin Head and around the next big headland, Dodman Point, before she'd need to change course for Falmouth. Working as quietly as she could she climbed out through the hatch and fitted the foresail. The night was dark but clear. The moon had not yet risen, but in the east, the sky paled heralding its imminent appearance. If she left it much longer, the moon would highlight her position.

The launch ahead of her was still in darkness. She dropped the mooring overboard a few inches at a time, so as not to make a splash, pulled the sail up and returned to the tiller.

The shore-scented breeze filled the sail and took *Cazutt* gently and silently down the river. She'd show no lights while the launch was in sight. Two could play at that game.

Hours later, bathed in moonlight, *Cazutt* sailed into the Fal Estuary between Black Rock Beacon and St Anthony Lighthouse. Pug stood up in the cockpit and stretched her stiffening limbs, exhilarated at having made her destination in such good time. That offshore breeze had stayed with her and the calm waters had made it an easy run. She cut across the river to the Port of Falmouth, dropped both sails and motored to the designated visitors' moorings.

Lights around the quay gave her a sense of homecoming. Their reflections in the water danced to the whim of the tidal flow. The breeze rustled the lightweight foresail – she grabbed it before it ballooned, and stuffed it into a sail bag. After she'd fixed the anchor-light, she took to her bunk to sleep through whatever was left of the night, rocked by the gentle flow and lulled by the sounds of halyards clinking on the masts of nearby boats.

* * *

25

Ratz woke her when the sun was high by pulling at her sleeping bag. The harsh cry of gulls penetrated her dozy state. She climbed out of the bunk, put the kettle on, and opened the hatch for her first look outside in daylight. The cranes of Falmouth Docks stood stark against the grey sky. Boats from small runabouts to the full-sailed Falmouth working boats ploughed the waters around her.

She turned to take in the view full circle and stopped. There, up against the quay sat the red and black launch she had left in Fowey. It had to be *him* – that space had been empty when she came in only six hours ago. She dropped a fist on the sliding hatch-cover. "Bugger!"

A man came out of the wheelhouse. She sat down suddenly to reduce her profile. He was dressed in jeans, dark blue anorak, a faded navy-blue seaman's cap, and wore a short beard. He looked nothing like Viktor Kohl. He locked up and stepped over the gunnels onto the quay. He walked away and disappeared amongst the buildings. Not once had he glanced in her direction. She turned the kettle off, threw on her shirt, jeans and anorak. Anxiety re-awakened the butterflies sleeping in her belly.

She untied the dinghy's painter. "Come on Ratz, let's go and see what he's up to."

If she gave Kathryn the name of his boat, maybe she could do a trace on it and find out who this man following her was. She rowed towards the launch to have a better look. Its black and red hull looked newly painted, its name clear on the stern read *Piglet* and its port of registry was Devonport. *Piglet!* What kind of a name was that for a boat manned by a stalker?

She turned and headed for a slipway crowded with small dinghies. Her first job ashore would be to check in with the harbour master. After that, she'd walk through the town. The shops were mainly on two sides of one long street, with any luck, she'd find *Piglet's* skipper along there somewhere.

Twenty minutes later, business with the harbour master completed, she walked, with Ratz on a lead, into the town's busy main street. Her quarry could be anywhere. She passed numerous cafes along the route, and peered down alleyways leading to the harbour, where she caught glimpses of the shining water. Too many other men wore dark jeans and anoraks, but not many of them had a seaman's peaked cap and fewer still had beards.

Finally, she caught up with him coming out of a chandlery. He now carried a red plastic shopping bag. She stood well back and let him pass, then followed him from shop to shop, the red bag flagging his movements. She watched as he approached assistants, or paid for his goods, and saw an easygoing man full of bonhomie, the occasional joke and friendly wave. Like the name of his boat, it didn't tally with the sort of man she believed was pestering her. Then she lost him in a crowd of tourists. She swept along behind them looking into every shop as she passed.

With hands shielding the light from her eyes, she peered in through the glass door of a bakery. At the same moment, the door swung inwards and there he was standing in front of her. Taken by surprise, she blurted out the first thing that came to mind.

"Why are you following me?"

His mouth curved up at the sides, and white teeth flashed. "Me – following you!" He gestured to indicate their relevant positions. "Don't you think it's the other way around?" His look was so direct she could see flecks of brown in his clear blue eyes. But, she could think of nothing to say.

"If I'm not mistaken, you've been dogging my heels all the way down the street." He glanced at Ratz. "He does rather give the game away, you know. Look, is everything okay? Is this a case of mistaken identity, do you think?"

His voice rich and full of concern, was not as she imagined it should be. Did she have the wrong man? This was the same man she'd seen getting off *Piglet*. Or, cringe, cringe, did she have the wrong launch? She hadn't actually heard its engine.

"Look, I'll tell you what," he said. "How about we go in there and have a coffee and talk it over?" He pointed to a coffee shop nearby.

Pug nodded. It made sense, and she might find out his last port of call and learn whether she had the wrong boat. She couldn't come to any harm in full view of the public.

133

Inside the café, with Ratz sitting by her feet, hidden beneath the table, Pug studied her mystery man as they waited for their coffee. He wasn't much taller than she was, with a stocky build and looked around forty or so. His quiet firm voice had a trace of a Cornish burr. He'd taken his cap off, and his brown curly hair showed flecks of grey, the same with his neatly trimmed beard. Deeply embedded crow's feet lined his face.

Noticing her scrutiny, he leaned forward, hands on the table. "I'm Gilford Trelawney, known variously as Guilty, Gil, Gills or even Fish-face by my friends."

She smiled, "Why Fish-face?"

"Fish have gills." In his soft laughter, she recognised his ploy to ease the tension.

"Right, then, I'm Pug Germaine, and before you ask, my parents named me after my two grandmothers. For years now I have used only my initials."

"So, what are your real names?"

"That comes under the official secrets act."

He grinned. "Alright, I won't pry. So, who is this fiend following you?"

"If I knew that, I'd know what I was up against."

"What made you think it might be me?"

She told him of the motorboat with the recognisable engine noise, and the places she'd been to and the fact that the same boat always followed her in. They both sat back while the waitress delivered their coffee. Then Pug continued.

"So, when I saw your boat this morning, I knew you'd done it again. It's too much of a coincidence." Her reasoning faltered. His friendly manner, his way of looking her straight in the eye, gave rise to serious doubts that Gilford Trelawney's presence had anything to do with stalking. As he was taking it with good grace, her embarrassment diminished.

He tapped the table with his fingers, deep in thought. "Look, I think I can relieve you of your worries. *Mea culpa,* I am the guilty party. I *was* at Fowey last night, but after a few hours' kip, I woke up and it was such a fine night I was ready to move on."

At least he hadn't lied, but her suspicions returned. Breath caught in the back of her throat, she waited for further explanation.

"Alright, alright, I'll tell you. I'm pub hunting. I have details from three estate agents. I'm going down the coast and looking at pubs for sale, preferably, in a holiday area. I'd like to find one freehold and free of tie, but they're like hen's teeth. Look, I can show you if you like, I have the info back on the boat. You can tell me if you've been in any of them." He smiled at her and sipped his coffee.

The warning her parents had drilled into her when she was a kid raised its ugly antennae. Was getting into a stranger's boat the same as getting into one's car? But for her recent history, she wouldn't have given it a second thought.

"So, why did you sail up the River Yealm without navigation lights?" she asked.

"Ah, so you were the boat ahead of me." He shrugged and put his coffee cup down on its saucer. "Look, I'd hit a problem with the electrics. I couldn't do it easily while under way, so I waited until I anchored. It was no big deal."

And, that, she could understand. Sailing on your own meant that occasionally things had to wait until you were in a better position to deal with them. They continued to talk boats. He told her how he'd spent the last two years renovating an old fishing vessel, and turning her into a seaborne home fit to live in. By the time he'd finished Pug was captivated. But still not game enough to take him up on his offer to show her his renovations deep inside his boat.

They walked back to the quay together and stood beside his launch. She couldn't deny she was tempted. But, she offered the excuse that she had calls to make by a certain time and that maybe she'd come aboard another day. In the meantime, she intended to get the hunky Gil Trelawney checked out by Kathryn. She watched as Gil went aboard and opened up the wheelhouse. He turned back to wave.

She responded and suddenly Ratz jerked the lead out of her hand and dashed forward. In a flurry of black and white fur and vicious growls he leapt onto the launch, disappeared between Gil's ankles and down into the cabin.

"Ratz!" she yelled after him. "Come back!"

"He's after the cat!" Gil disappeared down into his boat. Pug stepped aboard and followed the pair through the wheelhouse and down the unfamiliar ladder-like steps.

Down below she found Gil looking into his saloon. Ratz sat on the floor, eyes intent only on the tabby cat holed up in an open locker too high for him to reach. He ignored Pug's call and licked his lips. The cat looked enormous with all its fur standing on end, its green eyes wide. It yowled at Ratz. He wrinkled his nose and lips to show his teeth.

Gil picked up Ratz's lead and handed it to Pug. "No harm done," he said.

The irate spitting cat was nearly as big as Ratz. "What's his name?"

"She's called Moggy." He shrugged at the unoriginal name. "I've had her for years. Look, now you're here, how about a quick beer or a cup of tea?"

"Think we can keep these two apart long enough?"

"You hang on to him. I expect Moggy will stay where she is. That's her place, she feels safe up there."

While he poured the beers, Pug looked around in envy. He had far more space than she did. Mahogany panelling lined the sides of the saloon, dark red berth cushions and brass fittings gave the whole an ambience of warmth and cosiness without fuss. He even had a small wood burner built into a bulkhead.

"For those chilly winter nights," he told her when he caught her looking at it. No sign of a feminine presence. She wondered if he lived alone. It was too personal a question to ask on such short acquaintance.

"Why *Piglet*? Or, was she already called that?"

He laughed. "No, she had a series of numbers rather than a name. I was going to call her Babe, but somebody pointed out it could be misconstrued and seen as something other than a little pink pig."

He opened up the mahogany chart desk and took out a sheaf of papers from the real estate agents to show her. From inside the desk a splash of colour caught her eye. Bright orange, it reminded her of the insurance company files Dom had in his room.

"Look, here you are, I've seen these so far," he said, giving her those with comments written on the sides. As he'd told her earlier, they were all pubs located southwest of Plymouth. She felt an apology was in order, but sensed her earlier suspicions hadn't bothered him.

"Ahoy there, *Piglet*!" a voice called from outside.

Gilford looked out. "It's the bloke from harbour master's office. Come for his dues, I expect. Won't be a minute." He grabbed his wallet from a shelf and went out.

Curiosity won. She lifted the desk lid and looked inside at the orange folder. Although partly covered by a chart, the familiar TSIC's logo was plain to see. She slid the chart away. The name SPENCER

D. stood out in bold letters on the subject line of the folder. Dominic? What was Gilford Trelawney doing with a file on her dead husband?

The sound of men parting company reached her ears. No time to look further, she wanted out quick smart, at least until she'd checked with Kathryn. She dragged Ratz away from his Moggy-watching and helped him up the narrow steps into the wheelhouse. The powerful binoculars clipped to the bulkhead there took on a new sinister tone. Was Gilford Trelawney's pub hunting all a ruse?

Gil was on his way back. He stopped as they met at the door. "You going already?"

"Erm, I have to fly. Sorry, but I'd forgotten, I'm expecting a call at three. My phone's back there," she lied, hoping the damn thing wouldn't go off before she'd left his boat. She checked her watch, "It's nearly that now. Thanks for showing me around and for the beer."

"Oh, alright. That's okay. Anytime." He took a card out of his wallet and gave it to her. "Look, here's my mobile number, if you feel like a bit of company or dinner out, by all means call me. I'll be around for a while." He gave her a cheeky grin.

A quick glance at the card showed only his name and his number. She hauled Ratz back to the slipway and pushed the inflatable into the water. Gilford Trelawney – the man was so likeable, but she didn't know who to trust any more. She took up the oars and rowed back to *Cazutt*, disappointment heavy in her heart.

* * *

26

Kathryn opened the car window a couple of inches to stop the windscreen fogging. Ed sat in the driver's seat talking on the phone to the DCI, reporting the progress of the search. Fine drizzle misted the wet forest scene in front of them. A bobbing blue line of police officers crept across the ground, hunting for any clue that would indicate Viktor Kohl's van had been at this site recently.

She looked at Ed and saw the worry lines creasing his face. With the discovery of their suspect's blood in the back of the van, it was becoming increasingly clear that Viktor had not left the country on the day of the murders. Ed's case was taking a U-turn.

Known as Pine Ridges, this stretch of woodland was the second area named in the botanist's chart. Set back from the road, the clear ground beneath the pine trees made it a popular place for picnics. Towards the rear, the forest degenerated into scrub, the ground rough with fallen trees and dead branches. As Kathryn watched, an officer with a cadaver dog raised his arm. Other officers collected around one spot where a small assortment of branches lay. A cry went up, but too far away for her to hear the words. More officers converged on the group.

"They've found something," she said, fastening her long, belted mackintosh.

Ed finished his call. "Right. Let's go." He shrugged into a black anorak and they set off to join the group of officers pulling at the brushwood. A dank smell of the forest was stronger here – she touched her nose.

Truscott looked up as they approached. He indicated the heap of dead branches. "This stuff didn't fall naturally, it's been put there. Underneath there's newly dug earth." He pulled a face.

"Right. Seal off the area and let's look. Go carefully, hand tools only to start with." Ed stood, white hair plastered to his forehead, rain channelling down his face like sweat.

Officers removed the boughs and started by scraping the loose topsoil. Freshly dug it was easy to move. A smell permeated the air and set at least one officer gagging. Kathryn pulled the collar of her raincoat over the lower part of her face trying to avoid the stench.

Trowel by trowel, they moved the earth and placed it on a tarpaulin for later examination. They didn't have far to go. Tiny creatures scurried away from the corpse as they exposed it. A black plastic bag covered the head. The mud-covered body looked as though the earth had already started to absorb it. A touch of colour came from the pullover where shiny beetles climbed in and out through the holes they'd eaten into the dark red wool.

Socks, but no shoes, Kathryn noticed. If that was Viktor Kohl, she knew exactly where his shoes were. Inside a plastic bag and locked in the evidence room with human blood and vegetable matter stuck on their soles.

The officers stretched another tarpaulin over the body and the makeshift grave to preserve evidence from the effects of rain while they erected a tent around it. Others taped off the area. Ed rang in to report their find, and get the pathologist and his team out to examine the body in situ.

"Right. We can't do any more here until we've identified the body," Ed said to Kathryn, "Let's get out of here."

"It's pretty obvious that it's Viktor. His shoes are missing and he's wearing the same clothes that were taken from the laundry," she said.

Once back in the car, she changed the subject away from the disturbing mess in the grave and asked Ed how the second interview with Derrick had gone.

"Bloody waste of time. He was too quick with his 'no comments' and his solicitor continually bleated that we had nothing on his client. In the end, we had to let him go. We need more than circumstantial."

"What time did you let him go?'

"Around midnight. What's on your mind?"

"That was the night someone followed Pug Germaine up the River Yealm."

"It wasn't Derrick Kohl. We had a tail on him after he left us."

*

Not again – he offered up a straight fat finger to the newsreader. Wasn't there any other news in this frigging city? What with the TV

139

coverage plastered over every newsbreak, the world and its wife knew Viktor Kohl had been found. He watched the latest update – cops running around like farts in a colander, searching for clues – pity they didn't have something better to do. Too late now, he should've gone deeper – made a better job of it.

He packed his kitbag – time to move on. At least travelling light was no problem. How to get rid of his tail? That shouldn't be hard. They call that surveillance – he called it bloody laughable. Travelling home in his brief's car he'd tagged the tail within minutes of leaving the nick. They were still there, outside in the street, watching. But now Lady Luck had upped the stakes. They had a body. Any time soon they'll be banging on his door, ready to haul him in again.

He had his back to the wall. Even the search of the widow's new quarters had produced nothing more than paperwork. At least it proved he was on the right track. Why else would the silly cow carry copies of the merchandise? He'd pocketed the information to study later in case she'd left a clue there. If, against all rhyme and reason, she intended to ignore the plan and go solo, then maybe her pretty pamphlets would help her find a market. Not that it affected him – his buyer was ready and growing more impatient by the day.

Earlier, in the woman's house, her briefcase still in his hand, he'd felt the weight of his mobile in his back pocket. *They* hadn't phoned in a while. Moments later the house telephone had rung. Startled, he wheeled around and eyeballed it. The answering machine cut in; a woman's voice invited the caller to leave a message. He'd listened as the caller obliged, his grin getting wider. On his way out he'd dropped a little present for the dog.

Armed with new knowledge he paid a visit to the chandlers who fixed him up with the right equipment, and a carefully timed trip to the sailing club did the rest.

You gotta bloody win some of the time.

Now, as his own TV blared on, he knew he was running out of options. He set the indoor security lights to On/Off – irregular intervals, and left the TV going. He picked up his kitbag and climbed out of the dormer window at the top of his block of flats. Once on the roof, it was a simple matter to by-pass the surveillance, slip down to the far end of the terraced building and climb back in through the end dormer window, with its conveniently broken lock, and down to his car parked in the nearby shopping centre.

*

Ed's next early morning call took him to the mortuary. Apart from the cold, he hated the smell, the damp and the deadness of the place. Kathryn had already arrived and was donning a mask while talking to Denny.

The pathologist rolled the steel gurney out of the refrigerator. The body from the pinewood grave had been identified as Viktor Kohl by the four of its fingerprints still viable. The mound beneath a green sheet looked smaller than Ed had expected.

Denny uncovered the torso; Ed looked away for a moment. When he looked back the sight reminded him of Matt and the bloody remains of his head after the shotgun blast. Viewing the dead was a side of policing Ed had never been comfortable with, but since Matt's death, it had become a dreaded chore. He mentally shook himself and looked down at the body he'd come to view. The cadaver, although cleaned up, was still a gruesome sight, its head black, and what flesh he could see, sickly green.

He adjusted the mask to cover his nose, and caught Kathryn's uneasy glance across the body. "Okay, Bruce, tell us what you've found," he said.

Bruce Denny, without a mask, looked at ease in his place of work.

"Your man died as a result of blunt-force trauma," he said, pointing to areas around the back of the battered head. "It cracked his skull and caused intracranial bleeding. He also suffered a broken jaw."

Ed's hands retreated deeper into his pockets as he bent over to peer at the wounded head. "Any idea how the injuries occurred?"

"He took a heavy blow to the jaw. He could've been thrown backwards and cracked his head on something hard. It's the sort of damage we see from a fist fight."

Ed took a step back, considering the scenario. Viktor's killer had to be a man; few women could pack a punch like that. "Can you tell us when he died?"

Denny looked down, eyebrows raised and lips pursed. "His body's in reasonable condition. The torn bag on his head contained most of blood, but not all. Burial in shady ground kept him cool. Putrefaction has only just begun. No predator damage, a certain amount of insect activity present – black beetles. No fly eggs or maggots, suggests prompt burial. My best guess is that death occurred about three to four weeks ago. Could even be the same day his two victims died."

"How can you tell that?" Kathryn looked at Denny curiously.

Denny smiled at her. "What, that he killed them? Or that it was the same day?"

"Both."

"His clothing. Underneath the red pullover, his shirt had been saturated with blood. Lab results show it was a mixture of Dom Spencer's and Chantelle's blood. This fellow either murdered them, or was in close proximity at the time they were killed."

"If he died as the result of a fight, would his assailant be marked?" Ed asked.

"There are no further abrasions on the body, no undue bruising. So, the fight didn't last long. That one punch to his jaw could have bloodied the perp's knuckles, or even broken his hand. He'd be a big man, and strong to have decked this fellow with such force."

Ed nodded. "Right. Thanks Bruce. At least we're no longer chasing a dead man's trail. Anything else you want to ask, Sergeant?" He took a few steps towards the exit, eager to get out of the place.

"Is there any chance the assailant left skin particles from his fist on Viktor's face?"

Bruce chuckled. "You interested in a career change? With questions like that, we could do with you down here – stretch my team a bit. But no, we haven't found any yet."

"What prompted that question?" Ed queried as they walked out to the car park.

"That first day we talked to Derrick, he had blood on his knuckles. He said he'd scraped his hand down the side of the van. Remember?"

He hadn't remembered. He didn't say it aloud, but he was impressed that she had picked it up. "You think Derrick would kill his own brother – because?"

"Rage – again. But for a different reason. Chantelle took the opal home with her; she and Spencer planned to disappear with it. But when she died, nobody could find it. How would Derrick react when he learned his brother had just killed the only person who knew where the opal was hidden? It was sheer temper."

"Killing Viktor wouldn't help him find it," Ed said, looking for more.

"What if he didn't mean to kill him? He lashed out in anger. As a bouncer, and ex-army, he had the power to do damage. It could have been accidental."

"That won't get him off the hook. He buried the body."

"Didn't we ought to pick him up again? This time we could ask him what he knows about his brother's death."

"We sent someone in this morning. Derrick Kohl's vanished. He's gone AWOL and nobody saw a thing!"

* * *

27

The weather hadn't made up its mind which way to go. Leaden skies cracked occasionally to let short bursts of sunshine through. Pug slipped her mooring and sailed away from the town of Falmouth. The Fal Estuary had plenty of other interesting places to explore and time was of no importance other than for tidal movements.

She sailed past the dockyard wharves with their cranes black against the sky. The distant sound of metal hammering on metal rang out from a cargo ship in dry-dock. She turned into the main estuary and headed upriver into the Carrick Roads, a mile-wide stretch of water that sometimes saw huge ships making their way upriver to laying-up moorings near the King Harry Ferry. She manoeuvred *Cazutt* between a flotilla of sailing yachts, motorboats and ferries.

Her first port of call was a village on the left bank. It had a church, chandlery, restaurants and a few shops. There were empty places on the pontoons, but she preferred the security of a mooring. She picked up a visitor's buoy. With water all around her, nobody could step aboard her boat unannounced.

Eyeing up the best place to row Ratz ashore, she chose the slipway next to the old public quay, which now doubled as a car park. She locked the boat and dropped Ratz, over the side into the waiting dinghy. He stood in the bow watching the shore come closer and leapt out as soon as the nose of the inflatable touched land. Pug folded in her oars, stepped out and hauled her dinghy out to join others on the side of the slipway.

A ten-minute walk brought her to the long, narrow beach with its low sand dunes and ground vegetation. Ratz bounded after a heron poised at the edge of the water. It took to the air, tucking in its long legs. Clumps of dried seaweed littered the sand along with plastic bottles and lengths of frayed rope.

As she walked, thoughts of her future came knocking at her mind. The loss of her business still rankled. More than that, it was an ache that wouldn't go away. She tried not to think about it. The amount she had saved in her own account might last her for the rest of the year, but at some point, she'd have to start earning money to live on. Beach combing wouldn't cut it.

Kathryn hadn't phoned back. She fumbled around her canvas tote bag, to check her phone for missed calls. Her hand came out empty. She smacked the side of her head. *She'd left the bloody thing behind.* Damn it. She had intended to recharge it whilst lunching in the local sailing club.

Ratz galloped back to her with a stick, which he dropped at her feet. She picked it up and threw it, but her aim was off and it landed in the water. Ratz barked and waited for a wavelet to bring it in. He hated getting wet.

"Coward," she called, and found another stick to throw.

Her thoughts went back to Gil Trelawney's boat *Piglet*. Sometimes it disappeared for hours and she wondered if he'd finally gone. But eventually, she either heard him or spotted him in the distance. She had enjoyed his company at the coffee shop. The card with his phone number burned a hole in her pocket. It would be so easy to contact him. Earlier the temptation had her fingers tapping the table. But what was the point? How could she trust him when he'd lied to her, telling her he was pub-hunting?

If that was all he was doing, why would he have a TSIC file on Dominic on his boat? There had to be a connection. Once she'd had time to reflect how deeply Dominic had been involved in swindling his company, she wondered if Trelawney was investigating him for TSIC. If so, why would the investigation still be going on when they knew Dom was dead. Or, were they now gunning for her?

Another thought sent shivers up her back. If they found Dom guilty, could they demand restitution for the Blood Opal from Dom's estate? She might even now lose the boat. Trelawney could be trailing *Cazutt* to make sure it didn't escape their clutches. She stopped and stared out across the river studying the shadows of the tree-clad riverbank opposite. Where did he hide himself all day?

Her whistle brought Ratz racing back to her. "Change of plan," she told him. "We'll pick up supplies first and then go back to the boat. Okay? I need that phone."

She returned to the dinghy with salad rolls, fresh bread, milk and a rolled-up chart of the Scilly Isle she'd picked up from the chandlers. She placed the bulging bag in the stern.

"Ratz, come here!" He ignored her call – too busy tracking a scent. He spun around in short circles, his nose to the ground and hackles raised. He tracked the scent back towards her. She grabbed him and put him, growling softly, into the dinghy. "Stop fussing, we'll come back later."

The dinghy felt sluggish to handle as she rowed back to *Cazutt*. The tubular walls dimpled slightly indicating they needed more air. Next time she went ashore she'd take the foot pump. It was easier to do it on the slipway than on the boat, a few quick pumps should do it.

*

Kathryn clasped her coffee cup and threaded her way through a group of uniformed officers gathered for Ed's next briefing. Constable Jodie Bligh was entering the latest information on the whiteboard. Kathryn pulled out a chair and sat facing the board, studying the names and arrows crosschecking people and events, seeking inspiration.

"Morning." Truscott arrived and plonked into the chair next to hers. He was wearing one of his ill-fitting knitted pullovers again. He'd be in for more teasing when Jodie saw it. She smiled, "Mum's pullover?"

"Yeah, so?" He rubbed a hand across his chest defensively.

"A different one today, I see."

He gave her a sheepish grin. "I've got a drawer full of them. I've gotta wear them sometimes." He paused, tapped his head with a finger. "Mum's sick. Early onset of Alzheimer's, but she's still got knitting."

"I'm sorry to hear that. It can't be easy juggling a sick mother with the job."

"She's all right. Her sister lives next door, she's the official carer. But that's why I still live with Mum. Jodie says, it's very un-cool – and reckons I don't have to wear them outside the house. But that's not quite playing the game, is it?" He sighed then scraped a hand through his wiry red hair. "Have you heard? Derrick Kohl's done a runner."

"Yeah, I just heard. I hope you weren't the one supposedly watching him."

"Not guilty."

"Let's hope we get this Kohl brother back alive," she said. Celeste's words of warning whispered through her mind.

He nodded, his eyes appraising the figure in front of the board, rather than what was on the board. "Yeah, his vehicle description and number plate is on radio and the TV news," he said, distractedly.

DCI Hawke came into the room followed by Ed and the visiting officer from Exeter. The murmur of conversation died. Theo Pappas stood tanned and taller than those around him, smart in his charcoal pinstripe suit. A glance from his dark eyes swept the room. Was he seeking her out? Or was she kidding herself? As their eyes met, he smiled and acknowledged her with a dip of his head.

The DCI introduced him. Then Theo Pappas reviewed his side of the investigation. Kathryn listened but there was little there she didn't already know until he mentioned a couple of names. Then she started to pay more attention to his words and less to his magnetism.

"Have you heard the name Harry Norton?" Theo asked the group. "We arrested him yesterday. His wife said he'd gone abroad – what she meant was, gone to ground. He's the squealer inside the London Branch of TSIC's insurance office. It seems he's been selling sensitive information. Your man, Dominic Spencer, was not the only one he dealt with. When he heard about the murder of the courier, and your two victims, he panicked and fled. Now we've got him, and he's singing more sweetly than Maria Callas." Theo grinned showing a set of perfect white teeth.

Kathryn felt the heat rise in her face; she lowered her head and stared at the black shiny toecaps of her shoes. Chemistry, pure chemistry.

"Another name," Theo continued. "Gilford Trelawney. He's the insurance investigator from TSIC, who was already in the process of investigating Dominic Spencer. It seems Trelawney's trail led him to Spencer's Sunday morning sail in his yacht the day after the robbery. Later, Trelawney recognised the woman accompanying Spencer that day, as Chantelle Kohl, the third member of the robbery gang. When the widow, Ms Germaine, took up residence on that same boat, Trelawney made it his business to follow her, in case she was taking up where her husband had left off, by delivering the opal. As far as we are aware, he is still on her trail."

Kathryn raised a hand. "I had a call from Ms Germaine yesterday. She's met Trelawney and wants to know who he is. She insists he's stalking her."

"What did you tell her?" Theo asked.

"That I'd check it out and get back to her."

147

"If he hasn't told her who he is, it indicates he's still interested in her movements. And if that's the case, he must have a good reason. So, I suggest you think very hard before you blow his cover."

Kathryn shook her head. Pug was not the villain here. They were wasting time waiting for her to deliver. What was she going to tell Pug next time she called? Trelawney was not out to do her harm, but Pug didn't know that, what if she ran away from him into greater danger elsewhere?

Theo wound up his talk. The briefing closed and officers dispersed. The phone rang. Kathryn picked it up. She looked at Ed. "Front desk. There's a woman out there come to report she's seen the number plate we're after. Shall I deal?"

"On your way."

"Would you mind if I came along?" Theo asked.

"Not at all. Let's hope it's genuine." She caught a whiff of Hugo Boss.

Several people crowded the reception area. A noisy argument had broken out between one couple and a constable who tried to calm them down. A sprightly old lady in a purple trouser suit stood aside and watched. The desk officer dabbed his finger in her direction in answer to Kathryn's enquiring look.

Kathryn approached her. "Mrs Pamela Webster?"

The woman turned her pink powdered face towards Kathryn. Her eyes sparkled with interest. "My, my," she said, touching her tight white curls. "What an interesting place this is. I expect you get to see lots of exciting things here!"

Kathryn exchanged looks with Theo. *We've got a right one here.* "Would you like to come this way?" She ushered the woman into a side room away from the noise and distraction. Mrs Webster sat down, her glance sweeping the room as though she'd never been inside a police station before and was making the most of her outing.

"You have something to tell us?" Kathryn prompted, as she and Theo sat down.

"Yes, dear, I just thought I'd let you know, about the number plate. Don't you have to put your um, recorder on first? I've seen it on *The Bill.*"

Kathryn smiled. "We don't need to do that yet. If I need it, I'll tell you, okay?"

"Right you are, dear. Now, that number plate on the telly. I've seen it before."

"Yes, whereabouts?"

"In the park. I'm not very good with cars, but I do know a Land Rover when I see one. My husband used to have one before he passed away."

"Which park was this, Mrs Webster?"

"Whitely Park, where I walk my dog. We often go there of an afternoon, and sometimes I go and visit my friend. She lives over the other side of the park. That day it was her birthday and I was taking her a box of chocolates. There was this silver Land Rover parked up in the back corner under a tree."

Whitely Park was ringing bells in Kathryn's mind. "And what did you see?"

"That number plain as day – V074 PAM – and, well, as my name is Pam it just stuck in my memory. So, when I saw it on the telly this morning, I recognised it straight away."

"Well done, that's very observant of you," Theo said. The old lady beamed.

"When exactly did you see this?" Kathryn asked.

Mrs Webster rolled it off pat, the date and the time. Theo looked as disappointed as Kathryn felt. Two weeks ago was long before Derrick became a missing suspect. They thanked Mrs Webster for her time and assured her that every little bit helped.

"That wasn't much help," Theo said, as Kathryn returned from seeing the old lady out.

"I'm not so sure about that." She rifled through her notes. "Yes, here. On that date, Pug was staying at her mother's house. At the time mentioned the house was broken into and searched. Whitely Park backs onto her mother's garden. Mrs Webster's sighting puts Derrick Kohl in the frame for the break in."

"So, with that, a murder rap hanging over him and the opal buyer on his back, Derrick is under pressure from all quarters. He has nothing more to lose. How long before he catches up with Ms Germaine, do you think?" He paused, and then gave her a teasing grin. "Another prime suspect you've lost."

"You make any more funny remarks like that, Theo Pappas, and I won't take you out to dinner tonight," she said, with a threatening smile, knowing full well she'd walk over hot coals to take him out anywhere, anytime.

"Oh, I'm still going to get dinner, then?" his smile upgraded into a wide grin. "But if you're too busy, I won't hold you to it."

"No, a deal's a deal. You paid last time, now it's my turn. Which do you prefer, steak house or seafood? I know a nice little place not far away that does a mean job with langoustines in garlic butter."

"Sounds tasty, Ed coming?" He walked alongside her as they returned to the workroom. "I seem to remember the last time he reneged."

"I don't think he likes fish," she said with a shake of her head. It sounded like a good excuse. The last thing she wanted was Ed coming along.

They reached Kathryn's workstation. "Let me fill you in on Pug Germaine's movements. It'll give you the bigger picture," she said.

He half sat on the corner of the table, one leg swinging. "Where is she now?" he asked.

"Last location was Falmouth – that's where she met Trelawney. But she's not staying very long in any one place."

"It's my guess that's where Derrick Kohl is heading now that he's ditched his tail."

Kathryn looked up at him. "How would he know where to find her?"

"So, it might take him a bit longer. But he'll find her. We should watch her and see if he makes contact."

"What? Use her as bait, you mean?" she asked.

"Well, I wouldn't put it quite like that, but yes."

She didn't mind acting as bait, but as a police officer she knew her colleagues and trusted them to watch her back. Pug was not a suspect to be set-up.

"On what justification?" she asked.

"Apart from the opal robbery, we are looking at four murders. Derrick Kohl is more than a person of interest. He's our number one suspect and he's on the run. I understand from Ed that Derrick's girlfriend is a bit player. How much help is she really giving him? With Viktor gone, Ms Germaine is the only other major player left."

"Pug is a victim, not a major player," she said vehemently.

"Maybe. But judging by the places Derrick Kohl is looking for the Blood Opal he must believe she's connected. Kohl *will* go after her. She's his only link to the opal. What I'm saying is if you want him, find her – then sit back and wait it out."

At least, if they were watching Pug and Theo was right, they'd be in a position to protect her. "Okay, I'll run the idea past Ed and he'll need to clear it with the DCI."

28

Pug scraped the remnants of her lunch overboard to a waiting seagull, and then went below to spread the new Scillies chart out on the table. It looked like a sailor's nightmare with its rocks, reefs and wrecks. Absorbed in books and charts, she didn't notice the time slip by and jumped to her feet when she next checked her watch.

Loading her bag with her shower gear, she pointedly placed her dead phone on top of it.

"You ready, Ratz? Let's go." His claws clicked along the cabin roof where he had been dozing in the late afternoon sun.

About to release the dinghy's painter she did a double-take. Instead of the inflatable bobbing on the water astern of her, it lay partly submerged. Air filled some of its chambers, which stopped the whole thing from sinking, but others had emptied. No way could she use it to row ashore. What the hell had happened now!

She couldn't remember snagging anything on her way into the slipway that morning. This was more than a slow puncture. One pull on the painter drew the flaccid mass towards her. With its depleted buoyancy, it was too heavy for her to lift into the boat, and she couldn't use the pump while the dinghy was in the water.

If he were one of the good guys, now would be an excellent time for Gil Trelawney to turn up. She gazed around, but of course, men were never around when she needed them, and with her dead phone she couldn't even call him. No sign of any water-taxis she could beckon. They'd been thick on the water earlier, ferrying tourists to waterside pubs for lunch. Now she was stuck. As she examined her options, a flash from a car window caught her eye, but that was ashore and no good to her.

She could motor to the club marina but the pontoons were crowded and going in there with an unmanageable tow was not a good idea. Time, however, was with her. On the incoming tide, she could tie alongside the public quay. *Cazutt* would be okay there for two hours either side of high water, which gave her four hours ashore. The boatyard was only minutes down the road from the quay. Somebody there should be able to fix the dinghy.

Mind made up, she tied the fenders down the starboard side and took the mooring lines out of a locker. She started the motor, dropped her mooring buoy overboard, engaged the gear and gently headed for the stone quay. A lanky youth wearing the uniform of his peers stood looking out at her.

As she approached the jetty, she turned the boat slightly, cut the motor and let the momentum carry her forward. The boat glided to a stop alongside the metal bollards. The boy raised his hands. Quickly, she flung the stern line across. He grabbed it and attached it to one of the posts. She ran forward to the bow, lassoed the forward bollard and pulled her boat safely into the wall.

She checked the boy's seamanlike knot and smiled at him. "Thanks for that." He looked about sixteen or so. "What's your name?"

"Pete." He nodded to the boat, "Cool boat."

"Well, Pete, want to earn yourself a fiver?" It was one thing leaving an old battered dinghy on the slipway, but she was beginning to doubt the wisdom of leaving a thirty-thousand pound yacht up against a public quay unattended even for so short a time.

He stood back, eyes narrowed. "Depends. What've I gotta do?"

"Do you know the boatyard up the road?"

"Yeah, it's me dad's."

"Even better, you'll be able to explain my problem." She showed him the half-sunk dinghy. "I need to get it repaired."

"Sure, I'll fetch me dad." He shuffled off, hoodie up, hands in his pockets.

Pug sat on the wall, her feet dangling over the side occasionally brushing *Cazutt's* guardrails. The tide had two more hours to rise, so the deck would come up a little way yet, which would make getting on and off the boat easier. Ratz sat on the cabin roof looking up at her expectantly. "Stay there, too much traffic around for you to run loose."

Pete returned in the back of a small truck that his dad drove up to the edge of the quay. A wiry man with dark hair and darker eyes climbed out of the driver's seat. His weathered face broke into a smile.

"The boy says you gotta problem, Jack Cartwright, at your service." He held out a calloused hand for her to shake.

"Thanks for coming." She pointed to her lifeless dinghy.

Father and son worked together to haul the dinghy up the side of the wall. Jack spread the inflatable out on the quay and examined it. "Shouldn't all go at once like this. Reckon it's deliberate. I'll have to take it back to the workshop to check it properly."

"How long before I can have it back?"

"Depends how bad the damage is. You got a few hours left before you need to move. If I can't repair it in that time, I'll bring a spare for you to use overnight. Okay?"

He and Pete hefted it into the back of his truck. Pug handed Pete his fiver. He'd earned it, and he'd volunteered to recharge her phone in the workshop.

As afternoon turned into evening, the number of cars parked on the quay dwindled. Eventually only one remained in the open space. A couple of others stood sheltered in a group of trees at the top end of the car park. She locked the boat and took Ratz out. They walked across the road into the churchyard, out by another gate and back across the road to the slipway where she'd left the dinghy earlier in the day. At no time did she lose sight of *Cazutt*. Did Jack mean mindless vandalism, or did he mean that someone had deliberately targeted her? She wandered back through the car park. The solitary car was still there. The sky darkened, not just with the night, but with clouds and a promise of imminent rain.

Her wristwatch told her the tide had turned and was now dropping. She had an hour and a half before she had to move. If Jack didn't come back in that time, she'd motor over to the pontoons before it got too dark. A young couple walked across the car park hand in hand and claimed the solitary car. When they'd gone, the place looked deserted, but for the one remaining vehicle, a Land Rover, left in the wooded area on the far side of the car park.

*

For her evening out with Theo, Kathryn chose her unbleached linen suit with a black silk camisole top showing just a peep of cleavage. She'd lightened her blond hair and brushed it back into its own casual style. She'd spent an exorbitant amount of time on her make-up to ensure it looked natural, not plastered on, and battled with her choice of shoes. Theo was tall; she'd get away with her elegant high heels even though they were killers to wear.

153

She slipped on her grandmother's opal ring, twisted it around, taking pleasure in its changing pattern of colours. Inevitably, Celeste came to mind, with her rant about the Blood Opal. And even her own mother, so superstitious she would not sit down to thirteen at the table, had labelled all opals unlucky – such a shame they could not appreciate the beauty of these ancient treasures.

Theo Pappas suggested he picked her up, as she was nearer the restaurant than he was. Kathryn was happy with that, it felt more like a date and less like a working dinner. A quick glance around the flat showed nothing out of place, the lounge spotless, and the coffee maker ready on the kitchen top, the bed linen freshly changed. It had been her day to change it, anyway.

At the ring of the doorbell, she caught her breath. She opened the door and invited him in noting a reversal of their situations. This time he wore the same suit he worked in during the day. But his black curly hair was still damp from the shower and the Hugo Boss, fresher. His appreciative look as he ran his eyes over her figure made her smile. The effort had been worthwhile.

He stood back. "Kathryn, you look really lovely," he said. "I shall be proud to take you out tonight." He came no nearer to her, but glanced around room. "You have a nice place here, old but cosy, I think. Now, do you need a coat?"

"Yes, I'll just get it."

He took his mobile from his inside jacket pocket. "I need to phone the wife. Check how the boy is. Won't be long."

Wife! Boy?

"Oh, is your son sick?" Her words came out sounding normal to her ears. She barely heard his reply that the boy had started the day with a sore throat. His call was ringing. She raised her hand to indicate she'd leave him to it and slipped away into her bedroom.

Bastard. He was bloody married. Why didn't he wear a wedding band? The average Brit male didn't, but she thought all Greeks did. She'd checked both hands, but not even a ring indentation to warn her.

Walking over hot coals for a guy you really fancied was one thing, trampling over his wife to do so was quite another. Not her scene at all. She wanted to scratch the paint off her face, but pride and self-control kicked in. He hadn't seen the fantasies inside her head. She'd not compromised herself in any way. Thank God. It didn't lessen the ache in her loins, but now she knew she had to hide it.

Damn the man, he had no business stirring her up. She kicked off the wretched high heels, put on the middies and grabbed her coat. The ringing of her mobile saved her from any awkwardness as she rejoined Theo.

"Yes, Truscott? What can we do for you?" She listened while he told her Pug's phone had just come to life again, and gave her its location.

She relayed his words to Theo. He launched once more into his diatribe that someone should be down there observing Ms Germaine.

"Ed's sending a couple of guys down there tomorrow," she told him, easing back into work mode. At least their investigation was something they had in common.

* * *

29

One by one the streetlights lit up around the village. The yellow light in the deserted car park reflected off the slick asphalt, wet from the last shower. Pug paced the wharf, torn between waiting there for Jack Cartwright to return with her dinghy, and moving *Cazutt* down to the pontoons. She'd give Jack another fifteen minutes.

The next cloudburst caught her unawares and drenched her. She ran back and climbed aboard her boat, pulled off her wet gear and left it puddling on the floor. Half-naked and shivering, she stumbled through the main cabin into the forepeak where her clothes lay stacked in plastic bags. She heard the sound of a car drawing up nearby.

"Jack – he would come right now, wouldn't he?" she said to Ratz as she struggled to get her damp body into dry jeans and sweater. She scraped her wet stringy hair off her face and made her way back to the companionway steps.

The boat dipped to one side. Surprised that Jack would come aboard without the courtesy of announcing his arrival, she hurried to meet him. Ratz cocked his head, barked, dashed up the steps and out to the cockpit ahead of her.

Pug reached the hatchway at the same time as her boarder. In the half-light she came face to face with a man she saw immediately was not Jack, or Pete. Dressed in jeans and a black leather jacket he looked more heavily built than both of them put together. His face had a vaguely familiar look. She stood her ground on the middle step, disconcerted by his manner.

"Yes? What do you want?" she demanded.

"You know what I'm after. Let's not play games. I'm not in the mood." His voice was calm, and all the more sinister for that. "If you're sensible and hand it over quietly, you won't get hurt."

Derrick Kohl. A wanted man – a killer, this wasn't the time to play coy. The picture of the Blood Opal flickered in her mind. That is what he wanted. Dry lipped and tongue-tied, she stared at him. Ratz, out in the cockpit behind him, kept up his barking.

Without breaking eye contact Kohl said, "You shut him up, or I will."

Her breath caught in her throat. Was he the man with the poisonous snail pellets? She had no illusions about how this man would treat her dog. Ratz pranced around in a frenzy, his claws clicking on the cockpit floor, his barks high pitched and urgent.

"Quiet!" She had to repeat the command before he obeyed. Muted, his barking turned to a whine and he looked cowed. Where was Jack? If he would just put in an appearance, this man, a fugitive, would surely flee.

Kohl held his hand out, palm up.

She shook her head. "I haven't got it."

Kohl turned his hand and placed his palm squarely on her chest, as though to push her backwards. She remained standing on the cabin steps, holding on to the sliding hatch top, resisting the pressure he exerted.

"Your old man and his whore had it last. You *know* where they've bloody hidden it. Tell me and I'll leave you be. If not ..." His grip twisted the front of her pullover. Slowly he turned his fist, pulling the material around her in a tight knot, restricting her chest and cutting off her breath. Such was his strength that he almost lifted her off her feet.

"Hand it over, or take same as the others!" He thrust his face into hers smothering her with hot, garlic breath. Her hands slid off the hatch cover under his pressure. She grabbed the wooden handholds either side of the hatchway. Precariously she remained on the step. He drew back and released his hold slightly. Her knees bent. Sweat prickled under her armpits. Her lungs burned for air. If she backed down, he'd have her below decks where he could take his time with her. By staying put, Jack might arrive, or anybody for that matter. He tightened his grip again.

"Can't ... breathe," she gasped. Once more he released the pressure. She licked salt from her lips, and shook her head.

"Talk!" He shouted, shaking her until her teeth rattled.

"'kay. Know what you are looking for ..." she gulped another breath. "But hear me out. Dom was leaving me. No way was he going to give me that opal." She kept her tone level as she played for time. "I didn't know Dom was involved until the police told me. You're wasting your time here. Go and look around your brother's place. I've never had it, never even seen it."

Ratz's restraint was wearing thin. His snarl sounded remarkably loud and brave to her, but she dared not remove her concentrated gaze from Kohl's eyes.

"You lying bitch. You can't tell me you didn't know about it. I know you did!" He released his hold on her clothes. "Get back inside." He thrust his chest in her face. Towering over her he forced her to back down a step. As he raised a foot to climb over the top step and down into the cabin after her, Ratz grabbed the ankle of his jeans and tugged it back. The dog's slight weight had no impact.

Kohl looked around, lifted his leg and kicked it out sharply. With his tenacious hold, Ratz swung in the air, teeth locked onto the denim. Kohl lunged at his tormenter. "Ged off, you lump of shite," he shouted.

Pug regained her middle step, but was still unable to get out of the hatchway. She pummelled the man on his back, going for the kidneys. Kohl ignored her and went for the dog.

Ratz seized the opportunity, let the trouser leg go and snatched Kohl's hand. He jerked it backward and shook it, like he would a rat. Kohl yelped in pain and uttered a string of curses. Using his other hand, he grabbed Ratz by the scruff of his neck and squeezed until Ratz's jaws released their hold and freed the injured hand. Then, jerking his arm into the air, Kohl flung Ratz far out into the night.

"No-oo!" Pug's wail followed the small white form arcing through the air until it splashed down in the sea. Kohl spun around to confront her, blood dripping from his wounded hand, his face contorted with rage, before the blur of a fist sped towards her to deliver pain and blackness.

*

A faint scent of fibreglass resin reached her nose. She opened her eyes into semi-darkness. Pain and a sense of peril filled her head. Lying on her stomach, she took an inventory of her situation. Beneath her, she felt the touch of the boat's bunk cushion. Immediately in front of her was a curved wall that went up and over her, enclosing her in a tunnel-like construction. Pain centred on her neck, shoulders, the back of her head. Gingerly she moved both arms and legs. Somewhere behind her, she heard rustling. Ratz?

With a sickening lurch to her stomach, she recalled the man on her boat had thrown Ratz overboard. She jerked fully awake and tried to sit up, only to bump the top of her head on the roof of the tunnel. She waited for the dizzying stars to leave her.

In her tight space, she peered from side to side and realised where she was. The bastard had stuffed her the wrong way round down inside the quarter-berth. Her head was in the narrow place where the feet normally go. To turn the right way around to see what was going on in the cabin, would be like trying to reverse her position while lying in a closed coffin. Had to get out, had to find Ratz. But Kohl must still be on board; she could hear him moving.

How long had Ratz been in the water? Maybe he'd swum back to the boat and was even now paddling around the outside looking for her, seeking a way in. He was a spunky little dog. Even though he hated water, he knew how to swim. He'd keep going until his legs gave out. If she could get out of this berth without alerting Kohl, she could be up the steps and overboard before he realised she'd gone.

Pug caught the sound of things falling, breaking, locker doors slamming. Kohl was too busy to watch her. When she drew her knees up under her belly, the roof of the tunnel was only a couple of inches above her head. Mustn't come out of it feet first, or she wouldn't be able to see where Kohl was. If he heard her move, he could be standing behind her waiting to pounce – and he *was* a killer. The memory of Dom's body, the blood, the smell of death would be with her until the day she died.

Hot saliva swamped her mouth. She forced the bile back and wiped the sweat from her face with an arm. Only the mental picture of Ratz desperately clinging to life out there spurred her on. On knees, elbows and hands she inched backwards until the tapering tunnel grew wider and higher. Mindful of the teak chart desk at the head of the berth, she must turn before one of her feet kicked it, or the noise would alert Kohl.

Her first attempt at turning failed. With her head against one bulkhead, her bottom jammed against the other, she became stuck. In the moments of panic, her body cramped up and only released its grip as she fought back into her previous position. She opened her mouth wide to give the air free passage as she forced herself to breathe quietly. A few more inches in reverse and she tried the turn again. This time she made it and came to the opening of the quarter-berth headfirst. Exhausted, she lay still and listened.

All the lights in the boat blazed. A clinking noise now came from the forepeak. She eased her head around the chart desk to see the main cabin in chaos. The floorboards had been prised up, the freshwater tank visible, locker doors open and their contents spilled over the other bunks, the Calor gas bottle out of its cupboard. Beside her, the companionway steps were clear. A few more inches then she coiled ready to climb out of the berth and bolt up the steps.

Headlights turning into the car park reflected in the cabin. Jack? Then, she felt a bump on the seaward side of the boat, up near the bow. Kohl's searching noises instantly ceased. She heard him spew a mouthful of obscenities, then stumble over the chaos as he headed for the steps. He scrambled past her without a glance, anxious to make his escape. The boat dipped as he lunged across the deck and stepped up onto the quay wall.

The car's headlights were still moving towards her. From the seaward side of the boat the sound of someone shuffling down the outside became louder as they drew nearer. Pug scrambled out of the bunk and keeping a low profile, climbed into the cockpit. She grabbed a hefty stainless steel winch handle from its locker and stood up, ready to crown the next person attempting to board her boat without permission. A white hand appeared on the gunwales mid-way down the side of the boat. It moved back towards her, hauling its owner's dinghy towards the stern.

The car on the wharf stopped, its headlights remained on. The person on the seaward side was lost in the shadow cast by *Cazutt's* bulk.

Pug raised her weapon. "Stop right there. Identify yourself! Now!"

The answer came in a small whimper, and a bedraggled little dog appeared over the side of the boat. A hand dropped him gently into the cockpit.

"Ratz!" Her weapon abandoned, she gathered her dog in her arms. She cuddled him into her sweater, crooning baby noises at him. His watery black eyes regarded her with a forlorn mixture of relief and reproach. His body shook like it was gripped in a seizure.

With him safely in her arms, she looked over the guardrails to the dinghy alongside. Its occupant wore a dark anorak and a seaman's cap. When he stood, the car's headlights lit his face and she gazed straight into the eyes of Gilford Trelawney.

30

The strumming increased its beat, striving to reach a crescendo. Diners clapped their hands in time to the Greek music. Seated at a table near the band, Kathryn felt the heat of excitement rush to her face, as the rhythm of her claps grew louder and stronger and the dancers, arms outstretched, shoulder to shoulder, swayed and cavorted to the dance. She glanced at Theo – he responded with a jubilant smile. His eyes sparkled with delight; his hands loudly beat out the quickening tempo. She could see he was itching to get up and join the dancers. It was a floorshow and not for the public to partake. Pity – she would have enjoyed watching him, up there with the macho men, showing off his skills.

The Greek *taverna* she'd chosen for their meal had met with resounding approval from him. She'd heard they played the traditional Kalamatiano and Zeimbekika music. The fact that the restaurant provided entertainment was a plus for Kathryn, as it filled time where otherwise they would've had to make conversation. But she needn't have worried. Theo was totally at ease with her, as though taking a woman other than his wife out to dinner was perfectly normal for him.

"I'm going to have the roasted langoustines with avocado salsa," she said, reading down the list. Not exactly a Greek dish, but she craved the avocado.

"Sounds good. Make it two."

Later, after their plates were cleared away, they sat back and enjoyed the music, waiting for their main course to settle before tackling the dessert trolley.

Male dancers in colourful costume locked arms behind each other and danced in perfect unison. Bronzed and beautiful, their muscles rippled beneath pale blue silk shirts and tight pants as the tempo built. The music reached towards its climax and Kathryn stole another look at the handsome Theo to see how he was taking the competition. His rhythmic clapping grew louder as the musicians reached their closing moments. Lost to her, he was absorbed in watching one face in the line up. The gleam in his eye was not one she'd seen before. When the dance reached its explosive finale, Theo's applause was loudest of all. At the last bow, that one dancer's eyes, flushed face and radiant smile were for Theo alone. He responded in kind.

Then it struck her. Theo Pappas was gay.

Were the wife and son a smokescreen, a stock answer he gave to any woman who might show an interest? When originally he'd kept a certain distance from her, she'd put it down to professional etiquette, but now she knew it had a deeper meaning.

In the silence that followed the thunderous applause, she heard the phone ringing inside her bag. "Sorry. I need to get this."

Theo nodded, his face still creased in smiles. She left the table and headed for the ladies room where she hoped for sufficient silence to deal with Pug Germaine's call. When she returned to their table, the floorshow had changed. A solitary dancer acted the role of an inebriated man attempting to pick up a glass of ouzo from the floor. At this stage, the audience were laughing quietly at his antics while the tempo gradually increased. Theo raised an enquiring eyebrow.

"It was Pug. You were right. She's had a visit from Kohl."

Theo's expression changed. "That was quick. What happened?"

Now, he was all business. Kathryn hesitated; he hadn't even asked how well Pug had survived the encounter. "She's okay, a bit bruised and battered. She wants to know how Kohl knew where to find her."

"Well, don't look at me."

"Pug asked if I'd told anyone she was in Falmouth. The only person I told was you."

She'd thought Theo was too professional to have released such information, but remembered he was happy enough to use Pug as bait in order to catch their suspect. Would he have gone the extra mile and deliberately sprung the trap?

Theo leaned back, formed a pistol with his hand and pointed it at her. "You're after Kohl for the death of his brother, and possibly the death of the two other victims. I understand that. But Derrick Kohl is also my number one suspect for the opal robbery, and for the death of its courier. I want that man. I'll do whatever it takes to get him. But I have not told anyone of Ms Germaine's whereabouts. Quite apart from anything else, the timing was not right. We didn't have any backup in place for her. Had Ed's men arrived on the spot earlier, well, I might have been tempted. Kohl has pre-empted us and I'm not responsible for that."

Kathryn believed him.

He relaxed his stance. "So, what happened? Did they catch the bastard?"

"No. Someone disturbed him and he ran off." Kathryn went on to tell him everything Pug had told her – though she abbreviated the length of time Pug spent on her dog's misadventures. "The point is, we know to within twenty minutes where our suspect is. I phoned Ed and told him. He's organising roadblocks as we speak. Kohl won't get out of Cornwall easily."

"Did Kohl find what he was looking for?"

"Pug says no, she didn't have it. Look, I have to get back to the station. I said I'd meet Ed there ASAP. Do you think you could drop me off at home, so I can change out of these clothes?"

"Of course. I'll join you."

Kathryn beckoned a waiter and called for the bill. Whether her question of Theo's sexuality had merit or not, it looked like she would be spending part of the night with him after all, but not in the way she had imagined. She sighed. What a waste.

*

Pug wrapped a towel around Ratz and held him in her arms, trying to give him some of her body warmth. Gil came aboard. He held Ratz while she climbed out the other side onto the wall. On the quay he placed his anorak across her shoulders and a comforting arm around her back. He squeezed her gently. She gasped.

"What's up? You alright?"

"A bit bruised, that's all."

"What did he do to you?"

"Look, don't fuss. I'm okay." She pulled the front of his anorak around her to cover Ratz. In the distance she heard the police sirens. Jack came to join them. He offered her the front seat of his car to sit in while they waited for the police to arrive. She took up the offer and gradually Ratz's trembling slowed.

The lights of a local police patrol car swung into the car park and joined Jack's in highlighting *Cazutt*. Two officers piled out of the car pulling their caps on as the moved.

Pug climbed out of Jack's car and approached the little group huddled under the yellow light in the car park. One of the officers remained with Gil and Jack, while the other asked her about the attack. She told him briefly, then took him to the edge of the quay wall and indicated her boat.

"Have a look inside. You can see what he's done." The officer stepped down onto the deck and looked through the hatch at the chaos inside.

"Okay. Apart from the physical attack on you was there any major damage done, anything stolen?" he asked when he returned to her side.

"I haven't had time to sort it out yet." She gave him Kohl's name and briefly the history behind the assault. He left her to talk to the two men. Pug, still holding Ratz, followed on behind, checking her watch.

The tide was still dropping and she had no more than thirty minutes left before *Cazutt's* keel would touch bottom. They were cutting it too fine. She moved nearer to the group hoping somebody would remember she had a tidal deadline. Having said his piece, Pete was hanging around, hands in pockets, kicking a lump of wood.

She heard Jack tell the officer. "It wasn't till I was half way up to the boat I saw this bloke legging it back to his car. Soon as I clapped eyes on him, I knew summat was wrong. He looked shifty, like. Left me lights on, so's we could see what was going on."

"Did you get the car's registration?" the officer asked.

"Nah, he went off hell for leather, no lights, neither. Saw the car all right, a four-wheel drive. Land Rover. Soon as I heard this 'ere lady shouting, I knew there'd been trouble."

Gil told the officer. "The first sign of trouble was something white in the water. Put the glasses on it and realized it was alive. He looked as though he was nearly done for. I rowed out to pick him up and recognised the dog I'd seen on *Cazutt* earlier. I saw the boat tied up at the quay, so brought him back."

Pug noticed he didn't mention her threatening behaviour as he came alongside her boat. She looked from one officer to another getting more anxious with every passing minute.

"Excuse me, but the tide's going out and I need to move the boat down to the pontoons. Can I go now?"

The senior officer, obviously not a sailor and unaware of her dilemma, tapped his notebook with his biro. "Let's get you checked out in the hospital first, Ms Germaine. You've had nasty blow on the head. Could have concussion. I'll call the ambulance."

"No, don't. Please. I'm okay, really, but I do need to move my boat right now."

Gil looked at her. "It's all right. If you want to get your injuries checked, I can take your boat down if you like."

"No, honestly, I'm fine – I don't need to go to hospital."

"It's okay, love," Jack said, and nodded to Gil. "Him and me'll do it. You go with Pete." He looked at the senior police officer. "Maybe if my missus were to take a look at her? She's a midwife, she'll know if any medical treatment's necessary. Pete, you take her home, tell your mother what's happened. She'll know what to do."

The police officers exchanged looks. "Okay, sounds good, Ms Germaine, pop in the back, you too Pete."

Pug took Gil's coat from her shoulders and handed it back to him before she climbed into the police car. "Thanks for that, Gil. The key is already in the ignition. I'll see you later, perhaps?"

The senior officer waved them into the back of the patrol car for the ride down to Jack's house. On the doorstep, Pete explained the situation to his mother. She told the officers she would take care of Pug. If necessary, she would contact the local doctor. Reassured, the officers departed.

"I'm Aggie," Jack's wife introduced herself. "Now, you come on in. Let's hear it in your own words, what's happened? And who's this little fellow?" She put out a finger and stroked Ratz's paws folded over Pug's arm. Pete interrupted to tell the story of Ratz's dunking overboard, but his mother cut him short.

"We'll hear all about that in a minute, Pete. How about you make us all a nice cup of tea?" Pete shrugged and disappeared into the kitchen.

"Come on, love, this way. Let's have a look at you. Put him down if you like, we don't mind dogs."

Pug warmed to the short, dark-haired woman who had taken charge, and put her at ease. She lowered Ratz to the floor and followed Aggie through a small hall and into a comfortable sitting room. Ratz stayed close to her ankles.

Aggie indicated an upright chair. "Sit yourself down there and tell me where you hurt."

Pug pointed the back of her head and various other places. Aggie's fingers combed gently through her hair as she examined her scalp. "There's a small lump on the back of your head, but no lacerations. Let's have a look under this."

Pug opened her shirt to reveal the shoulder where Kohl's fist had landed. Aggie probed around and asked Pug to move her arm and shoulder in different ways. "Everything seems to be working all right. Do you feel nauseous? Or sleepy? Blurred vision?"

"No, no and no. Think I'll live?"

"The bruise is already starting to come out," Aggie said. "And, yes, I reckon you'll live. This is going to be cold. It's witch hazel – best thing for bruises. You're lucky the blow landed there, and not on your throat, or jaw where it would have done some real damage."

Pug winced as Aggie bathed it. "I saw it coming and turned away. I don't remember falling backwards, but I must have done to hit my head like that."

"From what you say, I think you got off lightly."

"I'd left the pile of wet clothes on the floor; they must have cushioned the fall."

"Right, let's go and have that cup of tea. I'll give you a Paracetamol for the headache, and you need to rest up to let your system get over it, that's my recommendation."

"Okay, thanks Aggie. I'll go back to the boat and turn in, how's that?"

Aggie smiled. "Not so fast. Concussion is a funny thing. I'll need to keep an eye on you at regular intervals for a few more hours. I suggest you stay here overnight. You can use our daughter's room. She's away, but I keep the bed made up."

The thought of leaving her boat to its own devices didn't go down too well, but on the other hand, staying the night with Aggie, Jack and Pete sounded a whole lot better than having to deal with the mess Kohl had left behind. Pug thanked Aggie. She felt over-emotional and their kindness brought tears to her eyes.

"That's all right, love. Now, I've got a nice beef casserole keeping hot in the Aga. We'll eat soon as Jack gets back."

"Mm, it smells wonderful."

Jack returned a short time later and passed the boat keys to Pug. "Nice little boat you've got there, missus." Before she could reply, Aggie called them out to the kitchen. Pete thundered down the stairs and joined them around the table. Aggie dished out portions of meat in thick brown gravy and handed the laden plates around.

"There's plenty more in the pot for seconds. Help yourselves to the vegetables."

166

The clatter of cutlery broke the busy silence. Jack finished piling his plate. He sat for a moment with his knife and fork held vertically in his fists either side of his plate. He looked at Pug. "Anyways, you don't need to worry about your boat tonight; she's tucked in next to a cruiser with a family on board. They'll keep an eye on her."

"Thanks for doing that, Jack. What happened to Gil?"

"He's gone back to his boat. Said he'd call by in the morning and show you where yours is. Quite concerned about you, he was. He put the gas bottle back where it'd come from, and some other things, so at least you can move around down below now. Before I forget, that dinghy of yours is still in me truck, didn't seem no point unloading it tonight."

"Oh Jack, I'm sorry, I forgot to ask how you got on with the dinghy. Is that why you were working late?"

Aggie shook her head and winked at Pug. "Don't you worry about Jack. He enjoys his work. Don't you, love? He'd work on boats all the hours day and night, if I let him."

"Look who's talking. Haven't noticed you stay abed when you get a call out in the middle of the night. I'm not the only one, you know!"

Pug listened to the banter between husband and wife with envy. It was a long time since she and Dom had enjoyed that sort of comradeship.

Jack turned back to her. "Like I said, reckon the damage to the dinghy was sabotage. Think it could be the same bloke as attacked you?"

Pug thought about that for a moment. "That man was looking for something he thought was on my boat. How could vandalising my dinghy help him?"

"It forced you bring the boat into the quay which gave him easy access."

"But he couldn't have known I'd do that! I could have hailed a water taxi, or got a lift from another boat. He wasn't to know."

"Ah, but you didn't. Chances were high you'd take the boat into the quay. He's probably been watching you." Jack doled out another spoonful of meat and gravy onto his plate. "Have you noticed anyone following you round?"

"He'd been watchin' her all right," Pete said. "His Land Rover'd been parked under the trees for hours – you don't get people parking up there when there's room in the car park, stands to reason."

Pug looked from Pete to Jack. "This guy comes from Plymouth, how could he follow my boat that distance if he was on land driving a car?"

Aggie reached out across the corner of the table and touched the back of Pug's hand. "Don't you worry about that tonight, love. From what I've heard, it strikes me you've had a lot of bad luck lately." She turned to her husband. "More than her fair share, wouldn't you say, Jack?"

* * *

31

Pug lay back on the daughter's bed, staring at the ceiling. After a supper of leftovers, Ratz lay curled up in the cardboard box that Aggie had found and lined with an old towel. Every now and again, Pug heard his feet scrabbling at the sides of the box as he ran in his dreams, or perhaps, she considered, as he swam for his life.

Thinking of Aggie's words about bad luck she recalled Celeste's suggestion that she get rid of everything associated with that *bloody* opal, as she was beginning to think of it, even down to her stock of stamps. Well, she didn't have them anymore. Someone had nicked them. But, her luck hadn't changed for the better. Had that someone been Derrick Kohl? He was more than welcome to her bad luck. Her mobile phone rang; it was probably Kathryn checking up on her.

"Hi, Honey-Pug, it's only me!"

"Hey, Celeste! Now it's my turn to say you must be psychic!"

"Well, you know me, honey. After your call, earlier, I did a bit more research on the Blood Opal and well, I have something that might interest you." Celeste's voice sounded bubbly as though she had difficulty containing her news. "I've found another story. Wanna hear it?"

Pug wasn't sure she did. Hadn't she heard enough? But she didn't want to relinquish Celeste's cheery voice. "Try me."

"Okay. This one comes from way back in the1950s, before the opal became world famous. It was still in Australia at the time. Its owner had intended to take it to the auction rooms in Sydney, but on the way, he had an accident, ran off the road and drove into a river. The river was in flood at the time and the car sank within seconds."

"Ooh, what happened to the driver?"

"He died. But hear this; a witness swears that instead of the car taking the bend, it left the road, drove straight towards the water, accelerating all the way. Later they found that the driver had died of a heart attack. The theory is that he put his foot hard down on the accelerator in his agony and the car kept going. Verdict: accidental death."

"And, you think this has something to do with the opal's curse?"

"It's another death you can add to the list. Inside the car, they found the briefcase full of water, and the opal wrapped in wet cotton wool inside a leather box."

"And, I suppose you're going to tell me opals don't like water, right?"

"Wrong. Solid opals actually contain water, something like five or six percent. If they dry out, they're subject to cracking, or even self-destructing. Now, get this, that particular owner thought the same as you did. He'd had the Blood Opal stored in a low-humidity bank vault along with his other treasures. Left there much longer, the opal would have dried out. So, you could say that dehydrated stone was mighty thirsty!"

Pug slapped a hand across her mouth to stop the sound of her laughter. She imagined the opal sprouting arms and legs like in the advert for M&Ms, and running around with a will of its own, grabbing the steering wheel and racing the car into the river.

"Good story, Celeste, but it's a bit far-fetched, isn't it?"

"That's okay; I know you're a non-believer. But think about it. Count the number of bodies you know associated with that opal. Just don't mock it, eh Pug? Whew! Now I've got that off my chest, tell me where you are now and what you're doing?"

Pug took a deep breath, lay back and told her friend the latest.

*

Pug woke, disoriented. Had she gone aground? Her bed didn't feel right; it wasn't rocking. Of course, she wasn't on the boat; she was in Aggie and Jack's house. In the silence, she listened for the sound of others but heard none. Not even a snore from Ratz. She looked down and in the moonlight saw he was asleep in the box beside the bed. Aggie's words whispered in her mind, *more than her fair share of bad luck.* Celeste's voice, *count the number of bodies.*

The first to die was Seamus Kelly, the miner who dug the opal out of the ground. His partner was killed in a pub brawl shortly after. The jeweller, who cut the opal open, burned to death in a wild bush fire.

170

Celeste's heart attack victim drove his car into the river in the 50s. The young woman, whose father entrapped the opal in a pendant, died in a light aeroplane crash. It was an impressive number of deaths already, and if you added this year's total, the courier, Dom, that woman, and now – Viktor Kohl.

Scary.

Even if there was something in Celeste's theory, about the opal hurting only those who had hurt it, and she still doubted that, she hadn't done the opal any harm, there was no reason for it to subject her to its malevolence. Unless...unless she really was harbouring the stone somewhere on the boat, albeit unknowingly?

Agitated, she got out of bed and went to the window. In the moonlight, she could see the glint of the river. Some distance away on her right, a forest of masts showed where the pontoons lay. Boats jigged on the incoming tide. Which one was *Cazutt*? Where on that boat could Dom have stashed an opal? A thing like that could go into the tiniest of spaces. It could take forever to find.

The light dimmed. She looked up, expecting to see a cloud passing over the full moon. Gooseflesh broke out on her arms. In the crystalline indigo sky, the moon was cloaked in a mist of red.

A Blood Moon – Blood Opal – what did it mean?

She clamped her shivering arms across her chest and dropped onto the bed. Tomorrow, when she got back to her boat, she'd strip the damn thing bare, if for no other reason than to prove to herself she did not have the opal.

* * *

32

The night shift was either out on patrol, or otherwise engaged. In contrast to the darkened general works office, the lights in the incident room burned brightly. Ed, with his radio in hand, walked up to the roadmap of the south-west of England that Kathryn and Theo were fixing to the wall. He'd known Kathryn was coming in – Theo's presence was an unexpected bonus.

"How well does Derrick Kohl know the area?" he asked Kathryn.

"The Kohls were born and bred in Plymouth. Viktor travelled Devon and Cornwall a fair bit in the course of his job, but we don't know much about Derrick yet."

"He can't be that difficult to find, can he?" asked Theo. "We have his departure time from a set location pinned down to within the hour."

"Depends how well he knows the Cornish lanes. Some are only as wide as a single vehicle, not the sort of place you want to engage in a chase," Ed said, more to himself than to them. The long peninsula of Cornwall offered plenty of hiding places. There were vast tracts of thinly populated wild land around Bodmin Moor, and the rugged north coast where a fugitive could lose himself until the heat died down.

Ed's stomach rumbled – he'd been called away from dinner earlier in the evening. He turned back to the table and picked up the phone.

"It's going to be a long night. I'm ordering a pizza. Anyone want to join me?"

Theo shook his head; Kathryn blew her cheeks out indicating she was already full. It was all right for them, they'd been out to dine.

"But a coffee wouldn't go amiss," Kathryn said.

Theo nodded enthusiastically, and Ed put in the order for immediate delivery.

"Make that four!" Louis Truscott appeared in the doorway. Dressed in a black tracksuit and soft-soled shoes, no one had heard him approach.

"Hey, Louis, I thought you were playing badminton with Jodie tonight," Kathryn said.

"Yeah, I was. She couldn't make it." He turned abruptly away from her and looked at Ed. "I heard the news on the police radio, thought I'd look in."

"Right. There's not a lot we can do this far away, the coordinators have it in hand. But they've promised to keep us in the loop, so at least we'll know what's going on."

Kathryn pointed out the relative positions on the map to bring Truscott up to speed.

"The hunt for Kohl started here in the village of Treganges where Pug's boat was tied up to a public quay."

"All we know so far is the local patrolling officers were called to deal with an assault," Ed said. "No one saw the index number of his vehicle, but it was a Land Rover. Ms Germaine claims the man who assaulted her was Derrick Kohl."

"Was she hurt?" Truscott asked.

"Not badly, but we don't know the details. The plan is to identify the route Kohl's taking, then set up a roadblock ahead of him." Ed did not know if Kohl was armed, but with a possible quadruple murder charge about to be laid at his door, he was certainly dangerous. Because of that profile, officers would not give chase on their own, but would work as a team.

Ed's radio came to life as he made contact with the coordinator of the search. He looked at Kathryn, and pointed to the map as he spoke. "He's on the A390. Sighted east of Truro; going through Grampound, travelling fast."

Kathryn pushed in another pin. Theo half sat on the corner of a table, one leg swinging. Truscott dealt with the coffee and pizza when it arrived. Ed ate ravenously as they waited for the next sighting.

"Thought you didn't like fast food," Kathryn teased.

He patted his stomach "The old engine needs stoking. We didn't all go out to a *gourmet* dinner, you know."

"Too bad you don't like fish," Theo said with smile. "The place we went to specialises in seafood. And the music was fantastic."

"Who says I don't like fish?" he asked indignantly, "love the stuff."

"Um, what do think Kohl's next move will be?" Kathryn interrupted, nodding towards the map, bringing their minds back to work.

173

Theo moved over to the map before he answered. "It's my guess he'll go north. He's not heading for home – he's running away. If he went the southern route, he'd have to cross the Tamar Bridge – too much of a bottle-neck, or use the ferry where he could be trapped."

The next sighting confirmed Theo's theory.

"Still on the A390 heading north-east for St Austell." Ed relayed information as he received it. "A patrol car's in position near the crossroads, ready to follow at a distance. They intend to stop him before he reaches the A30 dual carriageway. If they don't, it could end up a multiple chase."

Ed exchanged a meaningful look with Kathryn. That was the last thing they wanted. Nobody spoke while Ed waited for his next communication.

"Right, here we go. They've eyeballed his vehicle. He's ignored the A30 and gone straight on, still heading northeast towards Lostwithiel, fourteen kays ahead. They're in position, following."

Kathryn pulled a face. "The A30 would have been a faster route."

"He's taking the back roads hoping to lose his followers in a maze of lanes," Theo said. "Where're the bloody helicopters, haven't they been deployed yet?"

Ed repeated the question into his radio, and translated back the coordinator's disembodied voice. "The only one available is refuelling; it won't get here for twenty minutes." He continued listening to the latest information report. "Too late. They've lost him! He's sussed them and shot down a ring road at St Blazey."

Ed stood and joined Theo in front of the map studying the lay of the land and taking punts on which road he would come out on. At present, he was heading south back to the coast, but for Kohl, escape lay in the open roads of the north. He had to return to the main road or he'd be boxed in with the sea at his back. That would be an easy catch – too easy.

The radio broke in again. Ed nodded to the others. "Okay, he did the circle he's back on the A390 heading for Liskeard. Our guys are keeping traffic between them, but it's a bit sparse this time of night. Kohl's vehicle has a broken tail-light on the near side which makes it easy to pick him out."

They lost him again in the approach to Liskeard, picked him up after leaving the town still on the A390, heading for Tavistock on the edge of Dartmoor. Slowly the net was closing.

They'd set the roadblock just outside Gunnislake behind a sharp bend. Kohl would have to drop his speed to take the bend. He wouldn't see the block until he had driven into it.

Like a race caller describing the action around him, the controller's voice sped up. A muscle worked in Ed's bottom jaw. He held his breath as the coordinator's voice called it in, blow by blow. Kathryn moved up next to him, listening closely.

"Suspect's vehicle is approaching the bend. Trailing cars catching up, converging behind him, driving him into the ambush. Roadblocks straight ahead, he's braking violently, slewing. Yeah! We got him surrounded. Helicopter's arrived, now overhead. Suspect's stopped. Officers race towards his car. Door's opening. He's out and running, good vis in bright moonlight, heading for trees and river. Helicopter's searchlight pinpointing his position. Officers in full pursuit; one's got him down. Another two are on him. Okay, that's it folks – they've gottim. Not armed, repeat, the suspect is not armed."

Unbearable silence held the four of them rigid for a moment, and then Ed smiled at the quiet satisfaction in the next announcement – "Message for DI Ed Buchanan: we have your man."

"Well done, guys," he replied.

Theo made a fist in the air then grabbed hold of Kathryn's hands and together they did a little jig. Kathryn finally extricated herself from Theo, stuck the last pin into the map, and dropped into a chair. "They didn't even use spikes," she said.

"Not as far as I heard," Ed answered. "The geography did it for them. Okay, folks, go home; grab a few hours' kip. Thank you all for coming in. Tomorrow, Kathryn, you and Truscott interview Janine. Find out how her prints came to be on Viktor's van. If she kicks up, book her."

Truscott nodded and made no comment. Kathryn cocked her head, puzzled. "What time are we doing Kohl's interview?" she asked Ed.

"I'll take that with Theo. I need you in with Janine, play one off against the other."

Kathryn turned away. He sensed her disappointment that he'd chosen the visiting cop over her to interview the prime suspect. Possibly, even resented it, but that was too bad. Theo was as much part of the team as she was and Kohl was Theo's number one suspect for the opal robbery and courier's murder.

Besides, Ed was beginning to appreciate Kathryn's interviewing techniques. She may well get more out of Janine than he would.

* * *

33

In the morning, Pug arrived in the kitchen to see a note from Aggie saying she'd had to go out. As Aggie had laid the kitchen table with packets of breakfast cereal, dish and cutlery for only one, Pug assumed the others had already eaten. A coffee machine brewed on the side bench. She helped herself and washed up afterwards.

The kitchen door backed out into Jack's boatyard. His workshop stood on the far side. Several boats rested in cradles on the concrete, some with canvas covers to keep the weather out. She found Jack whistling while he worked on a piece of wood at his bench. He stopped when he saw her.

"Mornin', did you sleep alright?" he asked. He tilted his head back and peered into her eyes as though examining her for after effects. His lined leathery face registered satisfaction. "The missus had a call out. Said you was to help yourself to breakfast."

"Thanks Jack, I saw her note."

"Did you hear the news on the radio? They've got him, the man that attacked you. Seems he was a wanted man."

"Did they say why?" Her heart thudded against her chest as she recalled the power in his throw as he chucked Ratz into the sea, his hands screwing up her pullover, the violence in his face.

"No, didn't go into detail. Might be more, later."

"What are you working on?" she asked, to change the subject.

He chattered about this and that and his enthusiasm made her smile. Like Aggie said, he was a man happy in his work.

"When you get a minute, can you make up my bill for the dinghy repairs, please?" she asked him. "Don't forget to add your time for all that running around you did for me last night."

Jack stepped into a side office and brought her the bill he'd already printed out. It only had the repairs for the dinghy and VAT noted on it.

He beamed at her. "That's all right, my dear, 'tis a pleasure. Now, where can I drop your dinghy off? You don't need it on the pontoons; I could leave it at the club's slipway if you want, be safe enough there."

They agreed on that and she gave him a cheque. The money in her account was slipping away like dry sand in a holey bucket. There'd come a time, not that far away, when her bank balance would read empty. She'd have to get a job soon, any job, just something to replenish the coffers.

"Morning all," Gil Trelawney sang out, as he sauntered into the workshop.

Jack acknowledged him with a wave and returned to his sanding. Ratz raced across the yard and stood with his front paws on Gil's knees, tail wagging, and making the throaty noises he only did with people he liked. Gil fondled his ears. "You look a lot chirpier this morning, little fellow."

Pug watched the interaction between this stocky man in his well-worn seaman's cap, and her dog. Judging by his actions last evening, Gil was not the enemy. Without him, Ratz could have lost his life – for that she owed him.

"And how are you this morning?" he asked. His eyes looked straight at her, clear blue and probing. "Fully recovered?"

"Never better."

"Good. Like me to show you where your boat is?"

She was quite capable of finding her boat on her own, but she found herself looking forward to his company and that had little to do with gratitude.

"If you have nothing better to do, then yes, thanks. It's time I got to work on it. Are you ready now?" At his nod, she turned back to Jack. "Thanks a lot, Jack, I'll come and see you and Aggie later."

Gil fell in step beside her. "Your cabin's in one hell of a mess," he said, as they walked towards the club. "Like some help cleaning it up?"

Pug hesitated. It wasn't just a question of cleaning or tidying up; she needed to look for the opal in all the tiny places no one else would know about. She had no expectations of finding anything, but at least it would set her mind at rest. The thought of working together at close quarters with Gil on the boat brought the flutters to her belly. He gave off all the right vibes, and she so wanted to say yes. Her pace slowed and she came to a standstill. But … why had he lied to her? She bit her lip at her own indecision.

Gil, three steps ahead, turned back to look at her, eyebrows raised. "You have a problem with that?"

"Yes, Gil Trelawney, I have. Give me one good reason why I should trust you." She kept her tone light and bantering. "You're still on my tail; you have a file on my dead husband, and you lied to me about looking for a pub to buy." A silent groan squeezed her throat. As soon as the words were out she regretted them. Stupid, stupid, just when she wanted him to see her in a different light, those stupid words came out to taunt him. But the damage was done and she couldn't haul the words back.

He crossed his arms and looked mildly hurt. "You want me to tell you all that before you've even put the kettle on?"

She laughed. He'd not taken offence. "You'll be lucky if we can even find the kettle."

"As it happens, I can give you one good reason. I saved your dog from drowning. You owe me at least one cup of tea for that."

"You're on." But the hint of triumph in his smile indicated he had the upper hand. The damned man was mocking her. She strode past him and headed along the path towards the boardwalk and pontoons. She heard his feet striding to catch her up. They marched along in silence.

When they reached the boat, Gil pulled at the bow rope to bring it close enough for her to reach the guardrails. He put a hand out, inviting her to go first. She stood her ground, hands on hips, waiting for more. Wasn't he even going to apologise for his lies?

Gil surrendered. "Okay, I'll lay it on the line for you. I am not following *you*, just your boat. I do have a file on Dominic Spencer. I work for the same company he did, the same company that insured the Blood Opal. As you probably know by now, your husband was under suspicion of conspiracy to steal it."

"What's all that to do with you? I thought the police were handling it."

"They are. They're concentrating on the murders – and the robbery, that's their job. My job is to find the gem and return it safely to its rightful owner, and thus avert a hefty insurance claim against my company."

Pug took a moment to absorb it. "So, what's the boat got to so with it? Why follow the boat?"

"My investigations show that in the twenty-four hours before their deaths, your husband and Mrs Chantelle Kohl took this boat out for a sail. Once it became clear that Chantelle was the third member of the robbery gang, it seemed quite likely that she and your husband had colluded in hiding the opal. If it *was* hidden on the boat, then someone was going to deliver it, or someone else had to come and collect it."

"So how long have you been watching the boat?"

"To start with I was actually watching your husband, which is how I came to see Chantelle on the boat with him. Once I knew the names of the robbers the penny dropped and I realised the boat might have been the vehicle of delivery.

"I see. So, when they were murdered, you thought that I was going to take their place, sail off and deliver it myself?"

"It was a possibility." His smile carried a mild apology. "Though, I have given up that idea. If you'd been party to the theft, you would have long since gone, not dallied around all these home ports, with your game little dog, waiting for your ex-partners to catch up with you. And last night's shenanigans confirmed it."

"What about buying a pub? Or, do you excuse those lies as 'cover'?"

"No lies. I'm leaving the job at the end of the case, and using this trip to seek out the right pub to buy. Oh yes, it is a good cover – but it is not a lie." He looked so smug she could have kicked his shin bones.

She stared out over the water. It had turned the colour of molten lead under the grey skies. She shivered. "If you were expecting someone to collect it off my boat, how come you didn't you see Derrick Kohl arrive? I could've been murdered in my bunk when that thug came aboard."

He made a wry face. "*Mea culpa,* again. An overdose of inactivity lulled my senses. I heard the dog barking and came out to look. I was in time to see splash-down and the frantic efforts of some small creature swimming in the water. I wasn't sure what it was. I had to lower the dinghy and row out after it. It wasn't until I hauled him in that I recognised Ratz."

"Okay, while we're at it, let's hang all the dirty washing out to dry. If I hadn't brought this up, were you going to search my boat under the guise of 'helping' me, without saying anything?"

He smiled. "The jury is still out on that one. Which would have caused you least stress? Me quietly looking for it without your knowledge, or for you to know that a bunch of villains believed you were hiding that opal on your boat."

"Good point," she conceded. "I think I'd rather know up front. What were you going to do if you found it? Pocket the gem and collect the reward yourself?" Her verbal diarrhoea continued in spite of her efforts to stop. Why did this man have such a disconcerting affect on her?

He frowned, inclined his head to one side, his lips clamped together. She realised that this time, she really had gone too far.

"I'm sorry I didn't mean that. Sorry, sorry, sorry!" She put her hands out towards him. He took them and placed them against his chest, and held them there, his palms warm and dry. Beneath his jersey she could feel the beat of his heart.

"It's all right. I do understand," he said. "In the circumstances it must be difficult to know who to trust. But to answer your question, I am not eligible to claim any reward. It's *my job* to find it. If I found it on your boat, I would have to declare that. But, who knows, if we did find it, maybe you could claim the reward."

That was an interesting thought. She could do with money like that.

"So, where do we go from here?" she asked.

"Kohl's action spells good news for us. It confirms the opal is still undelivered. He obviously believes Spencer hid the opal on the boat, intending to deliver it himself. Now, as Kohl was unable to complete his search last night, I suggest we work together and both look for the opal before somebody else has another go."

She thought of the reward money and wondered what Celeste's reaction would be on the subject. Would she consider it clear of the curse, or would Blood Opal simply turn into blood money? Not a happy thought.

As for Gil – he still had her hands trapped within his. She took a step back and slowly he relinquished them.

She smiled at him. "Come on then, let's go and find that kettle."

* * *

34

The alarm clock woke Kathryn after a few hours sleep. She came to with a feeling of satisfaction in her mind. Something had gone right. Her memory clocked in. They had Derrick Kohl in custody. Today, they should get some answers. She showered, grabbed a coffee and returned to the station.

Ed was busy talking to the custody officer. Kohl had arrived some hours earlier. They'd placed him in a cell to sleep and await his solicitor before his formal interview. She went on through to the workroom.

Truscott stood beside the window, gazing into space. She glanced out as she passed to see what had caught his attention. Jodie was stepping out the passenger side of a vintage MG. She leaned back in, kissed the driver and waved him off. So, that's why Truscott looked so crestfallen. There was no way he was going to compete with a bloke who owned a car like that, and he knew it. Jodie and Louis might be only a few years apart in age, but a whole generation in outlook.

"Morning Louis, are you ready to move?" she called to him.

He turned back. "Yeah, Sarge, anytime you want." He left the window and trudged over to her workstation. He scratched an ear with the car key; his brown eyes looking wounded. Then he followed her out to the car.

Truscott knocked on Janine's front door. Elvis opened it. A tall skinny figure, he stood looking at them, his hair freshly spiked, a gold ring through his eyebrow.

"It's the Old Bill," he called over his shoulder.

"Well, don't leave 'em on our doorstep for everyone to gawp at," a disembodied voice reached Kathryn. Elvis stood to one side to let them in.

181

Janine leaned over the kitchen bench making up a lunch box. A white T-shirt emblazoned with the blue logo, "Surfers do it with a wave," hung down over her jeans.

"Oh, it's you," she said, looking pointedly at Kathryn. "What do you want this time? If it's about Derrick, I don't know where he is. Bastard's run out on me."

Truscott answered. "There are a number of things we need to discuss with you Mrs Kohl, not just Derrick. We'd like you to come down to the station."

"Sod it! You'll have to wait 'til I get the boy off, he still has to carry on his father's business, you know. I tell him, he's gotta get a manager in, he can't cope with all that on his own. Maybe get a partner. I thought Derrick might go for it. Seems I was wrong.

She packed Elvis off out of the door and turned back to them. "Right, what's all this crap about? Can't you say what you gotta say here? Save us both a whole lot of trouble."

"It's no trouble to us, Mrs Kohl," Kathryn said. "If it makes you any happier, we'll place you under arrest and formally caution you." This woman playing the innocent was getting right up her nose.

"On what bloody charge?" Janine stood back, hands on hips, a smirk on her face.

"Hiding your ex-husband's van, for a start," Truscott said. "That's concealing evidence."

"Oh shit! I knew that would bring nothing but trouble. Look, there's nothing to it. He just wanted to get the van out of the way for a time. Don't ask me why, I don't know."

"*He* being Viktor, or Derrick?" Truscott prompted.

A sullen look came over Janine's face. She wasn't going to fold that easily.

"Alternatively," Kathryn said, "we could charge you with the unlawful disposal of a body. Or, we could upgrade that to accessory after the fact for any criminal act perpetrated by Derrick Kohl on the morning in question. So, come on, get your coat before we think of more ways to put you behind bars."

"You wait. I'll get this sorted. I'm not talking to you, or anybody without a bloody brief. Right?" Swearing under her breath, she collected her black leather jacket.

*

Pug watched her possessions pile up on the pontoon as they shifted everything not screwed down on the boat. Ratz happily stayed ashore, romping with two small boys who had come off the cruiser tied next to *Cazutt.*

Gil started with the outside lockers. Then he opened the engine housing, examined the prop shaft and ran his fingers into every aperture large enough to accommodate the opal. Once Pug had cleared the main cabin, she stood back as Gil lifted up the floorboards to check around the flexible, bladder-style water tank that lay beneath.

Pug sat back on her heels, watching him sweep his hand around the floppy topsides of the tank. "What if it's fallen down into the space underneath?"

He shrugged. "The tank's too heavy to lift; we'll have to pump out the water. I hope to God it's not under there, what with the weight of the tank, the vibrations from the motor, it won't stand a chance. You have to treat opals like glass."

"Celeste told me that. She's into this sort of thing. She said even the vibrations from an ultrasonic cleaner will shatter them. But what if whoever hid the opal didn't know that?"

Gil rolled his eyes. "This is a million pound gem we're looking for. Who in their right mind would hide it in a place like this, anyway?"

Pug forced herself to think of Dom in this scenario. What would he have done with it? Would he have taken the trouble to lift the tank out and put it underneath, in a protective box, for example? For a lot less than a million pounds, Dom would sell his soul.

"Let's finish the rest of the boat; with luck we might not have to come back to this," she said, putting the kettle on for another cup of tea.

Gil replaced the floorboards and sat down on one of the cushioned berths to take a break. She handed him a mug and sat opposite him.

"So, how's the head this morning?" he asked. "Did you have any after effects?"

"Not unless you count seeing a blood moon in the middle of the night."

Gil laughed and shook his head. "Not last night, you didn't. It's the wrong time of the year. October's the month."

"Yeah? Well it sure looked spooky to me. The face of the moon was red. Doesn't that foretell something bad?"

"Back in ancient times, if the moon came up red it foretold a night of extra brightness. It meant that huntsmen could see their prey for longer and by a bigger, brighter moon than usual. That extended the killing time. The red stain on the rising moon's face represented the extra blood spilled. A blood moon usually happened on the first full moon after the harvest. That's around October in the northern hemisphere."

Pug felt a chill ruffle the hairs on the back of her neck. There had been plenty of blood already spilled in the name of that opal, they didn't need any more.

"Must've been the bump on your head, you were seeing things," he said.

Pug would very much like to dismiss her night shivers as the result of an overwrought imagination, but for the moment, she would say no more. She placed her empty cup back in the sink and looked around at the desolate cabin.

"Right, apart from under the tank, where haven't we looked?"

"There's only the forepeak left," he said.

Kohl had pulled most of the anchor chain out of its locker, but apparently hadn't finished the job when Gil's arrival interrupted him. Pug still thanked her lucky stars that Gil had bumped the boat and set the intruder blundering past her in his haste to escape.

Gil moved ahead of her into the cabin. His touch as he passed was fleeting and in the smallness of the space around them, inevitable. They'd given up apologising when their bodies brushed against each other as they worked.

They pushed five bulky sail bags up through the hatch onto the deck ready for stripping and opening up the space beneath the bunks. "I suppose we'd better empty the sail bags in case it's wrapped up inside one of them," Pug said.

"Let's finish in here first." Gil started on the second bunk. Kohl had left the anchor chain piled on top of the berth cushion, weighing it down. Gil pulled the remainder of the chain out to check for a hidden cache in the base of the locker. Pug watched him, unable to help, as there wasn't room for two to stand between the twin berths.

"Nothing in the bottom, except a bit of sand and a dollop of seawater," Gil's voice sounded muffled in the clank of chain links. "I'm putting it back now, okay?"

All she could see were his back and arms moving rhythmically, as metre-by-metre he fed the heavy chain back into its locker. She left him to it and went out to check on Ratz. He was still with his new friends. All three were on the boardwalk, bottoms in the air, eyes peering through the gaps in the wooden planks, the boys squealing with delight at shrimps darting around in the water beneath.

Piece by piece she collected the stuff stacked on the pontoon and returned it to its correct place. She was outside again when she heard Gil call.

"Pug!" Her stomach contracted. God, she was beginning to hate this opal. She hurried back to find Gil stretched out on one of the bunks. His head was down the far end, inside the anchor locker, resting on the chain and facing upwards.

He craned his neck to look back at her. "Can you bring a torch?"

She fetched one, slid onto the second bunk and crawled down towards the end where her bunk joined his at the point of the "A" shaped cabin and handed the torch to him.

"What've you got?" she asked, her breath shortening in anticipation.

He lay on his back, hands above his head peering into the topside of the locker. Leaving the torch balanced on the mound of chain, he pulled himself out to give her room.

"Up here, on the roof inside the locker, take a look," he said.

She lay on her back and wriggled in further until her head was inside the locker. She flashed the torch over the rough fibreglass.

"Gottit. A small black box," she tried to wiggle it with her fingers, but it remained firmly glued in. "What is it?" Surely, it wasn't the thing they were looking for.

He didn't answer. When she hauled herself back to his level, their faces were only inches apart. Fully stretched along one of the bunks, he lay on his side, resting on an elbow, watching her. Warmth emanated from his body in a clean man smell. He'd discarded his cap and anorak. His navy and white T-shirt stretched taut across the broad expanse of his chest, and his tanned bare arms spoke of workouts in the gym. His eyes locked on hers – his very masculinity filled the tiny cramped space.

Suddenly she became self-conscious of the mess she must look with her face damp, her hair stuck to her brow. She lowered her gaze to the bow shape of his full lips, neatly outlined by a trim dark beard. Tentatively, she raised her fingers and touched his face. His beard was softer than she'd thought. She put her hand behind his head and drew him towards her. Their lips met. Long dormant sensations, deep within her belly exploded with the pressure of their kiss. She closed an arm around his shoulders and held him tight against her before letting him go. He drew back, and once more their eyes met. The last time she'd seen a grin that endearing was on her old brown teddy bear, and she'd loved him to bits. She smiled back and for a moment nothing in the world mattered any more.

He came back for more and as their second kiss came to an end she pushed against him, he released his hold and sat back watching her and waiting her reaction. She knew so little about him. Until the day before, she'd had him on her list of dubious characters, and possibly even an enemy. Besides, for all she knew, he could have a wife and a handful of kids waiting for him back home. She extricated herself from his arms and slid down the bunk until she could sit upright.

"You're a good kisser, Gil, I'll give you that. Had me going there for a minute," she said flippantly.

"Any time you fancy another, I'd be happy to oblige," he said, matching her tone.

To quell the yearning he'd aroused in her, she needed to get things back to normal. She jerked her thumb towards the anchor locker. "What about this box? Is that it?" As she intended, he recognised her manoeuvre. It was back to business.

"No such luck. It's a portable marine tracking unit, battery operated. People use them to track their boats in the event of them being stolen. Did you or your husband put it in?"

She shook her head. "Not me, I don't know about Dom. Though, if he'd been spending money on the boat, I'm sure he would have said."

"They can also be used by someone stalking a boat. All they have to do is hide it where the owner is not likely to find it. It looks like somebody, other than me, has been tracking your movements."

She felt a cold draught shimmer down her spine as the implication hit her. That's how Derrick Kohl had known where she was all along. He could have jumped her anytime.

"Right, I'll soon fix that." She stumbled back to the toolbox and returned with a hammer and chisel.

*

Before their interview, Kathryn had directed Janine into a side room for a private consultation with the duty solicitor. There wasn't time enough to get on with anything else, so Kathryn took her cup of coffee and slipped into the observation room to see how Ed was getting on with Kohl.

Derrick Kohl sat back in the chair, his right ankle resting on his left knee. He wore a black sweatshirt, jeans and a few scratches on his face, presumably from his arrest last night. Kathryn noticed he had a new brief. Mr Waterhouse was a burly man in a dark suit. The black framed spectacles on his nose added weight to his leonine head.

Kohl's assault on Pug was sufficient to hold him. But more importantly for the investigation, Ed wanted to question him about Viktor, the opal robbery, the death of the courier, and the deaths of Dom Spencer and Chantelle. She arrived in time to see Kohl's lawyer having a spat with Ed. It looked as though things were not going as smoothly as Ed had hoped.

Waterhouse had an edge to his voice. "My client is here on one case of assault, not four counts of murder. If you wish to bring in other cases, then charge my client. But you'd better be sure of your evidence, because as things stand you have nothing. In the Spencer and Chantelle Kohl murders, my client has accounted for his movements until eleven o'clock of the morning in question. Shall we continue with this minor assault charge, or are you prepared to release my client immediately?"

Kathryn pressed her lips together. And there lay the root of their problem. They had a mass of information and intelligent guesswork, but very little in the way of proof. Janine's alibi had Derrick firmly pegged in her house until well after the victims' official time of death.

Unless they could break that alibi, Derrick was going to walk.

* * *

35

Kathryn returned to the interview room where Janine sat slumped at the table, nibbling on a thumbnail. Her solicitor, sitting quietly beside her, nodded that they were ready. Truscott, already seated, was checking out the video recorder equipment.

Questioning her in turns, Kathryn and Truscott touched briefly on the ground they'd already covered at Janine's last interview, about the way she disposed of Viktor's clothes. Her story was the same, and she maintained Derrick had been with her until eleven o'clock on the morning Spencer and Chantelle were murdered.

Kathryn started on new ground. "When did you last see Viktor Kohl alive?"

Janine sniffed. "Months. Me and my ex didn't exactly see eye to eye."

"Can you explain how your fingerprints came to be on his van?" Truscott asked.

Janine frowned then shrugged. "I could have touched it at some time in the past. Perhaps he hadn't washed it lately. How long do fingerprints hang around?"

"Was it your idea, or Derrick's, to wipe the number plate with mud?" Kathryn asked.

"You don't have to answer that, Mrs Kohl," Janine's solicitor advised.

"No comment."

Kathryn threw in a bluff to test the waters. "That's not what Derrick says."

"Derrick doesn't know his arse from his elbow. What's he say, then?" Janine asked.

"I want to take you back to the morning of May thirteenth. The day Viktor died, the day Dom Spencer and Chantelle Kohl were murdered, the same day you assisted Derrick in disposing of Viktor's body and hiding his van."

Janine straightened. "Stop right there! I had nothing to do with hiding his body, and if Derrick says different, he's lying."

"Your fingerprints are impressed on the mud used to blur the registration plate."

Janine shrugged. "Could've been accidental."

Kathryn pushed her point. "The earth you used has been analysed and is shown to have come from one of the rose beds surrounding the car park where we found the van. Several sets of your fingerprints are smeared all over the plate. That was no accident."

Janine pressed her lips together until they went white. It looked like silence was to be her next weapon.

"Okay," Kathryn said. "We know that before you hid the van, it was used to carry Viktor's body to his place of burial." When Janine remained silent, she continued. "Now, I want you to think very carefully about this. Someone killed Dom Spencer and Chantelle that same day. With Viktor dead and Derrick at your home with you until eleven that morning, neither of them could have done it. Likewise, Derrick vouches for you – so, who else could have killed Chantelle and her lover? Who else might have had a motive?"

Janine looked blank. "It could have been anyone off the street, who knows, who cares?"

Kathryn turned to smile at Truscott. "I think it's time we brought Elvis Kohl in for further questioning."

"What?" Janine jumped to her feet. "You leave my boy out of it. Elvis knew nothing about it."

"Knew nothing about what?" Kathryn asked. "And sit down."

Janine resumed her seat, narrowed eyes full of hate. "No comment."

"Elvis knew nothing? Someone used the incinerator behind his shop that morning to burn workmen's overalls and a leather attaché case. Are you trying to tell me Elvis knew nothing of what was going on in his own backyard?"

"Why should he? There's a storeroom between the yard and the shop. He could work all day in the shop and not know who was in the back yard. And if you're suggesting he killed Viktor, why would Elvis kill his dad? You're right out of your tree on that one."

Without knowing how deeply Janine was involved in the plot to steal the Blood Opal, Kathryn didn't want to reveal too much information at this stage. But Elvis was Janine's weak spot, and who knew what might pop out if she squeezed hard enough?

"We know that Viktor, Derrick and Chantelle were involved in a robbery recently. Elvis worked alongside his dad and his Uncle Derrick. Are you telling me he knew nothing about their plans for the robbery?"

"No comment."

"What if he did know their plans? What if Elvis discovered that Chantelle was about to do a runner with the loot *and a new boyfriend*? Would he try to stop her for his dad's sake? Could Elvis have killed Spencer and Chantelle because they were running off together with the proceeds of his dad's robbery?"

"No! I told you. He was at work all day."

"Janine, we've been unable to find a single witness to say your boy was in the shop those first couple of hours on May thirteenth."

"So what?" Janine held her hands out, palms up. "The fact that he had no customers that early in the morning is not unusual. A quiet day – doesn't mean anything."

Kathryn made a show of looking at her watch, then at Truscott. "Right, I think we'll take a short break. Meantime, let's get Elvis in and ask him what he *really* knows." She put her hand out towards the remote. "Terminating interview," and paused. Who would Janine sacrifice, her son or her lover?

"No, wait." Janine jerked her hands up, her face the colour of stale porridge.

The solicitor beside Janine spoke up. "You do have the right to remain silent, Mrs Kohl. You don't have to admit to anything that is likely to incriminate you."

"It's not me I'm soddin' worried about." Janine turned back to Kathryn; her voice raised an octave. "Look, Elvis doesn't know anything about it. He's not the brightest. The way you're going on, you're hell bent on droppin' him in the shit, and I'm not having it."

Kathryn leaned forward. "So, tell us the real time Derrick Kohl left your house that morning," she said quietly.

"You really are a bitch, aren't you?"

Kathryn ignored the insult and waited, finger tapping the table. Janine sat back, folded her arms across her chest. "He had a phone call around nine and he left then."

"Say that again. Who had a call around nine?" Kathryn sat back as Janine repeated her last words and this time naming Derrick.

190

"Who called him?" Kathryn asked.

"Viktor. I don't know what it was about, but it was trouble, and as usual Derrick had to go and sort it out. Later he called me. That's when he wanted me to pick him up from the car park. I didn't ask questions, I just went. He told me he needed to keep the van out of sight for a while. Okay, I helped him cover the number plate, not such a big crime is it?"

Kathryn thought of the untold wasted man-hours searching for a suspect that was already dead. But that would mean nothing to the likes of Janine.

"Where did you take Derrick after you'd picked him up?" Truscott asked.

"To the shop's backyard where he'd left his car."

"Did you know at this stage that Viktor was dead?"

"Look, it was an accident. Derrick's right – he said no one would believe him. That's why I helped him. That's why I got rid of Viktor's clothes to make it look like he'd packed and gone away. That's all."

"Did Derrick offer you any inducement to keep quiet?"

"All he said was he and Viktor had unfinished business. He said Viktor had a jewellery order ready for delivery. Only Derrick didn't know where he'd put it. He said if we could find it and deliver it to the customer's agent, then we could keep the money and it wouldn't have to go through the books. Sounded fair to me."

"Where were you supposed to deliver it?" Kathryn asked in a neutral voice, to keep Janine talking and her own building excitement hidden.

"He said it would mean a weekend in the Channel Islands. Well, I'm not one to turn down a fully funded weekend away. Far as I was concerned, it was worth keeping schtum." Her eyes blazed and she tapped her fingers on the table. "But not if you're going to start blaming Elvis, because my boy knew nothing about it."

She slumped in her chair, the bolshie look back on her face. It was obvious they were going to get nothing more. The silence grew deeper.

In a low voice Kathryn asked: "Did Derrick tell you what you were going to deliver?"

The woman shook her head.

"The Blood Opal."

Janine's eyes widened, her jaw dropped. And for the first time Kathryn spotted fear.

*

Gil Trelawney had pressed all the right buttons. Pug's heightened senses made her acutely aware of his presence in the confined space of the forepeak. She gritted her teeth as she chiselled the tracking device out of the locker. When it came off, she passed it to Gil, conscious of the warmth of his hand as it touched hers. He moved out into the main cabin and placed the device on the table where they could see it clearly. Pug followed him out. She regarded it much as she would have done a snake in the grass.

"I want it off this boat, now. What if we ditch it in a dumpster ashore?" she asked.

He put his hand up, palm out. "Not so fast, let's think about it a moment. Right now Kohl is safely in custody, but there's no saying a wily brief won't get him bailed. His next aim will be to find this boat and finish his search. As of this moment, he has no means of knowing where the boat is, but he can still see the tracker. If he gives them the slip, this would be an excellent way for the police to draw him in."

"What do you mean? You want to use my boat to catch him? Where am I supposed to go?"

His smile reached his eyes. "You could always share some cabin space with Moggy and me." The crows' feet deepened as his grin widened.

With the taste of his kiss still haunting her lips, the thought of them both together in his boat, sharing his cabin space was tantalising. Abruptly she turned her head away. There were other things to consider.

"What if he damages my boat next time?" The boat was all she had – it was her home. Gil appeared unaware of what he was asking of her.

"I was joking – about sharing my space," he said softly. She turned back to see his look of concern that he'd upset her. "They wouldn't need to use your boat," he explained. "They could stick the tracker in any old boat, tie it up to the jetty and wait for him to turn up.

"Okay, I'm with you now," she said, slightly embarrassed that she'd misread him. "Let's finish our search first before we get the police back in. If we do find the opal, then the whole nightmare is over. We can hand it back and forget it."

"And you can spend the reward money at your leisure."

"I don't care about the reward. In fact, I've decided, don't want it. It's tainted. It's blood money."

"Most people wouldn't care about that."

"I'm not most people."

He fell silent, looking thoughtful. The silenced lingered.

"Are you married, Gil?"

His smile softened. "No longer, I fear. My wife died some years back."

"Oh, I'm sorry." Foot in mouth again, she stretched a hand across the table and placed it on top of his. "I didn't mean to pry."

"I know that." He checked his watch. "I don't know about you, but I'm getting damned hungry. How about we take a break before we tackle the water tank? Have a pasty lunch and a breather. Then come back fresh and start on the sail bags and the tank, what do you say?"

"Sounds good, do you have somewhere in mind?"

"I know of a little pub just up the river. We'll take my dinghy. The outboard will get us there in no time."

Pug returned *Cazutt* to her designated mooring. Gil collected her repaired inflatable from the club's slipway and brought it out to join *Cazutt,* when she and Ratz transferred to Gil's dinghy. Having spent the last few hours inside her cabin, Pug welcomed the fresh air, the damp overcast sky, and the wind blowing in her hair. They sped through the water, past an old stone quay on the edge of Penwood Acres and followed the line of trees that hung over the riverbank, laughing as they crossed another boat's wake and spray cascaded over them.

Gil took a left turn, away from the main river and into a tidal creek. A pontoon stretched over the water; Gil tied his dinghy to one of its struts. Together she and Gil, with Ratz on a lead, walked towards a low thatched building with white cob walls.

"Welcome to the Ferryman," Gil said. "Bar, lounge or beer garden?"

"Oh, let's stay outside. It looks a bit crowded in there," she said, taking a vacant table beneath a Martini umbrella.

Gil went in to fetch their order of hot Cornish pasties and two half-pints of draught. The rich, savoury aroma of the filling inside the golden pastry cases had Pug salivating as she unloaded the tray. He'd also brought water for Ratz.

"When do you think Derrick gained access to the inside of your boat?" he asked.

"I've been thinking about that. Dom brought the boat into the club's pontoons the day before he died and left it there. Derrick could have climbed aboard any time during the following week. When I first checked it I found the padlock broken."

"Did you inform the police?"

"I did, but at that stage, I didn't know Dom's murder was connected to the opal robbery, and nor did the police, come to that. They checked the boat for clues to the murder investigation. The new charts showing Dom's proposed destination were of interest to them. But that's all. If anybody saw the black box in the chain locker, they would assume it was part of the normal equipment."

"When did you first decide to take the boat away?"

"The day Mother's house was ransacked." She gave him a brief account.

"So, that's the first day Kohl could have known you were sailing off in the boat."

"What are you getting at?"

"When he was in your mother's house, he could have heard the phone message from your solicitor, and learned you were about to make off with the boat. He probably put that device in while you were at the solicitors knowing you were out of the way."

Pug stayed silent. That made sense; Kohl could have been to one to delete Peter's call.

"If he's been watching me all this time, why didn't I sense it?"

"You did sense a watcher, but you put the blame on me." He chuckled.

"Well, I wasn't exactly wrong about that, was I, Gil Trelawney?"

"True, but at least I wasn't out to harm you." He finished his meal and held out the last small corner of pastry to Ratz. "Fancy an amble up the riverbank?" he asked.

Wavelets lapped the edges along the narrow shoreline as they strolled slowly side by side, with Ratz running free ahead. Drying seaweed added pungency to the air. Pug stopped to gaze out over the estuary teeming with water birds. A pair of swans glided by, shags and cormorants dived for fish; the raucous call of gulls rang in the air. She turned back to Gil. "It's so beautiful here."

"Yep, just the sort of place I'm looking for."

"Perhaps you should buy the Ferryman," she joked.

"I'm thinking about it," he said seriously. She stopped and stared at him, mouth open.

He laughed. "That surprised you, didn't it? I should've had a camera handy."

"Okay, one up to you," she drew a line in the air. "What does an insurance man know about running a pub, anyway?"

He pushed his cap further back on his head and continued his tramping along the shore. Pug thought he wasn't going to answer, then realised he was gathering his thoughts.

"I used to be in the pub game, long time back," he said eventually. His grin faded. "Gave it up when my wife got sick with cancer. I needed time to care for her over that last year. Afterwards, well, I didn't feel like going back into the business. I needed a change, and that's when I joined the insurance company."

Embarrassed that she may have stepped over the line and caused him pain, Pug put her hand out and touched his arm. They stopped.

"I'm sorry to hear that, Gil."

"Well, it was a long time ago, now. Somehow, in the interim, our friends moved on, or split and took up with new partners, and I lost touch. We had no kids; the empty house was full of memories. After a while, I sold up."

Pug could relate to that. "That's when you moved into your boat?"

"Yep, I took the cat and we moved into *Piglet*. As for Moggy, waited on her hand and paw, she loved the boating life. But now, I'm looking for a little *joie de vivre*. Cats are all very well, but it would be nice to have company without the fishy breath." He gave her a bright and easy smile. "Besides, I'm a bit disillusioned with the money market and the materialistic attitudes I have to deal with every day."

"I know what you mean ..." She tailed off as his arm went around her. He drew her towards him and hugged her gently, mindful of her bruises. Eventually, they disengaged, smiled at each other, and ambled back, hand in hand.

Back at the Ferryman they returned to their table and Gil went to the bar for more beer.

While she was waiting for him to come back, she saw three men come ashore and head for the pub. Like her, they'd come in a dinghy with an outboard. So, they probably had a yacht out in the river somewhere. As they drew nearer, she recognised one, returned his wave, and watched as he followed his companions into the bar.

Zebedee was the owner of her local boatshed at home. He was the one who'd seen Dom on the boat the day before he died.

She wanted a word with him.

* * *

36

Once Janine had signed her new statement, Kathryn sent her back to the holding cell to await further interrogation, should it prove necessary after Kohl's interview. She sent a note to Ed, informing him of their breakthrough on Kohl's alibi. Derrick's solicitor called for a halt in the proceedings to consult with his client. Kathryn was pouring herself a coffee when Ed came looking for her.

"Well done, Sergeant. You did a good job in there."

She smiled at the warmth in his voice – he actually meant it. Praise indeed. She held the coffee jug up and he nodded for her to pour him one. A nearby fax machine rattled through its latest message. He took the steaming cup from her.

"Let's go to my office. It'll be quieter in there," he said.

She followed him and took a seat not cluttered with paperwork. Ed sat on the swivel chair at his desk. He linked his hands behind his head and pulled a face as he tried to disguise a yawn.

"It's going to be a long haul with Kohl. It's like pulling teeth from a rhino. But in breaking his alibi you have given us a point of leverage. That man has a lot more explaining to do."

"Do you think Derrick could the take the place of Viktor as our prime suspect now?" Kathryn asked.

Ed shook his head. "Forensic comes down more heavily on Viktor being the killer of the two in the bedroom. But Derrick Kohl doesn't know that, so we can use that as a bargaining chip. By the way, Theo's brought the enhanced CCTV photos from the lab."

Kathryn raised her eyebrows. "Any good?"

"Good enough." He loosened his tie and ran a finger around the inside of his collar.

Theo stuck his head around the door. "We're on again."

*

Back in the interview room, Ed nodded for Theo to switch the recorder on again. He'd decided not to start with the broken alibi. If

Waterhouse had been fed the same lie as the police, no doubt Kohl's ears would still be ringing from his brief's indignation. Ed hoped the delay would unsettle him still further. Kohl slouched at the table, ankles crossed, arms folded. His facial expression continued to be mulish. He wasn't going to chuck the towel in easily.

Ed opened the file on the table in front of him and extracted a photograph of Derrick Kohl sitting between two smiling people, each with a raised glass in hand. Ed pointed to it. "Would you identify the man and woman either side of you, please?"

Derrick shrugged and named Chantelle and Viktor Kohl. Ed smiled as he produced a second photo. "And this woman?"

After a fleeting glance, Kohl shot a look straight at Ed. Having just identified his sister-in-law in the first photo, he could no longer deny her full-face identity in the second.

Ed held it up the better for Kohl to see. "This one was taken by a CCTV camera in the car park of the Market Place. Here, Chantelle Kohl, carrying a bulky shopping bag, is seen leaving a white van." Derrick shuffled his feet. "And then there's this one." Ed produced a third photograph with a smile. "Here we are, man of the moment, Derrick Kohl himself." He tapped the photo. "This one places you outside the emergency exit of the market place, getting out of the same white van your sister-in-law was driving. The dates and times correspond to the time-slot of the robbery that took place in Centurion House, a few minutes drive away."

Kohl remained silent, eyes shifting between Ed and Theo and back to his brief.

Waterhouse stirred. "Inspector, what do you hope to gain with these innocuous photographs?" he asked in a tired voice. "All they show is my client at the market on Saturday afternoon, a fact he has never denied. His proximity to the crime-scene is co-incidental."

Ed turned back to Kohl. "What it *does* show is you lied about the time you last saw Chantelle. You lied to the stall-holder who was looking after your stall. You also lied to us about your whereabouts on the Monday morning. Your story is unravelling. What other lies are about to trip you up?"

Waterhouse sighed. "So, reprimand my client for lying, and let's all go home." Theo Pappas tapped a pen against his notebook, his patience also wearing thin.

Ed ignored them both and concentrated on Kohl. "Which one of you brought the opal home? You, your brother, or your sister-in-law?"

"Told you. It's all news to me."

"My money's on Chantelle. The size of that plastic bag she's carrying would have nicely disguised the attaché case," Ed said.

"It's bollocks," Derrick said to Waterhouse. "He's on a fishing trip. All he's got is a crock o'shit. He can't prove any of it." His brief looked more guarded.

"Ah, that's where you're wrong, sunshine," Ed said. "Inside your incinerator we found identifiable remains of the courier's attaché case. His widow has identified the medallion as coming from her husband's case. It directly links you and your brother to the crime.

"And … it wasn't my incinerator."

Theo slapped the table at Derrick's continued rebuttals. Ed willed him to hang on there a little while longer. He knew how to wear Kohl down. That Theo Pappas should interrupt him at this stage surprised him. He and Theo had agreed that Ed would direct his interrogation towards the murder of Spencer and the Kohls first, while Theo would concentrate on the robbery and murder of the courier in the next session.

Theo bent forward towards their suspect. "Stop arsing about. I don't care whose bloody incinerator it was. One of you three brought the case home from Exeter and burned it." He dabbed the table with his fingers. "What did you do with its contents?" Theo sat back and waited.

Kohl scraped his chair backwards, folded his arms across his chest, feet flat on the floor. Ed feared much more of this and they would lose ground. But before he could add a soothing word, Theo spoke out again.

"Just tell us what you did with the bloody opal!"

Kohl raised his voice an octave. "Or what? Will you lose your pretty little temper with me, gay-boy?" he said, mimicking an effeminate voice, jiggling his body from side to side. Theo was on his feet and around the table close enough to catch the man by his shirtfront and pulled him out of the chair.

Ed raised a palm towards them. "Okay, that's enough, Pappas."

Theo came to his senses, released Kohl and stepped aside. "It's a simple enough question!" Gathering his self-control, he returned to his seat, and sat down.

Ed scraped a hand through his hair. Theo Pappas was more wired than he'd allowed for – his outburst could have wrecked the interview.

If Pappas did have sensitive issues, then it was time he grew a thicker skin.

"Right, Kohl, back to your seat." Ed's calm voice was the only sound in the room as Derrick Kohl, a mocking smile on his face for Theo, sat down.

"Now, we come to the alibi you gave for the time Dominic Spencer and Chantelle Kohl were murdered." Ed started again. "In your statement you said you got home around seven that morning. Unloaded the van then you went to Janine's where you stayed until eleven o'clock. That was a lie. We now know you left Janine's around nine that morning."

"She's lying."

"You had this panicky call from Viktor, who said you were to meet him in the backyard of the shop."

"I said – the cow is lying."

"Don't you think that with four counts of murder to be taken into consideration, a little more co-operation on your part might make it the better for you?" Ed asked reasonably.

"Four? That's crap. There's not even one – how'd you get four?"

"After the courier, those extra hours without an alibi, nicely puts you in the frame for the murder of Dom Spencer and Chantelle."

Anger flared in his face. "No. That wasn't me."

Ed leaned back in his chair. "Right, let's take it from the time you arrived home after that weekend. Where was the attaché case?"

"Dunno – I didn't have it."

"I suggest that Chantelle brought it home, removed the contents and either took them to her new boyfriend, Dom Spencer, or hid them away herself. You, or maybe Viktor, found the empty case and burnt it along with the overalls you both wore for the robbery.

"Wasn't me."

"Right. Then, it was Viktor." Ed waited for the denial, but it didn't come. Maybe he had isolated one fact out of the debacle. "Okay, so Viktor finds the case. It's empty. He sees someone's done him over. Can't be you – you were with him all the time. His wife? He can't believe that. What about Spencer, the fourth member of the gang, the delivery man. What did he know about the missing opal? Viktor decides to pay Spencer a visit. But when he arrives there, he sees his wife's car nestling in the garage. What do you think went through his mind? He didn't arrive intending to kill his wife. But when the light dawned, he grabbed the nearest weapon and before he knew what he'd done, he'd killed them both." He paused for a moment to let that sink in. The silence stretched between them.

"Or, maybe it wasn't Viktor. Maybe you got there first?"

"No, I bloody didn't. You can't pin that one on me."

Ed paused. Did that mean he could pin it on Viktor? Was this fact number two? Was this how Derrick wanted to play it? Admit nothing and accuse nobody.

"We do know you were in that house sometime after it happened."

"You might guess, but you can't *know* that," Kohl scoffed.

"Wrong again," Ed bent to the floor, picked up a package and placed it on the table. "These are Viktor's shoes. Forensic evidence shows us they completed two separate journeys through Spencer's house. You walked into places we knew the killer had not been. It was you that searched the house, not Viktor. When you wore those shoes, you picked up the stains from the soup *you* emptied on the kitchen floor, long after the victims were dead. In deliberately leaving these shoes in the outhouse at Viktor's home, instead of burning them, you were laying a false trail to throw us off the scent, by suggesting Viktor was responsible for the search, as well as the murders."

Derrick washed his hands over his face. "What if I did? It couldn't hurt Viktor. His footprints were there anyway."

Ed paused. He'd squeezed an admission at last. "So, how did Viktor meet his death?"

"By accident. We argued. One punch, he fell over backwards and hit his head. He didn't get up."

"So you buried him."

"*It was an accident.* You can't do me for murder on that one."

"That is something we'll let a jury decide."

*

Kathryn had entered the observation room in time to see Theo's confrontation. She switched the speaker on and listened as Ed's unhurried voice filled the tiny room. She was surprised how quickly Kohl had picked up on Theo. As far as she could see, Theo showed no overt indications. Yet Kohl had picked it up within a couple of hours.

Both Ed and Theo had that end-of-a-hard-day look, ties loosened, jackets discarded. Kohl's lawyer remained cool and occasionally glanced at the ceiling, or studied his fingernails, his expression growing more wary as Ed delved deeper. She wondered at the DI's patience with Kohl – she would have strangled the man by now.

The door into the observation room opened. Louis Truscott came in. Her glance slid over his athletic figure, dark cords and light blue polo shirt, and no sign of his mother's knitted pullovers. He raised his eyebrows in greeting. "How's it going?" he asked quietly and sat on a chair beside her.

She gave him a brief summary. "With three of our villains dead there's not much of a case left. Derrick is pleading accidental death for Viktor."

The silence in the interview room lengthened, until Kohl broke it once more. "Look, these murders, you've got the wrong guy. It was Viktor. And if you ask me, his bloody missus got what was coming to her. As for the courier, Viktor did that one an' all."

Kathryn exchanged a knowing glance with Louis. "Well, he won't get away with that one, even if we can't prove the others," she said. They may not be able to prove which of the robbers killed the courier, but the death of Gordon Drysdale was a felony murder, which meant that both robbers were equally guilty, no matter which one of them wielded the weapon."

Theo asked quietly. "So where is the opal now?"

Kohl gave an indolent shrug. "Figured I'd missed it and that Dom Spencer's missus, whatsername," he waved a hand in the air, "must've taken it. After me, she was the next one on the scene. Why don't you ask her?"

"And this is where we come back to the assault of Ms Germaine." Ed exchanged looks with Theo, and then turned back to Waterhouse. "I think we'll take a break here. When we come back, Detective Inspector Pappas will ask the questions." Ed checked his watch, "Interview suspended …" gave the time and turned off the videotape.

Ed and Theo rose and made for the door. Kathryn switched off the speaker.

"It looks like they're going on into the night," Louis said. "Are you planning on staying to hear if Theo can get the opal buyer's name out of him?"

"Don't think so. I've seen enough of Theo for one day. Besides, his business is not our jurisdiction. Our suspects are the ones who did the hands-on work." She nodded towards Theo as he passed by the window. "Our visiting DI nearly blew it – I thought we were going to have a punch-up there for a moment."

Louis grinned, "What did Ed do?"

"Stayed remarkably calm, I don't know how he did it. It was amazing watching Ed work. While he extracted information from Kohl, Theo only jerked his chain."

"You're not so bad yourself," Louis said quietly. "Remember, I was there when you interviewed Janine. She's not an easy subject to interrogate. I thought you handled her well. You found her weakness and she just folded."

Two compliments in one day; she was doing well. She smiled at him. "Thank you, Louis." A spark of interest ignited between them. She caught her breath and held his gaze.

He cocked his head to one side as he returned her smile. He raised his hand in a drinking gesture. "Fancy a drink to round off the day?"

"Yeah. Why not?" She couldn't believe she was doing this. Louis – he was five years her junior. So what? Take a chance for once, woman. "Where shall we go, the usual pub?"

His warm toffee brown eyes locked on hers. "Or, maybe we could try out the new Thai restaurant down the road, a bottle of wine to celebrate."

"Celebrate? We don't need an excuse, let's just go out and enjoy ourselves."

* * *

37

Pug kept watch on the Ferryman's open door to make sure she didn't miss Zebedee when he came out. His boatyard, back in the River Tamar, was *Cazutt's* winter home, the place where she and Dom had bought their marine supplies and did their maintenance on Zeb's laying-up beach. Gil came back with the drinks.

Reluctant to stir old memories, Pug steered clear of mentioning Gil's wife, and instead got him to talk about other pubs he'd seen so far, and how the search was going. He looked thoughtful, and she was about to ask him what was on his mind, when the three men she'd seen earlier came out of the pub's door and made for a table nearby.

Zebedee picked up his drink. He said something to his companions then left them and walked towards her. She smiled as he approached; pleased she didn't have to seek him out.

"Zebedee!"

"Hey, Pug!" He put an arm around her shoulders, giving her a little squeeze. "It's good to see you. What are you doing down this way?" His touch on her bruised shoulder nearly had her gasping, but she managed to hold it back. His smile creased his wind-burnt leathery face. He looked the same as ever, his curly grey hair tied back in a ponytail, and his beard showed signs of a rough but recent trim. She and Dom had known him for years.

She introduced him to Gil and they shook hands.

Zebedee turned back to her, his face solemn. "I heard the news, Pug. I was so sorry to hear about Dom. Couldn't believe it when I heard. I was only talking to him the day before it happened. You been all right?"

She told him she'd sailed *Cazutt* down the coast to get away from all the fuss. "I spoke to Nobby Clark before I left; he told me Dom had been to your place. I just wondered why. Was everything all right with the boat?"

"Sure, you got no worries there." He dismissed her concern with a wave of his hand.

She didn't allow him to fob her off. "I know Dom wouldn't have visited the boatyard without a reason. So, what services did he need? Look, I know the woman was with him, if that's what's worrying you." She still had difficulty calling the woman by her name, a name made it painfully personal. "I want to know what needed doing, that's all."

"He'd come by to fill the water tank and top up the diesel. You obviously know by now, he was preparing for a voyage."

"Did you happen to notice if he emptied the water tank before filling it up?"

He looked to one side as though thinking about it. "Funny question. Not that I saw. Why would he do that? Had it got contaminated?"

She shook her head. The refuelling made sense, but she wanted more.

"The only other thing he asked about was if he could use the crane. I was running late, and couldn't stop to help. But young Terry, the painter, was around and Dom said he could manage well enough with the lad's help." Zebedee raised his glass and drank.

"The crane? Why did he want that?" There was only one reason she could think of, but why would Dom want to lower the mast only hours before a planned voyage?

Zebedee shrugged. "Didn't ask. Dom knew his boats and if he needed a crane, so what? He was perfectly able to handle it. He said something about a twisted halyard at the top of the mast, but nothing major. I left him to it."

A twisted halyard? Pug exchanged a puzzled glance with Gil.

Zebedee told them a little about his voyage up from the Med. Sailing luxury yachts home from exotic places, for owners too busy to do it themselves, was all part of his job.

On the way back to their boats, over the noise of the outboard, she brought up the possibility that Dom had hidden the opal inside the mast.

"Then, we'll have to lower the mast, same as he did," Gil said.

"Let's go and ask Jack where we can hire a crane for an hour or so," she suggested.

"Okay if I drop you off at the slipway? There's something I have to do. I'll pick you up in half an hour. I'm sure Jack will be able organise something. Just let him know I'll be on hand to help."

204

Pug walked down to Jack's workshop, surprised Gil wasn't tagging along with her. But he seemed to have something on his mind, and right now, he wasn't sharing it with her. While in Jack's workshop, waiting for him to come off the phone, she heard the news on his radio that Derrick Kohl had been charged with one count of felony murder, one count of murder and had further charges pending. Although much relieved to hear that Kohl was still in custody, she was slightly miffed that the assault on her didn't even rate a mention. They did say the whereabouts of the Blood Opal was still unknown.

She didn't want to go into detail with Jack as to why she wanted to get the mast down. If it got out that they were looking for the opal, it could attract the wrong kind of people, like those wishing to claim the reward. As it turned out, Jack didn't question her. He gave her a long look, as though he sensed there was more to it than she was prepared to admit, then he nodded. He fixed it with the harbour authorities for her to use the public crane on the wharf around eleven the next morning.

Gil picked her up on time and took her back to *Cazutt*. He remained in his dinghy after she'd climbed out. "Coming in for a coffee?" she asked.

"Can't stop now, something I've got to do. Tell you what – I'll bring breakfast tomorrow. You like croissants?"

"With black cherry jam?"

He smiled and clicked his fingers. "Done."

She watched him motor back to the quay and wondered after all his days wandering around after her, what was so important he suddenly couldn't spare the time for a coffee.

*

After a restless night, Pug woke early and took Ratz for a morning run along the riverbank. The air smelled fresh – clean and unused. When she returned aboard, she glanced at *Piglet*, swinging ahead of her on the next mooring. Gil appeared on deck and she gave him a wave. She was still curious as to what had taken his attention at such a crucial point the day before. An unwanted niggle of doubt stirred. She stamped on it. Of course, she could trust him. He was the one person fully entitled to claim the opal on behalf of his company.

Ratz stood in the bow, his lips wrinkling over his teeth as he growled. His eyes fixated on Moggy as she performed acrobatics on the roof of Gil's wheelhouse playing with swinging cords that tied equipment down.

Gil waved a bulky paper bag in the air. "Put the kettle on, I'm coming over."

She watched him row the short distance between them. She grasped the warm bag of fresh croissants and smiled at the jar of black cherry jam he handed her.

"There you go, knives and coffee are all we need," he said.

They sat in the cockpit warming in the sun and planned their next manoeuvre – the removal of the mast. The subject was soon exhausted and Pug sought a more interesting topic.

"How far have you got with the negotiations on the Ferryman?" she asked him.

He gave her a smug smile. "I've given them a counter offer. They're considering it. The agent is hopeful that it'll all go through."

"Will you be able to run a pub like that on your own?"

"That's the beauty of it. It's a walk-out-walk-in job. I even keep the same staff. All, except the son." He coughed awkwardly and looked aside. "There could be a job for you, if you're interested."

Pug was desperate for a job, a waitress or barmaid's job for a couple of months would be good, but it was not high on her list of permanent career choices. She thought about her earlier plan to sail on down to the Scilly Isles – but the chances were their holiday jobs would already be taken.

Gil tilted his head as though understanding her reluctance to commit herself. "If you didn't like the job, you could pack it in. It comes with a free mooring for your boat and a cottage behind the pub at a peppercorn rent."

Wow, she'd even wear a bunny tail and long pink ears for that. "What's the job?"

"Fancy skippering a water-taxi?"

She felt her mouth drop open. "You're kidding!" That beat waiting on tables any day.

"The current owners are going to Australia. The son has been running a small water-taxi business ferrying people from Falmouth and St. Mawes to the Ferryman and back. There's a ferryboat, licensed for twelve passengers, included in the deal. I'm quite sure your boating expertise will see you through whatever commercial license you'd need."

It sounded too good to be true. She swallowed hard. "You're one big tease, Gil! You don't even have the place yet, and you're offering me a job like that. Negotiations could go on for months and still not come to anything."

"Uh-uh. They have a deadline. That's why I had to see the agent yesterday. He thinks we could even get a reply today. But would you be interested?"

"Of course I'm interested."

"So, where's the enthusiasm?"

"Because, I can't believe this is just going to fall into my lap. Can we wait until you get confirmation before we crack open the Champagne?"

"Is the bad-omen thing bugging you again?" He smiled. "You mustn't be greedy. You can't have all the bad luck all the time. By now, you must be due for a change. Perhaps this is it. Come on, give us an answer, or I'll offer it to someone else."

She laughed. "You do, and I'll never speak to you again Gil Trelawney!"

* * *

38

At eleven o'clock, Pug brought *Cazutt* into the harbour and lined her up against the wharf beneath the crane. The wind had increased marginally and the occasional white caps decorated the wavelets in the river. Gil leapt ashore to tie the warps as Jack arrived to help.

Pug shut Ratz down in the cabin. They didn't want any accidents with him running around their feet once the mast was swinging free. When Gil came back on board, he brought a boatswain's chair made of webbing which he clipped to the mainsail halyard.

"Right, let's get started. Got a good head for heights?" he asked, as he helped her step into the canvas seat and adjusted it to her size, ready to haul her up the mast.

"Better I go up than you, I'm lighter," she said. Pug had done this job once before with Dom. She'd hated it then and wasn't looking forward to it now, but she needn't let these two men know her stomach had turned to jelly.

Pug swung in the air as Gil winched her up. The deck beneath her looked horribly far away and the swaying movement of the mast was greater than she expected. She placed the sling around the mast and under the crosstrees as directed, and made the loop ready for the crane's hook to take purchase.

The sun reflected off shiny metal in places and blinded her. She turned her head away and glimpsed a speedboat sweeping up the river behind her, trailing a huge wake of white water behind it. Too late to signal Gil to bring her down – she hooked an arm around the mast. The expanding wave of white water, from the speedboat's wash, reached *Cazutt*, hit the wharf and bounced back, causing the boat to swing violently from side to side. Pug held on to the metal mast, travelling with it on its outward arc as the deck beneath her blurred into turbulent water. Disoriented, she closed her eyes and held on as the mast swung back towards the wharf. When she dared look again, she saw the crane's metal hook looming large and heading straight for her face. Time fragmented – she followed the trajectory of the huge metal hook in slow motion – Celeste's voice in her head rang out. "I told you."

Slowly, slowly the hook veered away from her as she swung back and the motion of the mast lessened. She became aware of another voice shouting. Her mind snapped back into real time.

"Let go of the mast, Pug. I'm bringing you down, okay?"

The swaying of the boat had reduced to a comfortable level. The hook was out of the way but still she was reluctant to let go.

"What's keeping you?" Gil's voice hammered into her. She let go and he lowered her to the deck. "There, that wasn't so bad was it? You did a good job up there," he said.

Pug stepped out of the boatswain's chair. She took a deep breath and clenched her hands into fists to hide their trembling. "I was okay until the speedboat kicked up a wash, and then the boat went all to hell! Doesn't he know there is a speed limit in the harbour?"

"What speedboat?"

"What do you mean, 'what speedboat' – that one." She pointed upriver but the speedboat had already gone.

Gil shook his head. "It wasn't going that fast. I didn't think it kicked up much of wash."

He didn't look the slightest bit perturbed. She glanced ashore to see Jack waiting – he wasn't even working the crane. He stood, one hand casually shading his eyes.

She turned back to Gil, indignation burning her throat. "It's alright for you. You weren't bloody well up there."

Jack raised his hand. "Shout when you're ready," he called.

"Are you okay?" Gil asked. "You look a bit wobbly."

How could they have missed it? She'd been seconds away from disaster and they hadn't seen a thing. She looked from one to the other – had she imagined it? Had her higher vantage point exaggerated the scene below?

"I'm fine," she snapped. She wouldn't say another thing. They'd think her bonkers if she told them what really happened to her up there. "Let's get on with it."

More than ever, she wanted this job over. If the opal was on the boat, she wanted it off. Now. She was certain she could feel its malevolent presence.

They released the various stays and shrouds that held the mast upright, while Jack prepared to take its weight onto the crane. Slowly he turned the mechanism and brought the gold anodised mast, with its clanking wire rigging, to rest horizontally along the length of the wharf. He left them to it and returned to his workshop, saying to call him when they were ready to put it back again.

Apart from Gil, no one else was on the wharf. People strolled around the village and along the riverbank with kids and dogs, and out on the water in boats. But no one was near enough to observe their actions. Gil stood waiting for her to join him. He'd pushed his cap up at a rakish angle. His blue eyes sparkled and she sensed an underlying excitement in his glance.

"Come on, let's get it over with," she said. "This is make-or-break time."

The top of the mast took only seconds to examine. It had no place to hide anything larger than a bean. The bottom of the mast looked more promising. It was much wider, but anything stuffed inside it would have interfered with the working of the halyards. They found a space below the wheels, cogs, and interior workings, where the base of the metal mast was hollow.

Gil slipped a hand inside. "If they've kept it in the original box, it could have fitted in here. Nothing. It's empty."

Pug left the wharf and stepped back onto the boat. She looked down into the great empty hole on the deck where the mast had slotted in. A distant memory surfaced. She had been there when they first put the mast up. Beneath the shoe, the area into which the mast fitted, there was a cavity deep enough to take her forearm. Dom had made a joke of it at the time, saying it was a perfect smuggler's hole.

To examine it properly she had to crouch on the deck and lean over the collar, which encircled the foot of the mast when it was up. The boat dipped as Gil came aboard. He squatted beside her, watching her face.

"You found something?" he asked.

"There's space down there." She squinted into the dark gap.

"Wait a tick," he said. Fumbling in his jacket pocket, he produced a penlight. "See if that'll pick up anything."

She turned it on and directed its narrow beam into the gap. "Something's down there." She put her hand through the narrow opening at the base of the shoe. Her fingers touched a smooth, slippery surface and caused a shudder to rock her body. She jerked her hand back as though she'd touched slime. "Yuk!"

"Are you okay? You're as white as a sheet. Want me to do it?"

210

Pug shook her head. This was her boat, her job. Once more, she stretched her arm down and this time grasped the slippery bundle. She had to turn and twist it to get it out through the narrow opening. She placed it on the deck between them and studied the bulky plastic zip-lock bag. "Is this *it* do you think?"

Gil's voice caught in his throat. "It's the right size for the box."

She felt sick just looking at it. "Are you going to open it, or am I? Or, do we just hand it over to the cops as it is?"

"We need to check the contents before we tell anyone. Think how much trouble we'd be in if we opened it in front of the police and found a stash of heroin."

The thought made her laugh. "Okay, let's do it together. You take off the bag."

Her heart pumped at twice its normal rate. Did she want it to be the opal or not? Celeste said the Blood Opal only wrought evil on those who harmed it. Pug hadn't harmed it. And what *was* that business up the mast? Was it a glimpse of what it could do to her? She wished Celeste was here.

Gil had divested the package of its bag and inner wrap to reveal a tooled leather box. His triumphant grin crinkled the crow's feet either side of his shining eyes. He put it back down on the cabin top, they crouched either side of it.

"This is it. You open it, but don't touch anything inside. If others have handled it, we want their prints," he said.

Pug used a fingernail to release the catch on the box and the lid sprang open. A thick pad of white cotton wool covered the contents like a duvet. Gil hooked the padding with the point of his penlight and lifted it off.

Pug drew in a breath through puckered lips. Gil gave a low whistle.

Pressed into an inset lined in rich black velvet, gleamed the gold filigree pendant. Its heavyweight chain, also indented, looped around it. Encased in its centre, lay the legendary Blood Opal.

Entranced, Pug leaned forward to examine the stone more carefully. It was the length of her thumb, black at the sides shading to dark red, to lighter red. The stone's rich colouring shone from its core. As she moved the box, a spear of sunlight struck the domed centre of the stone and from its depths flickers of blue, scarlet and yellow rose like flares in a miniature furnace.

No sound penetrated her giddiness. Once again, inside her head she heard Celeste's distant voice calling on her to destroy the stone, to break its curse. Aware only of the burning midday sun on her head, the back of her neck, she was unable to tear her eyes away from the Blood Opal's radiance. As she watched, the blaze died. A hairline crack appeared on its blood red face. She drew in a sharp breath.

Once started, the crazing continued until the dome resembled the broken leavings of a spider's web. In front of her there came a low wail. She'd forgotten Gil was there. She lifted her face to look at him. Their eyes met and he shook his head in anguish.

"Is it dead," she whispered.

"Thermal shock."

"What?"

Gil's flagrant disappointment lined his greying face. He spoke, slowly with care, as though he was reciting from a book. "If an opal becomes dehydrated, it may craze there and then. Or, it could be unstable ever after. Any sudden change, particularly a change of temperature, can alter the critical moisture balance and cause it to self-destruct."

Pug recalled Celeste's words. *"That stone was mighty thirsty."* According to legend, the stone had dehydrated prior to its dunking in the river. But it had stayed together until she, Pug, had taken it from its cool hiding place and opened it to bask in the hot sunlight. Inadvertently, she had caused the opal the greatest harm of all. She had destroyed it.

"So, is that the end of it?" she looked a Gil. "What happens now?"

Gil sighed, still shaking his head from side to side. "Not entirely. The company will be able to recoup some of its losses. The gold pendant and the chain is undamaged and worth a tidy bit. And look here," he pointed to the small cairn of fragments with no more life than red and black peppercorns. "Some of these are still useful sizes, they could be salvaged."

The churning in her stomach returned. Surely, Gil would not resurrect the Blood Opal. She watched with growing dismay, as he pointed out sizeable stones left.

His voice, a monotone, continued. "It'll never regain its former glory, but some of the coloured pieces are big enough to use for earrings or dress rings. And these smaller ones could be used to set other stones off in bracelets and brooches. It won't be a total write-off."

Pug thought of the amount of blood spilled in the name of this opal. From the first miner who dug it from the ground, to Dom and Chantelle. There, in her mind she'd said the name – Chantelle.

If, as Gil suggested, they used the remaining stones and turned them into other items of jewellery, would each one of these carry the curse? How many more people would it affect? She searched the sky for inspiration. *Celeste! Tell me what to do.*

She glanced down again. The broken remains of the Blood Opal, caught in a ray of sunshine, winked back at her like black and red diamonds. No longer dead peppercorns, they were alive again and ready to wreak more havoc. She'd been warned. Would she be its first victim? The answer lay in her hands.

She grabbed the leather box, stood and hurled it out to sea as far as she could throw.

Gil's mouth opened in shock and surprise. She turned away from him expecting his anger and covered her face with her hands. The squeak of his shoes on the deck told her he was moving. His arms encircled her, and gently he turned her around to face him. He hugged her to his body, patting her back as he might have done to a hurt child. And already she was regretting her hasty action. Since when had she believed in bloody curses, anyway?

"I'm sorry," she whispered.

"Don't be." He held her out at arms length. "Anyone else would have grabbed it and run for the reward. You – you throw it into the sea!" His laughter was so genuine it started her off, hesitantly at first and then the two of them were rolling around slapping each other like drunken sailors. As the hysteria waned, Pug could feel the tears running down her face. Gil pulled her towards him, wiped away her tears with his thumbs before he bent his head to hers. His kiss, when it came, was hot and firm and all consuming. Together they stayed, locked cheek-to-cheek – soul mates.

In time Gil looked over her shoulder in the direction she'd thrown the beast.

"You do know I'm going to have to dive for that, don't you?" he whispered in her ear.

She moved back to study his face. "Couldn't you tell your people it turned into dust?"

"You want me to lie?"

Touché, Gil, she thought, trapped by her own earlier ethics.

"Make me understand why I shouldn't go down there and look for those stones," he said.

"Because, they are too tiny to be any good, and they are not much use to anybody. And because they are back where they need to be, where they were made millions of years ago, beneath the sea in the days when the outback of Australia was covered by water."

He looked deeply into her eyes. "If I declare the Blood Opal lost at sea, I'd have to chart the area it was lost in. We'd have to accept the chance that another diver would discover more than just the gold pendant and its chain."

"I'll go along with that," she said.

"Then that is what we'll do."

*

Hours later, the mast duly restored to its place upon *Cazutt's* deck, Pug watched Gil take bearings and note them down, charting the approximate area where the opal was lost.

It was a risk of course that some stones may be found, but one small item she hadn't mentioned, might save the day. The box, when she threw it, was open. The stones would have scattered over the sea bed, and only the gold chain and pendant would be large enough to be found. One day, perhaps she would tell him, but right now he didn't need to know that.

They motored back to *Cazutt's* mooring. Gil picked the buoy up and looped its chain over the forward bollard. Pug turned the motor off. On his way back to join her in the cockpit she heard his telephone ring. He fumbled around in his kit bag to find it. Ratz, released from captivity, sat on the bench and cocked his head from side to side at the unfamiliar sound.

Pug went below to give Gil privacy, she watched him through the hatch. Was it the real estate agent? His eyes met hers. He nodded, grinned and gave her the thumbs up.

She beamed back at him, opened her wine locker, took out Dom's bottle of Champagne and waved it in a triumphant salute.

The End

Other Books by Carole Sutton

FERRYMAN Published by YouWriteOn 2008

One man's quest for justice, a detective with a conscience, a woman's betrayal and a powerful businessman with a sinister secret are just some of the intriguing characters that populate this Cornish tale – set in 1970s.

AAA American Author's Association: Book Review – *Ferryman* – Recommended by *American Author's Association* for all mystery and thriller lovers.

Ferryman pulses with action, intrigue and mystery. *Todd Fonseca* (Goodreads)

..., the ground shifts again, the plot takes another turn, always very convincing, you just don't see it coming. *Edith Parzefall* (Nurnberg, Germany)

Wonderful Who-Dunnit, *Randall Radic* (Alvah's Books)

A compelling tale – fast paced, well written... *Jassy Mackenzie* (South Africa)

AND THE DEVIL LAUGHED Published by New Generation Publishing 2009

Undercover cop, Hannah Ford takes on a drug surveillance job in Draper's Wharf. But when she arrives there, the town is in shock after the rape and murder of its local barmaid. Hannah, a rape survivor with a career to salvage, needs to prove to herself and her boss that she can hack it.

Sheer entertainment in the palm of your hand. *Stuart Ross McCallum* (Australia)

Murder in a small Australian coastal town – an entertaining and engaging read ... *Todd A Fonseca* (Goodreads)

A rollicking good read – Reviewed by *Randal Radic* (Alva's Books)

~

ACKNOWLEDGEMENTS

I would like to extend my heartfelt thanks to my two stalwarts, for their time and invaluable assistance over the years, Patricia O'Neill and Felicity Young, and to Chris Nagel our long time mentor. All three have played an important part in honing my work.

Thanks also go to family and friends for their support, draft reading and uncomplaining computer assistance whenever needed – believe me – it is much appreciated.

~

Carole Sutton

Carole Sutton

www.ingramcontent.com/pod-product-compliance
Lightning Source LLC
Chambersburg PA
CBHW020656030726
47498CB00002B/532